Ballykissangel
The New Arrival

Hugh Miller

*Based on the hit TV series
created by Kieran Prendiville*

BBC BOOKS

This book is published to accompany the television series entitled
Ballykissangel which was first broadcast in 1996. The series is a
Ballykea Production for World Productions for BBC Northern Ireland.

Executive producers Tony Garnett and Robert Cooper
Produced by Joy Lale
Directed by Richard Standeven and Paul Harrison

Published by BBC Books
an imprint of BBC Worldwide Publishing
BBC Worldwide Limited, Woodlands
80 Wood Lane, London W12 0TT

First published 1997
© Hugh Miller and Kieran Prendiville, 1997
The moral right of the authors has been asserted

ISBN 0 563 38327 5

Designed by Harry Green

Set in Plantin and Peignot
Printed and bound in Australia by
Griffin Paperbacks, Netley, South Australia

Hugh Miller was born in Scotland but has lived for more than twenty-five years in Warwickshire. He is the author of a number of books, among them the acclaimed Mike Fletcher crime novels and *The Silent Witnesses,* a study of the work of forensic pathologists. He also wrote the bestselling *Casualty.* His books have been translated into most western languages. Hugh lives in Warwick with his wife, Nettie.

Kieran Prendiville, a former journalist and broadcaster, has been a television scriptwriter for ten years. He has written for many popular drama series, including *Boon* and *The Bill.* As well as *Ballykissangel,* he also created *Roughnecks,* the hit series about life on a North Sea oil rig. He is 48 and lives in London.

ONE

It was a spring Saturday, bright and clear, with high patchy cloud over the Wicklow mountains and not a hint of rain. The sun warmed Peter Clifford's face as he gazed out of the bus window, relishing the vastness and colour, the sweep of the passing countryside and the occasional glitter of a distant lake. When he leaned near the open panel above the window he caught the scent of new growth on the trees and hedgerows.

After Manchester, this was nearly too much.

The bus rounded a bend and the gradient became much steeper. The driver, Gerard Lenihan, engaged a low gear, making the old vehicle shudder and rattle before it picked up speed again. Peter looked round, ready to smile at the handful of other passengers, but so far they seemed not to have noticed him.

Timmy-Joe Galvin, a young man with a ponytail who was sitting near the front of the bus, leaned forward sharply, staring up ahead as something hurtled down the hillside on their right, scattering sheep before it.

'Mother of Jayz…'

The thing was shaped like a giant wardrobe, a crate made of sturdy slats that were splitting under the impact as it rolled end over end, tumbling down the hill to the road. At the fence it hit a ramp of impacted earth and took off, spinning once before it hit the road three yards in front of the bus and rolled down the field on the left. Gerard slammed on the brakes.

'Did you see that?' Timmy-Joe jumped to his feet, pointing through the window. 'Did you see it?'

Peter and the others were out of their seats, staring at the thing as it rolled against a hummock and stopped in an upright position.

Gerard opened the door and got out. He swung his leg over the fence and made his way down to where the object had settled. The others followed at a careful distance, Brendan Kearney, a big, cheerful-faced man, called out, 'If it wants to know who our leader is, that's you, Gerard'.

They shuffled nearer as Gerard put a hand on the side of the crate, feeling the rough wood, stroking it. He reached up and pushed tentatively on the stout lid.

'What are you doing?' Kathleen Hendley demanded. She was a prim and humourless woman in her 60s, given to frowning from habit.

Gerard looked at her. 'Do you not want to know what it is?'

'I don't want to know what's inside it.'

'What?'

'Kathleen,' Brendan said, 'it's not a coffin.'

She sniffed. 'How do you know what it is?'

'Sure, look at the size of it.'

'Unless there's a heifer inside,' Siobhan Mehigan said. Siobhan was a vet, a big strapping girl in her 30s with a robust manner and a well-maintained sense of humour.

'Or an old sow,' Timmy-Joe offered.

'A flying pig,' Brendan said, nodding. 'Why didn't I think?'

Gerard was over his shock now, standing back and shaking his head at the crate. 'Nearly parted my hair and that's a fact.'

Peter asked where it came from, and felt the pause as they registered his English accent and ran a swift inventory of his boyish looks, his neatly cut hair and his hiker's clothes.

'From the back of a lorry, I'd say.' Gerard pointed. 'Up the mountain.'

'Out of the sky,' Brendan said darkly.

'Do you think he knows it's fallen off his lorry?' Peter said.

Gerard shrugged. 'He would if I got hold of him.'

Brendan asked if Gerard wanted to wait.

'Indeed and I don't. We'll report it. I have a schedule to keep.'

They headed back to the bus. 'Home, Gerard,' Brendan muttered, 'before Dracula himself opens the lid.'

As the others clambered back on board Peter stood by the door, his face tilted up to the sun. 'I think I'll walk,' he told the driver. 'It's too nice a day to sit on a bus.'

'Suit yourself.' Gerard reached inside the door and hoisted out Peter's rucksack. 'You'll have a long wait for the next one.'

'I don't mind. I like walking. How far is it?'

'To Ballykissangel?' Gerard hefted the rucksack, gauging its weight before he handed it over. 'Three miles.' He smiled. 'You have a grand day for it, anyway.'

Gerard got back on the bus and shut the door. As he pulled away, Peter slung the rucksack on his back and started walking. He was approaching the first bend when an Isuzu low-loader came trundling down the road, the driver and his mate anxiously eyeing the crate standing in the field 100 yards away ...

Peter strode on, getting himself up to hiking pace, swinging his arms and filling his lungs. This was the life, he thought, and this was the very place to live it. Poetry got written about spots like this – undulating landscape, vistas stretching to infinity, a ribbon of road winding round mountains that touched the clouds. On every side he could see and smell the splendour of nature as God decreed and designed it, every inch swept by the sustaining winds of heaven.

As interpretations went, he decided, that was definitely a bit too florid. But in these parts the colourful view was likely to come closest to the reality. He had heard more than one Irishman pining for God's own island, and already he believed he could imagine the bleakness at the core of their melancholy. It was simply the loss of this enchanting place, the terrible exile from perfection. That was what made grown men misty-eyed and choked up the more they tried to articulate their suffering.

As Peter strode along he felt a spot of rain. He looked up at the darkening clouds and caught another drop straight in his eye. A moment later he was enveloped in a downpour of monsoon proportions. In ten seconds he was soaked – head, arms, chest and legs, sopping and cooling rapidly.

He blinked through the downpour at the landscape, drab now, half-obscured and so dark it looked like nightfall. 'You have a grand day for it,' he muttered, aping the bus driver. Peter was not a swearing man, but one or two curses made it as far as his back teeth. He leaned into the rain and quickened his step. After a while the pounding on his forehead got so intense he had to shield it with his hand to stop the pain.

The wind shifted suddenly and his right ear seemed to fill with water, so he didn't hear anything the first time a horn sounded alongside. At the second peep he stopped and turned, seeing a small blue van.

The window slid down and a young woman peered out. Peter wiped his eyes and smiled at her. She was strikingly beautiful.

'Can I give you a lift? I'm going to Ballykissangel.'

'Oh.' Peter swelled with gratitude. 'That's perfect. Thank you.'

She told him to put his rucksack in the back and get in. As they pulled away he looked at her again: dark red hair to her shoulders, a fine oval face, buttermilk skin, sensitive features that belonged on a Botticelli nymph. She saw him staring and looked away sharply.

'Here...' She reached behind his seat and produced a small towel. 'Give your head a rub.'

He thanked her again and began towelling his hair. He noticed how she frowned as she drove, looking almost angry, her face close to the place on the windscreen where the rain parted in the path of the wiper blade.

'This is where the 40 shades of green come from,' she said.

'I'm sorry?'

'It's a song. Forty shades of grey would be more accurate, but there's the image to consider.'

Peter smiled politely. She asked him if he was staying in town.

'I live there. Well, I will be. I'm starting a new job.'

'Is that so?'

'At Saint Joseph's,' he said. 'I'm the new priest.'

The girl laughed softly.

Peter frowned. 'What?'

'Nothing,' she said. 'You'll be very welcome, I'm sure.'

He stared at her, puzzled.

'One thing this country needs', she said, 'is priests from England.'

He had expected some kind of comment like that, though maybe not so soon. 'We have enough of yours,' he said.

'We have enough of ours.'

A silence settled between them. Peter broke it by introducing himself. 'I'm Peter Clifford.'

'Assumpta Fitzgerald.'

He half-smiled, half-frowned. 'I'm sorry?'

'Fitzgerald.'

'No, no,' he said, 'your first name.'

'Assumpta,' she mumbled, obviously uneasy about it.

'Assumpta?'

She looked at him sidelong. 'Yes.'

'I've never heard that before. That's a beautiful name.'

'It's just a name.'

'I'll bet it isn't. It's to do with the Assumption, isn't it? The Assumption – '

'Of the Blessed Virgin. Yeah, big deal.'

'That's beautiful,' Peter insisted.

'Mother of God,' she groaned, 'A hippie priest.'

The rain stopped as suddenly as it had started. The sky began to clear and Peter's spirits rose again. They turned a bend on to a tree-lined stretch of road that led over a stone bridge into a handsome little town.

'This is Ballykissangel?'

'This is it.'

He couldn't help smiling; the place was so pretty. It sat snugly alongside the river, the long main street sloping down towards the bridge a full half-mile and rising gently again at the other end of town. There were rows and clusters of small houses, tidy shops and regular patches of green common land. The houses thinned out across the rising land behind the town's main stretch, with only smallholdings and farmland and wooded hill-sides beyond.

'Beautiful,' Peter murmured.

Assumpta took no apparent notice. They crossed the bridge and took a left turn past a bar called Fitzgerald's, the name painted in big white letters on a bright blue front.

'That you?' Peter said, pointing.

'That's me.'

'Don't let me take you out of your way.'

She drove on. 'We're used to carrying the clergy,' she said.

Peter smiled wearily.

Assumpta swung the van round another bend and pulled up in front of St Joseph's. 'This is you.'

Peter got out, grinning, forgetting to shut his door. He stood staring at the old stone church, admiring it, untroubled by the scaffolding and tarpaulins on the roof.

'Beautiful,' he said again.

Assumpta smiled tightly. 'You were made for each other.'

Peter got his rucksack from the back of the van and thanked her for the lift.

'Uh-huh.' She looked at him for a long moment, a noncommittal deadpan stare. Then, abruptly, she drove off to her bar.

✝

At the back of the church Peter genuflected and crossed himself, then stood for a moment, looking around. St Joseph's was a bright, well-tended church. In spite of the presence of workmen with their clutter and mess, the wood and brass were polished and gleaming. The floor was spotless and there were fresh flowers in every vase. A mingling of life and brightness and hope, he thought, automatically sermonizing, allowing himself to be florid again.

He turned at a sound near the confessional box. A ladder was set up there, leading up past a clear polythene sheet to a sizeable hole in the roof above it. A priest was coming down it, his clothes smirched with brick dust. Peter went across and helped him as he got to the foot of the ladder. The man was somewhere in his fifties, silver-haired and sternly handsome. Peter noticed he was built more like a boxer than a cleric.

'You've got the builders in,' he commented.

The priest nodded, slapping at the patches of dust on his arms and chest. 'I swear they're building a nest up there.' He cocked his head at Peter. 'You're not a Catholic by any chance?'

'Does a priest count?'

The older man stared. 'Father Clifford?'

'Father MacAnally.'

'I thought when you didn't get off the bus you weren't coming until tomorrow. How long have you been here?'

'I've just arrived.'

'How did you get here?'

Peter started to answer; Father MacAnally put up

his hand and said, 'Never mind. Come on.' He took Peter by the elbow and led him to the door. 'Let's get some tea.'

Peter nodded at the roof as they were leaving. 'That's some hole.' They strode out into the sunlight. 'Why did you ask if I was a Catholic?'

'I would have asked for a donation,' Father MacAnally said. 'But you can't afford it.'

Two

Assumpta parked the van in front of Fitzgerald's and took a cardboard carton with her shopping from the back. She elbowed her way into the bar, lugging the box, narrowly missing the heads of customers at tables near the door. Brian Quigley, a local businessman, was sitting at the bar, eating a sandwich and reading his paper.

'Morning, Brian.'

He grunted without looking up.

'Niamh…' Assumpta called to the girl behind the counter and pointed to Quigley's sandwich. 'Do me one of them, will you?'

'If you don't mind waiting while she orders it from Dublin,' Quigley muttered.

Niamh glared at him. 'Don't leave a tip, Dad. It only encourages me.'

She followed Assumpta to the kitchen at the back. Deftly and without preamble, while Assumpta put away her shopping in cupboards and drawers, Niamh was back on the topic which lately she would not leave alone – her plans for the advancement of her relationship with the young man of her choice. As she buttered the bread for Assumpta's sandwich she delivered a breathless summary of her tactics, then stopped what she was doing and stood with her head on one side, waiting for an opinion.

'Niamh, what does it matter what I think?' Assumpta was keen to get on with her work so she needed to sidestep a full-scale heart-to-heart. 'This is your life. If this is what you want to do, do it.'

'And what if he won't?'

'What if he won't?' Assumpta shrugged. 'Dump him.'

Niamh looked shocked, and she was well equipped for doing that. Depending on the angle of her gaze when she looked at another person, one eye drifted a fraction off centre, so that when she stood close, staring with her mouth half-open, she had the skewed look of a person struck by affront or alarm.

'Have you ever been in love, Assumpta?' she demanded. 'I mean, you know...'

'Oh, why ask me then? Ask the new priest, why don't you.'

'He's here?'

'Uh-huh. He's English.' Assumpta smiled mischievously. 'He looks about 12.'

Niamh was startled. 'He's here?' She looked at her watch.

'Uh-huh. See if you can find him a train set.'

Niamh finished making the sandwich, got her coat and hurried away. Assumpta went through to the bar where Quigley had his ear jammed to his mobile phone. At the other end of the line, Liam, one of his employees, was trying to convince him that a certain large crate that should have been in Ballykissangel by now had been delayed because it came off a later train.

'What later train?' Quigley scowled at the mouthpiece. 'There's no later train.' He stopped himself on the verge of shouting and turned away from the bar. 'Liam, I don't want to hear about it. Just get it here. It's supposed to be in place before the new fella arrives.'

Assumpta heard that. 'The priest?'

Quigley stared at her. 'What about him?'

'He's already here.'

He was motionless for a second or two, then he snatched up his cup, gulped down his coffee and hurried out of the place, just as his daughter had. He was in such a hurry that he didn't see Peter and Father MacAnally coming from the direction of St Joseph's.

'Let me ask you something,' Father Mac was saying. 'Why are you here?'

'This is where I was sent,' Peter said.

Father Mac took that to be an evasion. 'You don't have to tell me.'

Peter smiled. It was a vexation to priests in country parishes that they were often burdened with assistant clergy who had been troublesome elsewhere.

'You've nothing to worry about,' Peter said.

'That's good, that's good. Only that's what the last fella said and he was gone in three weeks. I swear he only came for the suit. Lost his vocation, he said. Three weeks in Ballykissangel and…' Father Mac spread his fingers like a magician and extended his arms, as if he was making something disappear.

'If it makes you feel any better,' Peter said, 'I lasted three years in the inner city and my faith is stronger than ever.'

'Good man.'

Peter noticed they were approaching Fitzgerald's. 'Are we going in there?'

'Is something wrong?'

Peter said no, but he sounded doubtful all the same. 'I've met the landlady.'

'Assumpta?' Father Mac chuckled. 'Well, she makes a good pot of tea, and I like to watch her seethe at my presence.'

The instant the door opened Peter liked the place. It was cosy but not cramped, with a good long bar, an excellent selection at the pumps and enough in the way of homely touches – armchairs, framed pictures, shaded lamps – to make people behave themselves.

'Assumpta…' Father Mac stepped up to the bar, smiling amiably. 'How nice to see you.'

Assumpta gave him a blank look. When she spoke, it was to Peter. 'You notice', she said, 'he doesn't spend more time up there than he has to.'

Father Mac held on to his smile. 'I'll put a hole in your roof one day, see how you like it.'

'You can make a pepperpot out of it, Father, you still won't get me in there.'

Peter shifted his feet awkwardly.

'A pot of tea and a plate of sandwiches if you please, Assumpta,' Father Mac said, 'And if you could summon up a little respect...'

She jerked her head at Peter. 'I hope you're not going to make him pay. You know, he doesn't even have a car.' She went through to the back.

'We'll find you something,' Father Mac told Peter.

'Oh, it's all right, I don't drive.'

'You don't drive?' Now Father Mac looked mildly alarmed.

'I never needed to.'

'So in emergencies you took the Blessed Sacrament by taxi, is that right?'

Peter laughed. 'No. By bike.'

'By bike?'

'Mountain bike.'

'Mountain bike?'

'It was just as quick.'

'In the city,' Father Mac said drily.

'Well, yes...' Peter couldn't help sounding defensive. 'But mountain bikes are designed for mountains.'

'No, Father, goats are designed for mountains and mountain roads are designed for motor cars.' Father Mac frowned. 'What kind of people do you think we are? Look, come over here.'

He led Peter to a framed, elegantly hand-drawn map on the wall. 'This is where you are...' He pointed to Ballykissangel, then to the nearby town of Cilldargan: 'Here is where I am most of the week'. His finger traced a wide circle: 'This is the entire parish of Cilldargan which I, as parish priest, am responsible for. I cannot be everywhere. This is why there is a priest in Castlecomarty' –

he jabbed the map – 'another in Dromane' – he jabbed it again – 'another in Ballykissangel, and so on.'

'Yes, Father.'

Father Mac made a circle around Ballykissangel and the surrounding hilly country. 'This is all you. Not just the town. And you're quite right, Father, some of your parishioners do live on the tops of mountains. Like Tommy Hassett. He's on his last legs and there are plenty more like him…'

'Yes, Father.'

'…only by the time you got there on your mountain bike, they could be throwing another sod of turf on the fire for the Prince of Darkness.'

The two men stared at each other. Assumpta came back, carrying a tray with the tea and sandwiches. She looked from one to the other. 'Making friends? That's good.'

✝

At roughly the moment Father Mac began pouring the tea, Brian Quigley was standing outside the gates of St Joseph's, watching as a low-loader with his company name on the door, Quigley Developments PLC, drew up with a big, battered-looking crate roped to the back. The driver, Liam, and his mate Donal got out. Recent exertions to get the crate back on the lorry with the aid of a mechanical digger had left them sweaty and more dishevelled than usual.

'Where have you been?' Quigley demanded.

'Sure I told you,' Liam said, 'the train was late.'

'Leaves on the line,' Donal offered.

Quigley sighed. 'In spring?'

Donal thought for a second. 'Global warming.'

Although Quigley worked at being a civilized man – he was urbane, well-groomed, moderate in his speech – he remained attached to a brutish streak that he had done nothing to tame. Liam and Donal saw a flash of it now as he glowered at them, first one then the other, and stabbed a finger in the direction of the big crate.

'Just get it off.'

✝

Fifteen minutes later, Peter and Father Mac left Fitzgerald's. As they crossed the road to where Father Mac's hatchback was parked, he dug in his pocket and fished out a couple of keys on a ring. He handed them to Peter.

'Your house is the one under the church. You can't miss it.' He opened the car door and smiled thinly. 'I know this is dropping you in at the deep end, but it wasn't me that asked for an Englishman.'

Peter found the house, a neat cottage with a bright red door and a lion knocker. He let himself in and put down his rucksack in the living room.

For a minute he took stock. It was a cool, bare-looking room with cream walls, scuffed furniture and one or two bad landscape prints in cheap frames. There was nothing demonstrably heart-warming about the place, rather it was drab and serviceable. Yet Peter liked it already, much as he had taken to Fitzgerald's.

From his early childhood the odours of any new place had coloured his first reaction and ever afterwards the memory would be recalled by similar smells. The aromatic quality of this house took him back immediately: he detected lavender polish, old rugs, sun-warmed wood varnish and a faint suggestion of cooked cabbage. It conjured up a neighbour's house, a woman he had called Auntie, whose home had provided him with a sense of snugness and safety throughout his boyhood.

He crossed the room, touching the backs of the plain solid chairs and the cracked polish of the table, feeling the floorboards move softly an instant before they creaked. It had a sunny, south-facing window that looked out on to a tiny garden at the back. As he bent to peer through he heard a sound from the kitchen.

'Hello?' he called.

A young woman put her head out of the kitchen door. 'Hello,' she said, and ducked back out of sight.

Peter went through. 'Hello,' he said again.

She was turning the gas up under the kettle. 'Father Clifford?'

'That's me. Father MacAnally never mentioned a housekeeper.'

She turned. 'I'm not the housekeeper. You are.'

'Oh.'

'I'm Niamh Quigley.'

'Peter.'

They shook hands.

'My father owns this place.'

'Owns it?'

'That's right.' Niamh put two cups on saucers on the kitchen table. 'He wanted to welcome you himself, but he had business to take care of.'

'Please thank him.' Peter frowned. 'I thought – '

'You thought the Church owned it?'

'Well…'

'Up until last year it did, then my father made an offer for it.'

'Right.'

'He wants to turn this place into a holiday home for American tourists.'

'And throw in their own padre,' Peter murmured.

'What?'

'Nothing. Um, when are these people arriving?'

'Oh he hasn't anyone yet, so you're fine for now.'

'Your father's a generous man.'

Niamh made no attempt to agree. Instead she picked up the boiling kettle and poured water into the teapot, which she then began to stir.

'Tea'll be ready in a minute, Father.'

He'd already had two cups at Fitzgerald's, but a steady intake of tea was part and parcel of being a priest. 'I'll get changed while that's infusing,' he said. 'I presume my bedroom's upstairs?'

'First door at the top.'

Five minutes later he came down the stairs transformed. The easy-going young man in jeans and checked shirt was now an eager-faced young curate in a sober black suit, black shirt and clerical collar. As he descended, Niamh brought the tea things in on a tray.

'Can I ask you a question, Father?'

'Go ahead.'

'Have you ever had a girlfriend?' She looked at him earnestly as she put down the tray. 'Have you? Ever had a girlfriend?'

'Come again?'

'Seriously?'

'I don't know that I know you well enough to answer a question like that.'

Niamh poured the tea.

'Why do you ask?'

I might have asked your advice.'

'Take it off the rent,' Peter said, accepting his cup of tea. Niamh smiled. He told her to go ahead and ask.

'No.' She shook her head.

'OK.' Peter sipped the tea and glanced around the room. 'It's a nice house.'

'My boyfriend says he wants to get married,' Niamh said, letting the words out in a rush. Then she paused. 'There are strings.'

'Ah.' Peter nodded. 'He wants you to go to bed with him.'

'No, Father. I want him to go to bed with me.'

Peter blinked.

'I want to know what he's like – to live with. I want to know what to expect. He's a good man, but I need to know. Can he take out the rubbish without being asked? Will he tarnish his elbows with Fairy Liquid? Does he grip an iron like he's holding a rattlesnake?'

'The important things.'

'You think they're not?'

'I'm not sure what to think,' Peter said.

'How do you mean?'

'I'm a Catholic priest. What do you expect me to say? I can't encourage you to have sex before marriage. But I won't condemn you if you do.'

'I don't agree with divorce.'

'No.'

They were silent for a moment, sipping tea.

'I just want to be sure,' Niamh said.

She went back to the kitchen. Peter followed her, realizing she was genuinely troubled. He watched her take a biscuit from the tin by the bread bin and break it absently between her fingers.

'What does he say?'

'He says I don't know what I'm talking about.'

It was probably a matter to be dealt with at length. Peter would pursue it if she wanted him to, but she would have to prove to him she was willing to face facts squarely and accept plain truth, however unpalatable she found it. His tactic for testing determination was to let the man or woman concerned stew for a while.

'Niamh, I'm going to go up to the church. Stay if you want to talk this through. Let yourself out if you want to go. I'd like to help.'

'I do love him,' Niamh said in a small voice.

Peter was sure that was true. 'I'll be back,' he said.

As he turned to the door his parting words came back at him in the unmistakable tones of Arnold Schwarzenegger. He winced and let himself out.

THREE

Brian Quigley badgered his men steadily as they pushed the huge crate on a wheeled pallet along the path at the side of St Joseph's, aiming it shakily towards the main doors. As the front wheels hit a bump the crate ground against the tarmac, making the whole unit rattle and shake.

'Careful!' Quigley yelled. 'Careful! Do you know how much this thing cost?'

'I do,' Liam shouted back, 'and it's madness.'

Donal concurred. 'You could buy a car for the same price.'

With more struggle and muted cursing the crate was brought right up to the church doors. As Peter approached from the house, Liam, Donal and several others were using hammers and crowbars to prize off the slats. Peter recognized the crate the instant he saw it.

Quigley turned, frowning. 'Ah! Father.' All at once he oozed goodwill. 'Welcome to Ballykissangel. Lads, this is our new priest.'

The men muttered various greetings; Peter told them he was pleased to meet them.

'From England, I believe?' Quigley said, with the kind of tone that suggested the fact was regrettable, but sufferable.

'Peter Clifford.' Peter held out his hand. Quigley did the same and they shook.

'Now is everything all right for you down below, Father?'

'Yes, thank you, you're very kind.' Peter nodded at the crate. 'What's this?'

'Do you know what it is?' Quigley put on a cunning little smile and narrowed one eye like a knowingly generous uncle about to reveal the nature of a marvellous gift.

'I know it can fly,' Peter said, making Liam wince.

Quigley looked puzzled. 'What?'

'Nothing.' Peter indicated the crate again. 'What is it?'

'It's a confessional.' Quigley's voice had a note of reverence.

'A confessional? Don't we have one?'

'We've two now,' Liam piped up.

'I promise you, Father,' Quigley said, 'Saint Joseph's has nothing like this. Nowhere in Ireland has anything like this.'

'Uh-huh.' Peter gazed at the tall, long, grey structure emerging from its slatted cocoon. 'Like what, exactly?'

'Well it's difficult to show you at the moment Father, because it's not plugged in.'

Peter stared at him. 'Plugged in?'

'Yes.' Quigley walked around the confessional, examining it for marks. 'To operate the sliding doors, you know?'

'And the soundproofing,' Liam said.

'The soundproofing?' Peter knew he was parroting but he couldn't help it.

'And the air conditioning,' Donal added.

'Air conditioning?'

'Oh God yes, Father...' Quigley came round the other side of the confessional. 'Some of them mountainy men have a fierce pungency about them.'

'Yes, but...' Peter felt that while it was rather soon to be overlaying his opinions on events in Ballykissangel, he could at least voice a misgiving or two. 'Aren't we losing sight a little – '

'Father,' Quigley cut in, 'who would sleep on the floor if he could have a bed?'

'Excuse me?'

'It's all cleared with Father Mac.' Quigley watched the

men wheel the confessional into the church doorway. 'I wouldn't have gone to the trouble of importing it from Italy if I didn't have his authority.'

The confessional stopped moving abruptly and Liam shouted, 'It's not going to fit, Mr Quigley!'

For a long moment Quigley stared, as if he was willing the confessional to alter its dimensions.

'No problem, no problem,' he said finally. 'We'll, um… we'll get it in through the roof.'

Peter marched down to Fitzgerald's to use the pay-phone. He was half-aware that Assumpta, going about her business behind the bar, was listening as he relayed his complaints to Father MacAnally. He first of all condemned Quigley's innovation on grounds of sheer bad taste, then went on to question the relevance of any kind of leisure-enhancing hi-tech within the framework of a religion that cherished both tradition and gradual change. He wound up on a soundly prac-tical note, with his worries about the harm the new confessional might do when it was lowered through the roof of St Joseph's.

Father Mac said he failed to see what all the fuss was about. 'If Quigley damages the roof,' he told Peter, 'he'll put it right. They're his men on the roof already.'

'But Father, we don't need that thing.'

'Oh is that right?'

'Nobody needs a monstrosity like this. Leather uphol-stery, sliding doors…'

'What have you got against the twentieth century?' Father Mac sounded testy now. 'What's so monstrous about a bit of comfort in the confessional? Would you be saying that if you were 70 years old and had arthritis in your knees?'

'No, Father.'

'No Father. And I would remind you that Brian Quigley already has my permission for this.'

'Yes Father.'

'He is a good friend of the Church. You'd do well to remember that.'

Peter put down the phone and caught a small mock-pitying look from Assumpta. He finished his Coke and went out, screwing up his eyes against the sudden sunlight.

He saw Niamh come across the road towards him. She looked sheepish now, but at least she wasn't avoiding him. He asked if she was all right.

'I'm fine, Father.' She lowered her eyes. 'Can we just...'

She wanted to drop it. He knew and he understood. In the few short years he had been a priest he had known plenty of young people, men and women, pull back from the brink of seriously examining their wants and motives.

'If you want me, you know where I am.'

Niamh nodded and smiled, grateful to be off the hook without a struggle.

'I met your father,' Peter said.

'Ah.'

'What does he do, exactly?'

'My father? All kinds of everything. Why do you ask?'

'He's supplying us with a new confessional.'

'Oh it's arrived, has it?'

'You know about it?'

'First of many, he hopes.'

'What?'

'In Ireland. He has the sole importing rights.'

Peter smiled. Every community had its hustling entrepreneur and Quigley certainly dressed and acted the part. There was something, too, in his unwavering gaze and the hard line of his mouth that suggested he was born to the work. Peter decided he would have to watch Brian Quigley, if only with a view to avoiding trouble.

'So don't forget,' Niamh said, moving off, 'before you start cleaning up this town, it's important to my father that people go on committing sin.'

Peter walked up the road to the church. A small crowd had gathered outside the railings to watch as the new confessional, dangling from the boom of a crane, was lowered towards the hole in the roof of the church. The crane operator was delicately manoeuvring his load while Brian Quigley hung through the side of the cab, issuing orders and warnings, waving his arms like an demented conductor. A television news crew was there, too – cameraman, soundman and female reporter – taping the event.

At the front of the crowd was the vet, Siobhan Mehigan, shading her eyes as she stared up at the swaying confessional. She nudged Timmy-Joe Galvin standing beside her.

'Does that look familiar to you?'

Timmy-Joe nodded. 'Last time I saw it, it was going an awful lot faster.'

Peter stood in the road, staring, bemused by the entire event, unaware that Assumpta had joined the onlookers. Brendan Kearney came freewheeling along on his bike and stopped beside Peter. 'Nearer my God to thee,' he murmured.

Peter turned to him. 'Are people going to think this was my idea?'

'Ah well now, Peter,' Brendan said, using his name with easy familiarity even though it was the first time, 'that very much depends on whether it's a success or not.'

'Terrific.'

They watched as the local police officer, Guard Ambrose Egan, asked the TV team to move further back from the church. Ambrose was young, lean and earnest. He had strong eyes and a prim mouth, a useful combination in a policeman, especially when he had to be simultaneously forceful and righteous, which Ambrose was being at that moment.

'What's your problem?' the reporter demanded, resisting Ambrose's instructions.

'I'm responsible for safety,' he told her.

'Are we in danger?'

'Well, now, if that thing fell down...'

'Well if it fell,' the reporter said, 'then we'd have made our last confession, wouldn't we?'

Having offered token resistance she waved for the camera operator and sound recordist to follow her. She stepped up to Peter and touched his arm.

'Father Clifford, is it?' She pointed to the camera, which was already trained on him. 'Could we have a quick word?'

'I think, um, Brian Quigley over there is the man you want. He's the brains behind all this.'

'It's your church.'

'Oh I don't know about that...'

'Come on, Father,' she coaxed, 'Two minutes and we'll be out of your hair.'

Brendan whispered in Peter's ear. Peter brightened at once and squared up to the reporter. 'Actually, I'm not allowed to give interviews,' he said, full of amiable regret. 'Not without the permission of my parish priest, and he's in Cilldargan.'

'Father MacAnally?' she said.

'That's right.'

'He said it was fine.'

'Oh. Did he?' Peter felt adrift.

'So would you like to do it for me?'

'Well...'

'I'll show you where to stand.'

He allowed himself to be led to a spot with a better background. The reporter stood in front of him and to one side of the camera.

'Look at me, Father. Are you rolling, Richard?'

Before Peter knew it the interview was under way.

'Now, Father Clifford, tell me about the new confessional.'

Peter had a flash memory of his first time in a pulpit,

facing a congregation. He did now what he had done then: he took a deep, lung-filling breath and held it for a second, mustering composure. The tactic would have worked better if he hadn't caught sight of Assumpta watching him.

'Well…' he cleared his throat. 'An opportunity came to take advantage of the latest technology.'

'What's so special about it?'

Well it has, ah, sliding doors, soundproofing – '

'Leather upholstery,' the reporter said.

Peter frowned. 'It's more comfortable.'

'In fact there's an armchair in there,' the reporter pressed. 'Isn't there?'

'Well…' Peter smiled uncertainly. 'I think calling it an armchair is overstating it a little.'

'What would you call it?'

Peter wet his lips. 'Look, as I say, what comfort there is is for the benefit of the community, many of whom are elderly and suffer from arthritis – '

'The armchair is for you though, isn't it?'

'I haven't actually seen inside it yet.'

'I see.' The reporter spoke briskly, the last trace of friendliness leaving her voice. 'Going back to your elderly arthritis sufferers, what would they want with a fax machine?'

'What?' Peter was bewildered.

'There's a fax machine in the confessional, isn't there?'

'Is there?'

The reporter chose to end the interview on that perplexed note. Peter marched off to the church, where Brian Quigley was overseeing the lowering of the confessional into place beside the old one. Peter demanded to know if there was a fax machine in there, and if there was, what possible justification there could be for such a thing.

'That's what it came with,' Quigley said. His flinty

stare melted to a look of sublime innocence. 'It comes as standard, you know. Like a car.'

'Brian, a fax machine! In the name of God – '

'What?' Now Quigley managed to look wounded. 'What's the problem here? A fax machine is only a method of communication. Sure, they have one in the Wailing Wall in Jerusalem.'

'What?'

'Without a word of a lie. Telecom Israel or whatever they're called put it in last year.'

'It's not the same.'

'Because they're Jews?' Now the wounded look became indignation. 'That's very ecumenical, that is.'

'We're talking about the sacrament of confession here, Brian!'

'Father, look...' Quigley put up his hands, placating, soothing. 'Why don't we have this conversation in a couple of days. See how it goes, see how the punt- – the faithful – like it, eh?'

One of the workmen called. 'I promise you, Father,' Quigley said, moving off, 'in a few days you'll be the most talked-about priest in Ireland.'

Peter wandered back out into the sunlight. Assumpta called to him from the road.

'Do you fancy a pint, Father?'

'No thanks,' he said. 'They've probably got it on draught in the confessional.' He shook his head. 'Where am I, Assumpta? The Twilight Zone?'

'No, Father,' she said, showing a glimmer of something he hoped was sympathy. 'You're just out of your depth.'

FOUR

The town's petrol station was a modest enterprise, a couple of buildings with a narrow forecourt, two pumps and a goat tethered on a patch of grass. Late in the afternoon Peter came by and stood looking in at the open door of the small shopfront. Among the tyres, gas cylinders, car batteries and folding roof racks there was a second- or third-hand 50cc Honda motorbike. He studied it for a while, then went in.

A man was turning from a confectionery rack behind the counter. He had dark curly hair and the lightly debauched features of a drinker who could take his liquor. His smile lit up his whole face. 'Father Clifford,' he said.

'Everyone knows my name.'

'They certainly do.' The man held out his hand. 'Padraig O'Kelly,' he said, pronouncing it 'Poraig'. They shook. 'What can I do for you?'

'I need some transport.'

'You want to leave town already?'

'I'm not much use if I can't get about. It says in the local paper, Mr O'Kelly – '

'Padraig.'

'– Padraig, that you have a motorbike for sale.'

Padraig was not keen to confirm this.

'You do have a bike for sale?' Peter pointed to the one he had been looking at. 'That one, is it?'

'Well now I'm not sure it's the thing for you, Father…'

'What's up with it?'

'Nothing. Nothing really.' Padraig lit a cigarette, in

spite of the 'NO SMOKING' signs. He scratched his head awkwardly.

'Can I have a look at it?' Peter said.

'I suppose so. But you have to remember they're tricky things, these little bikes. They don't have the smoothness or the built-in safety of the bigger models.'

After a minute sitting astride the machine, revving the engine and waggling the handlebars, Peter couldn't see the problem. Padraig, however, was shaking his head, rejecting this particular conjunction of man and machine.

'Padraig, if I can ride a bike, I can ride one of these, surely?'

'I was thinking more of your dignity,' Padraig admitted.

'Jesus entered Jerusalem riding on a donkey.'

'He'd have been quicker.'

'Well…' Peter shrugged. 'I have to have something.'

'You'll still need a licence for it.'

'A provisional?'

Padraig nodded. 'You'll have to go to Wicklow to get it.'

Peter switched off the engine, climbed off the bike and handed the keys to Padraig. 'I won't take it until I'm legal. Just keep it for me.'

✝

At 6.00 pm Peter entered the church from the sacristy, genuflected before the altar and crossed himself. He turned and walked to the back of the church, where the new confessional was now installed and plugged in.

As he passed he smiled at the three rows of penitents waiting in the pews. He felt more like groaning. A smaller number on his first day would have been nice. At the back, one man sat alone, first in the queue. It was Ambrose, the town policeman, looking even younger without his hat.

Peter stepped up to the confessional, pushed a button

and stepped back. The door opened with a deep rumble that vibrated the whole structure and reverberated through the church. He stepped inside and the door rumbled shut, giving Peter an unavoidable mental image of a stone rolling across the mouth of a tomb.

He eased into the creaky leather seat and pushed a button on the console in front of him. Outside, a green light went on above the penitents' door. Ambrose got up, pushed the appropriate button and was let in. As soon as he was inside the door rolled shut and a red light went on outside.

'Bless me Father for I have sinned. It's a week since my last confession.' There was a pause. He cleared his throat. 'It's not easy.'

'There's no rush,' Peter told him.

Another long pause, then Ambrose said, 'I think I'm going to commit a mortal sin.'

Again the silence. Peter heard a long sigh, followed by sniffing, which threatened to persist. There was a box of tissues in a recess beside Peter's chair. He pulled one out, opened the gilt fretwork grille and passed the tissue to Ambrose. He took it and blew his nose loudly.

'Thank you, Father.'

A moment later Peter was startled to see the grille open again and the tissue poked back through. He took it and dumped it before Ambrose realized what he had done.

'Sorry,' he mumbled.

'Don't worry about it.' Peter closed the grille. 'Come on, let's sort this out.'

Ambrose took a deep steadying breath. 'I'm a single man…'

'Yes.'

A pause. 'I think I'm going to have sex.'

'Who with?'

'I can't give you her name, Father.'

'No, no. I meant what's your relationship?'

'She's my girlfriend.'

'You seem very sure it's going to happen.'

'She's very keen.'

'You don't sound enthusiastic.'

'It's a mortal sin.'

'Do you love her?'

Ambrose sighed. 'With all my heart.'

'Does she love you?'

'I'd say so.'

Peter wondered if he would ever grow numb to this, his awareness of pain transmitting itself from one side of the confessional to the other, the pangs of a man or woman grappling with impulses that threatened to run ahead of the Christian formalities.

'Do you believe in marriage?' Peter asked.

'Oh, we do, of course,' Ambrose said.

The ease with which Peter could identify a frailty made him feel older and wiser whenever he was in the confessional. He understood now what an old parish priest in Manchester had meant, late one night after a few brandies, when he tapped his clerical collar, belched softly and said, 'This damned thing makes a Methuselah out of you.'

'But', Ambrose added now, 'she wants to find out if we're suited.'

Peter believed a penny had just dropped. 'Suited sexually?'

'She wants to know what I'm like to live with.'

'Whether you wash up,' Peter murmured.

'Whether I what?'

'Nothing. So, if you live together, and you are suited, then you'll get married?'

Ambrose nodded behind the grille. 'That's the idea.'

'What do you want?'

'I want to get married,' Ambrose said, deeply sincere. 'I don't want to live in mortal sin.'

To Peter's astonishment, and annoyance, the fax by his

knee buzzed into life and began to disgorge a printed message.

'That's why I'm here, Father.'

'Sorry – say again?'

'I want absolution.'

'Well...' Peter stared as the paper inched out of the machine. 'I can't give you absolution for a sin you haven't committed.'

'But if you know I'm going to commit it...'

'I don't know that. Not everything is so... ', the fax machine beeped to signal the end of the transmission, '...black and white.'

He waited for some response from Ambrose, but there was only the tense silence again, the small anguish of a decent Catholic boy wanting to do the right thing by God and his girlfriend.

'I think,' Peter said, 'God is more understanding than we sometimes give him credit for.'

Ambrose sighed again.

'Look, if you're unhappy about this, don't do it.'

'I have to do it.'

'OK, OK...'

Peter thought for a minute and had an idea. As far as he could tell it wasn't wildly practical, but it was worth throwing out, since a lifeline was clearly what Ambrose wanted.

'How about this: move in together, just don't have sex.'

Ambrose was silent for a moment. 'What?'

'You do all the things that couples do, just leave out one of them.'

'That's brilliant.'

'Well...'

'That's incredible.'

'I don't know whether she would agree,' Peter cautioned.

'She wouldn't have to know,' Ambrose said.

That baffled Peter.

'At first,' Ambrose added.

Peter had a premonition. It wasn't picturesque. He began to regret making the suggestion.

'It's not a recommendation,' he said. 'I really think you ought to discuss – '

The door on the other side rumbled open and closed again. Ambrose was no longer receiving messages.

'Let me know how it goes,' Peter murmured.

He tore the message from the fax machine and peered at it. The single word *FATTURA* was printed along the top, followed by a series of separate items, all in Italian, each with a figure opposite. A double-underlined figure at the bottom was, presumably, a total. He stared thoughtfully at the sheet, hearing the next penitent enter the confessional. Peter's Italian was not extensive, but he did know that *fattura* meant invoice. He folded the sheet of paper and stuck it in his pocket.

✝

That night, exhausted by so much change, by all the upheavals and by the good mountain air, Peter slept like a child. It was an enveloping, dreamless sleep that lasted for close to three hours. He was awakened sharply by the ringing of the telephone on his bedside table.

He pushed himself up on one elbow, fuddled but calm, accustomed to having his sleep broken. As he picked up the receiver he noticed it was a little after 2.00 am.

'Father Clifford speaking.'

A rush of words came at him, the accent strange, a woman's voice with the unmistakable tremor of grief. Nothing else was clear.

'Slowly, please. I can't understand what you're saying.'

The woman stopped and started again. It was Mrs Hassett. Tommy, her husband, was fading fast. The doctor had been called already. Would the priest come too? She was sure in her heart he would be needed.

Peter said of course he would come. Patiently, he scribbled down the details of how to get to where the Hassetts lived.

'Right, I'm on my way – oh!' It dawned on him he had no transport. 'Before you go, what's the doctor's phone number?' He wrote it down. 'Thank you, Mrs Hassett.'

He hung up and dialled again. A woman's tired voice answered.

'Hello, I'm sorry to trouble you at this time of night. Is the doctor there?'

'I'm afraid not. Is that the new priest?'

'Yes, it is.'

'You've just missed Dr Ryan, he left on an urgent call a couple of minutes ago. Can I give him a message?'

'No, no message. Thank you.'

He threw down the phone, leapt out of bed and began dressing at the double. Four minutes later he left the house and ran all the way through the town, down past Fitzgerald's to Padraig O'Kelly's garage. The sound of his feet set a couple of dogs barking but otherwise there were no signs of life in Ballykissangel.

He got to the garage panting and gasping. He battered on the door until his hand hurt. There was no response. He ran round the back and tried the door. It was locked. He grasped the handle and shook it fiercely, making the panels rattle, but it stayed locked.

He went to the shop door at the front again, stood a few paces back from it, took a deep breath and lunged with his foot, trying to kick it in. It was old and flimsy, but it held.

In a frenzy, determined to remove this one thin barrier, he shook the door again, harder than before, violently rattling it back and forth, using all his strength to make something, anything, give way. And all at once, with all the battering, the inside bolt slid down and the door opened.

Peter dashed inside, grabbed the motorbike and

wheeled it out to the forecourt. He ran back inside, found the keys and came out again. Straddling the bike, he turned the key in the ignition, kick-started the engine, and heard it die as soon as he turned the throttle. He started it again and this time it only turned over four times before it cut out. After that it wouldn't start at all.

He looked at the petrol gauge. Empty.

Running with the bike, he got it to a petrol pump, twisted off the fuel cap, unhooked the nozzle, pushed it into the tank and pulled the trigger.

Nothing.

He was seething. He knew he mustn't panic. There had to be a reason for this. A straightforward reason. He looked up and found it on a sign above the pumps:

THESE DISPENSERS ARE NOT
SELF-SERVICE. AN ATTENDANT
WILL BE WITH YOU SHORTLY.

He stepped back from the pumps and stood for a moment with his hands clasped, forcing himself to be calm.

After a count of 20 he glanced at his watch, took a deep breath and began running back into town. The stretch between the garage and Fitzgerald's was mostly downhill and as he ran he picked up so much speed he had to flail his arms to keep upright.

At Fitzgerald's he skidded to a halt and banged on the front door. He kept at it until an upstairs light went on and Assumpta came to the window in her nightdress.

'We're closed!'

'Assumpta!' Peter looked up, panting. 'Please!'

'What do you want?'

He took a second to catch his breath. 'I want to borrow your van.'

'My van?' Assumpta was still woolly with sleep. 'For what? You don't drive.'

'I know.'

'Then what are you standing there...?' It dawned on

her all at once. He wanted to borrow van and driver.
'Oh, great…'

'There's a couple of things that I need to pick up
from the sacristy,' he said, moving off. 'I'll be back in two
minutes. Oh…' he paused; 'Thank you.'

He ran up the hill to St Joseph's. Assumpta shut the
window and shuffled across the room to find her clothes.

✝

The drive to Tommy Hassett's smallholding took them
high to the north above Ballykissangel along narrow
twisting roads with mountains on either side. Five minutes into the journey Assumpta still hadn't spoken. She
was clearly angry and she threw the steering about at
every opportunity, making the tyres squeal.

'I'd do the same for you,' Peter said at last, fed up with
the wedge of silence between them.

'Give me the last rites?'

'I wasn't being facetious.'

'You were being a bit bloody hopeful.'

'I don't want an argument,' he said.

'Oh read my lips…'

'OK, OK.'

Assumpta swung the van round a bend and for a
moment the road in front of them seemed to disappear.
It came back as the van went down a dip then started
climbing again.

'You'd come anyway, wouldn't you?' Assumpta said.
'Knowing you weren't wanted.'

He looked at her. Her eyes were fixed on the road. 'I
may not know that,' he said.

'I just told you.'

Peter shrugged. 'Things change. You may not be able
to speak.'

'I'm speechless already.'

The final stretch was down a dirt path through a
field to a battered, rundown, single-storey cottage. The

door was open and a light was on inside. Assumpta stopped behind a saloon car parked near the front of the house.

The car's boot was open; a man, obviously the doctor, was rummaging inside, his overcoat flapping in the stiff breeze. He straightened and turned into the beam of the van's lights. He was in his early 50s, dapper and bald, with a close-trimmed fringe of grey hair at the sides and back. He tipped a few tablets from a plastic tub onto his palm, which he then transferred to a smaller bottle.

Peter jumped out of the van and ran across.

'Before you ask, Father,' the doctor said, 'these are for her, not for him.'

'Oh.' Peter looked at the small woman standing forlornly in the open doorway.

'I'm sorry. There's nothing anyone could have done. You're Father Clifford, yeah?'

'Yes.'

'Doctor Ryan. Michael.'

They shook hands mechanically. Peter was openly distressed.

'When did it happen?'

'About 10 minutes ago. Father – '

Peter didn't wait for the doctor's understanding. He strode to the house and put his arm around the little woman, ushering her inside.

Assumpta got out of the van, hugging her jacket about her.

'Assumpta…' The doctor looked surprised to see her.

'Don't ask,' she said. 'Were we too late?'

He nodded. 'Sure, it's no place for a person in poor health to be living, way up here. Did you know him?'

'I did not.' Assumpta looked at the house. 'I hope he didn't suffer.'

'I'd say not.'

'Well,' she made a wan smile, 'let's hope God is not as severe as he's said to be.'

The doctor nodded. He patted Assumpta's shoulder in farewell and got into his car. As he drove off she stood for a moment, looking in at the window, seeing the woman hunched forward in a low chair as Peter knelt and prayed by the body of an old man lying on a brass bed.

Assumpta walked back to the van. She knew what the score was here, she fully understood Peter's hurry. Catholic Christianity places store by preparing the dying for a good death. Ideally, the dying person would make his last confession to a priest and he would receive absolution; he would then be anointed with consecrated oil. Nowadays it was called anointing of the sick, but Assumpta's granny had called it extreme unction.

'Mumbo-jumbo,' Assumpta muttered, but at that precise moment her heart wasn't up to mockery.

She sighed and leaned on the van. Belief was all some people had, ill-founded or not, and a solid faith was a rampart against despair. Anybody who denied that was just an idiot. When Assumpta was a student she had devoured accounts of folk customs and tribal beliefs, appreciating their attraction, understanding why it was necessary for them to exist and to be told and retold.

There was one medieval belief she still found haunting. It held that the last moments of life were the most hazardous, because demons and goblins lurked around the deathbed, ready to snatch the unprepared soul as it emerged with the final breath. To be adequately prepared and immune to demons, a soul needed the last-minute attentions of a priest. Nonsense, of course, Assumpta always thought, but the story was still eerily persuasive.

She got into the van and waited out of the wind. When Peter eventually appeared she got out again. There was nothing appropriate she could say, but her silence was some measure of sympathy.

'I should have been there,' Peter said.

'You wouldn't have been, even with your motorbike.'

'Yes I would.'

'No you wouldn't,' she insisted. 'You'd be halfway round Glendalough by now, and that's if you hadn't fallen in.'

'I should have been there.'

'To hear his last confession?'

'Among other things.'

'The confession of a mountainy man?'

Peter didn't catch on. 'Do you think I care – '

'You wouldn't have understood a word that man said. You'd have given him absolution if he'd asked you for a glass of Power's.'

'At least he would have got it.'

This was beginning to annoy Assumpta. 'What difference does 10 minutes make?'

Peter looked at her. 'It makes a difference', he said, 'to his wife.'

He walked past Assumpta and got into the van.

FIVE

There was a good turnout for Peter's first Sunday Mass at St Joseph's. He was gratified by the numbers, but as he stepped up to the pulpit in his green and white vestments he couldn't help noticing that Assumpta was not one of those present. He had no grounds at all for expecting her to be there, but nevertheless he felt disappointed.

At the pulpit he made sure the microphone was switched on, then he waited for the coughing to die down. Brian Quigley, he saw, was sitting right at the back, beside the new confessional.

'Good morning, everybody. My name is Father Clifford – and before I ask you for your prayers for Tommy Hassett, who died last night, I just want to say thank you for making me so welcome.'

He smiled at the rows of attentive faces.

'You don't need me to tell you how beautiful this place is. The hand of God is everywhere – '

Everyone jumped as both doors of the new confessional rumbled open suddenly, stayed like that for a second, then closed again with a thump. Quigley shifted uneasily, his eyes darting everywhere but at the pulpit.

'And if this is his idea of a joke...' Peter said, deadpan, causing a few grins and smothered giggles. He put on a thoughtful look, exaggerating it for dramatic effect. 'On the other hand, maybe he's trying to tell us something. Brian, would you mind just pulling out the plug?'

Everyone in the church turned and watched, relishing Quigley's embarrassment as he got out of his seat, walked to where the power point was situated, pulled the plug and strode back to his seat, glaring at Peter.

Peter nodded. 'Thank you.' To the congregation he said, 'Is this what you want? If it is, say now. It doesn't have to end here. I could order a cappuccino machine. What about a sunbed?'

They looked disconcerted. Brian Quigley was fuming.

'I'll tell you what,' Peter said, 'for every three Hail Mary's, a course of aromatherapy.'

The congregation stared at him. Then the telephone began to ring. Everyone looked round.

'It's all right, Brian,' Peter said, 'I've left the answering machine on.'

Quigley's neck was turning red.

Later, when Mass was over and everyone was filing out of the church, Quigley stopped for a moment beside Peter. 'If it's all the same to you, Father, can we keep jokes out of the Sunday sermon?'

'I wasn't trying to be funny,' Peter assured him.

'Oh, I know what you were trying to do.'

Quigley stalked off. When Peter had said goodbye to the last members of the congregation he went back inside the church and leaned into the confessional. Another sheet of paper was hanging from the fax machine. He tore it off and took it to the light. There was a big printed header as before – *FATTURA* – and the same scattering of figures underneath. This time they were printed extra black, which he assumed was the fax equivalent of a red final demand.

As Peter stared at the paper he had a thought. More than that, he felt: it was a surge of inspiration. It would have occurred to him anyway, but in the circumstances it was focused with great clarity, and he felt a strong urge to act on it. He needed to score moral points to make up for the ones he lost by arriving late at Tommy Hassett's cottage.

Back at the house, he folded the latest invoice in three,

put it in a white envelope and addressed it carefully in capital letters, using his fountain pen. He sealed the envelope and checked the bus timetable. There was a direct service to Wicklow Town at 10.10 am. That gave him time to change into civvies – jeans, a T-shirt and a windcheater – and then gulp down a cup of tea before he caught the bus.

The journey was a miniature adventure of discovery, like the one that had brought him to the area, though it lacked the dramatic content. The bus took the winding road to Wicklow through lush, spring-fresh countryside, past villages, farms and hillside cottages so appealing they looked as if they had been transcribed directly from a children's picture book.

Wicklow Town itself had a cleaned and polished look, and as Peter walked the streets he fancied he caught echoes from a past long before his own. Pressed to be more exact, he would say he felt strong intimations of something uncommonly benign. He decided it must be something to do with the way life was conducted in these parts.

In the cathedral precincts he found his way to the Bishop's house. He walked smartly up to the door, slipped the envelope through the letterbox, and left again without ringing the bell.

He had coffee and a bun at a cafe, then in a town-centre shop selling motorbike accessories he bought a red crash helmet and a pair of motorcycling gloves. An hour and 10 minutes after he had arrived, he caught the next bus back to Ballykissangel.

✟

At 5.30 pm that evening Father Mac paid an unexpected call on Brian Quigley in his offices at the headquarters of Quigley Developments PLC. The building was a discreetly converted two-storey house on a neat little terrace, Quigley's private office looking out over the main street of Ballykissangel.

The office furnishings were basic and strictly functional. The one sign of human warmth was a framed photograph of Quigley and his late wife, with Niamh six years younger than she was now.

When the parish priest walked in, Quigley was at his desk in shirtsleeves, tie loosened, puffing on a cigar. Father Mac took the chair he was offered and came straight to the purpose of his visit.

'Are you out of your mind?' he inquired, sounding serious and rather angry.

'What?'

'You swore to me that this was a gift.'

'What?'

'The confessional.'

Quigley nodded. 'It is.'

'Then what have you invoiced the Bishop for?'

'I haven't invoiced the Bishop.'

'Well the manufacturers have', said Father Mac, 'and he's not a happy man. Especially after all that talk on the television about leather armchairs and air conditioning.'

Quigley rolled his eyes at the ceiling.

'He wants it out, Brian, and if I quote him accurately, "before that chancer Quigley puts advertising on the doors".'

Now Quigley was staring. 'I've only just put it in.'

'You're not listening, Brian.' Father Mac looked grim. 'He wants it out and back in Italy before the paint dries. Capice?'

Father Mac got up and left without saying goodbye. Quigley went to his secretary's office and put his head round the door.

'Marie. That confessional, it's on approval, isn't it? Sale or return?'

She appeared to think for a moment. 'Do the Mafia do that, Mr Quigley?'

He gave her an old-fashioned look.

'I think you took the agreement home,' she said.

He put on his jacket, left the office and got into his Land Rover. His ranch-style house stood in its own extensive grounds a five-minute car journey from the office. As he came down the drive towards the front door he saw Niamh hurrying out carrying a suitcase. Ambrose, in civilian clothes, followed her carrying another bag.

Quigley braked, cut the engine and jumped out. 'What's going on?'

'I don't want an argument, Dad, OK? I'm sorry.'

Again Quigley found himself bewildered. 'What?'

'I'm moving in with Ambrose.'

'What?'

Niamh trotted off. Ambrose paused, smiling nervously.

'It's all right, Mr Quigley,' he said. 'Father Clifford says there shouldn't be a problem.'

Shortly after 6.00 pm Quigley marched into St Joseph's, crossing himself as he went, and strode straight up to the confessional. A man was standing there, waiting for the door to open. As it did, Quigley barged in past him like an aggressive queue-jumper. The door closed behind him. He glared through the grille at Peter, who was sitting with his head back against the wall, eyes closed, waiting to hear the next penitent's confession.

'Did you tell Ambrose Egan it was all right to shack up with my daughter?'

Peter's eyes snapped open. 'Pardon me?'

'Did you – '

'I heard what you said', Peter hissed, 'and please don't raise your voice to me.'

'It's soundproofed. I'm waiting.'

'Then wait outside! This is a confessional!'

'Answer my question,' Quigley snapped.

'Do you want me to call the guards?'

'Ambrose Egan is the guards, and he'll confirm it.'

Peter resisted the urge to shout. 'Please leave,' he said.

There was no response, no hint of movement from the other side of the box. 'Brian, you know I can't discuss another man's confession. Now please, let's talk outside.'

He waited. 'Please!'

'I can't.' Quigley said. His voice was sullen.

'Why?'

'The door won't open.'

'Oh, come on…'

'I'm telling you, the door won't open.'

'Hold on.'

Peter pressed the door button on his side. Nothing happened. He tried it three more times. Still nothing.

'What do you hope to achieve by this?' he asked Quigley.

'I didn't do anything, I swear. It's just a fuse or something.'

'Wonderful,' Peter sighed. 'Well…' he looked about him, '…perhaps we could fax for help.'

There was a pause, then the grille opened. 'I'll give you my card,' Quigley said, passing it through the opening.

Peter took it. Maybe this was the Twilight Zone after all.

✝

It was late evening as Assumpta ran up the hill to join the crowd of onlookers outside St Joseph's. It had to be the best laugh anybody had had up this end of town in years. Even Ambrose Egan, always keen to keep an aloof distance between himself and the rest of the voters, had joined in the hilarity. The source of it all was the raising of the new confessional through the roof of the church on a crane for eventual transportation to a yard where the appropriate heavy machinery could be used to open the doors.

Inside the confessional as it swayed gently on the end of the jib, Brian Quigley provided illumination with his pen torch, shining it through the open grille and lighting up Peter's exasperated features.

'Is the house all right?' Quigley inquired. His tone was diffident.

'The house is fine, Brian, thank you,' Peter said stiffly.

'Only if there's anything you need, you know – '

'I'll let you know.'

'And there's enough turf in the shed?'

'There's plenty of turf in the shed, thank you.'

I heard you needed some transport.'

'Brian.' Peter spoke the name sharply, putting it up like a shutter. 'I'm fine for transport. Oh, and while we're here...'

'Yes?'

'It's just a small thing.'

'Oh no, no,' Quigley said generously, 'go on ahead.'

'Well, when we're in here...'

'Yes?'

'I ask the questions.'

Six

On Tuesday the bus pulled into Ballykissangel right on time at a quarter past midday.
Among the passengers who got off was a stranger, a
young woman in jeans and a windcheater carrying two
zippered bags over her shoulders. She was slim with
large, expressive eyes and unruly dark hair that dropped
down over her forehead.

When the bus moved off she took a slip of paper from
her pocket and read the address on it. Looking around her,
right and left, she stepped into the road a little way, spotted
the bar opposite and put the paper back in her pocket.

In Fitzgerald's, Assumpta was washing glasses and listening to the sporadic conversation at the end of the bar
where Brendan Kearney was studying form in the company of Padraig O'Kelly. Standing between them, bil-
ious-looking and pale, was the vet, Siobhan Mehigan.
She had just ventured a prediction about a horse that
would be running that evening at Fairyhouse.

'Siobhan, would you stop,' Padraig grunted. 'Roxy's
Cracker couldn't win over five furlongs if it set off last
night.'

Brendan nodded. 'Racing tips from a vet,' he muttered, throwing Siobhan a scathing look.

'A vet with a hangover, at that,' Padraig said, laughing.

The young woman who had just got off the bus came
into the bar and stood by the little reception desk.
Assumpta went across, smiling.

'Good afternoon.'

'Hi. My name's Clarke.' The accent was middle-class
English. 'I booked a room.'

'Indeed you did.' Assumpta checked the register. 'Two nights, is that right?' She put a tick on the entry. 'Flying visit, then?'

'Well…'

Assumpta turned the book round and handed the guest a pen. 'Just sign here, would you?' She watched the signature spread confidently along the line. 'Have you come for the scenery?'

'Not exactly, no.' The girl put down the pen and looked squarely at Assumpta. 'I've come for the priest.'

Assumpta could think of no adequate response. She handed over the key and pointed upstairs. The girl thanked her, picked up her bags and went to her room. Assumpta carried on with her chores, wondering.

A few minutes later Miss Clarke came back down and took a stool at the end of the bar near the door. She ordered a coffee, which Assumpta made at the Gaggia. When she brought it she asked if the room was all right.

'Everything's fine, thank you.' Miss Clarke took a sip of the coffee. 'How's he settling in?'

'Father Clifford? I'm not really the one to ask. Not all of us believe in fairy stories.' Assumpta gave a little laugh to soften the remark.

'Do you know where I can find him?'

'Where would Father Peter be now?' Assumpta asked Padraig.

'Above at the park, I heard, taking some exercise with the lads.'

Assumpta nodded. 'Male bonding, is it?'

'I believe they still call it football, Assumpta,' Brendan murmured.

'He has confession at four,' Siobhan put in.

Padraig looked at her. 'He won't want to miss yours.'

Brendan did an impersonation of a bleating sheep, which made Assumpta and Padraig grin, but appeared to depress Siobhan.

'I'll catch up with him later,' the girl told Assumpta. 'No woman comes between him and his football.'

✝

At roughly that moment Peter was dodging from side to side between the goal posts, dressed in black tracksuit bottoms and a grey T-shirt. He was under attack from a clutch of determined young men who snarled and panted a lot as they closed on him. Peter checked his flanks with a swift right and left jerk of the head, then dived forward into the attackers, snatching the soaring ball before they could get their hands on it.

He ran to his left, crouching, sighting his own men. His arms shot forward and the ball flew from his hands. It landed at the pair of feet he had intended and was taken safely into play at the other end of the field.

Peter straightened and wiped the back of a muddy hand across his forehead, trying not to let anyone see how hard he was breathing. He had underestimated the level of fitness required to take part in this kind of conflict. It was Gaelic football, played with 15 men a side. Handling of the ball was permitted, although players were not allowed to throw it. They could dribble with hand or foot, and they could punch or punt the ball toward the opponent's goal. The goal posts extended above the crossbar; a team scored a single point for putting the ball between the posts and over the bar, and three points for putting it under the bar and into the net. It was probably the most taxing and exhilarating game Peter had ever played.

From the sidelines Brian Quigley, wearing a tracksuit, a whistle and a Donegal hat, had just shouted something disparaging to the men who missed their chance to score.

'Learn to move your arse!' he yelled. 'You're not out there to study nature! Put some beef into it – this is football, for God's sake!'

He turned and glared at Ambrose Egan, who was standing beside him in shorts and a football jersey. Ambrose looked openly displeased.

'I suppose you think that was a lucky save,' Quigley said.

Ambrose pointed to where Peter was standing in the goalmouth. 'What's he doing there?'

'He's there because he's keen, because he's good, and because I said so.' Quigley moved close and lowered his voice. 'Have you talked to my daughter yet?'

Ambrose looked flustered.

'Well?'

'No,' Ambrose said, 'not yet. I'm waiting for the right moment.'

A small muscular adjustment turned Quigley's expression into a threat.

'I'll do it, OK?' Ambrose wet his lips. 'Today, definitely,' he promised.

Quigley returned his attention to the game. 'He's good, isn't he, the padre? Lot of bottle.'

Ambrose said nothing. He was scowling at Peter.

'What's the matter?' Quigley demanded. Ambrose kept scowling, saying nothing. Quigley sighed wearily. 'Go on, get out there, make yourself useful.'

Ambrose brightened at once. He ran on to the field and quickly involved himself in a fresh attack on Peter's goal. The flurry of bodies and outstretched arms was perfect cover for sabotage. Ambrose got close to Peter's left side. They leapt for the ball at the same time. At the height of the leap, Ambrose's elbow shot out and connected hard with Peter's ribs.

Peter howled and landed on his back, writhing in pain. Ambrose grabbed the ball and punted it into the net.

Peter got to his knees, then slowly to his feet as the players performed an impromptu victory dance around him.

'Jesus saves,' shouted Timmy-Joe Galvin, 'but Ambrose Egan tucks away the rebound.'

He did a high-five hand slap with Ambrose, who was smiling amiably at Peter.

'I thought this was supposed to be a kick-about,' Peter said, breathing carefully and clutching his ribs.

'That's right, Father,' Timmy-Joe said, 'you got kicked about.'

The others laughed. Ambrose put up his hands, appealing for order. 'Come on now lads, a bit of respect. Are you all right there, Father?'

'I'll live.'

There was a shrill blast from Quigley's whistle as he came on to the field and in among the players. 'Swap over, lads,' he shouted. 'Defenders attack, attackers defend. Thank you Father, we won't be needing you any more.'

'I'm happy to go on,' Peter said.

Quigley stared at him. 'Do you want to see a grown man cry?'

Ambrose stepped forward, grinning. 'Are you after my job, Father, or what?' He took up Peter's place between the posts.

Peter stepped graciously aside and tried not to wince too much as he picked up his sweater and kitbag from behind the goal. As he hobbled away he saw a young man crouching nearby, watching the game. Peter had heard someone call him Edso. He had ginger hair and a beard, both rather long, which gave him a wild look. He was on his hunkers with his arm around a bright-eyed collie, which appeared to be watching the game as intently as he was.

'You'll feel that in the morning,' he said to Peter.

'In the morning?' Peter put the arms of his sweater round his neck and knotted them in front. He winced again as he lowered his arms. 'Aren't you playing?'

'I can wait,' Edso said.

There was a frustrated howl from Quigley as Ambrose let through the ball.

'The Ancient Mariner,' Edso said.

Peter smiled and nodded, recognizing the gag. 'He stoppeth one of three.'

'If that fella threw himself under a bus', Edso said, 'it'd go between his legs.'

Quigley descended on the goalmouth. 'Ambrose,' he shouted, 'are you completely useless or is it a trick of the light? What do you need – an invitation to come for it? You are allowed to challenge for the ball, that's why we put you there.'

'Ambrose probably gave him a parking ticket,' Peter muttered, hobbling away.

He went home, washed painfully but thoroughly, and got into his black suit and dog collar. At the sacristy he swallowed two aspirins with water, then went into the church to take confession.

The first penitent was Siobhan Mehigan, who confessed that last night she'd had a good thirst on her and had indulged it without stint.

'You got drunk,' Peter said.

'My back teeth were afloat.'

'It's nothing to be proud of.'

'I'm not proud of it.'

She paused, began to speak again, then stopped herself. Peter waited. Nothing seemed to be forthcoming.

'Did something happen?' he prompted.

'Yes.' Siobhan sighed. 'I'm sorry, this is embarrassing.'

'Don't be embarrassed. Let me see if I can help. Would I be miles out in saying that you didn't sleep alone?'

'No,' Siobhan said huskily.

'And you're a single woman?'

'Yes.'

'And this person that you slept with – '

'It wasn't a person I slept with, Father, it was a sheep. Several sheep, in fact.'

'Hang on a second…'

'Father, I woke up in a field. I was so drunk I couldn't make it home.'

Peter hoped she didn't catch his smile. 'How do you feel now?'

'Stupid. Hung over.'

'Call it your penance.' Peter raised his right hand and signed through the cross-shaped opening in the partition. 'I forgive you in the name of the Father, the Son, and the Holy Spirit.' He turned and tipped two tablets from his bottle onto his palm and offered them through the opening. 'Here, take a couple of aspirin.'

'Thank you, Father.' Siobhan took then gratefully. 'Will you let me do something for you?'

'Well...'

'A small contribution to the missions.'

'Of course.'

'In the 8.15 at Fairyhouse Roxy's Cracker should go very close.'

✝

After confession Peter decided he should visit the doctor and have him look at his damaged ribs. He entered the waiting room as a young mother was coming out of the surgery carrying her baby.

'Hello,' he said brightly. 'What a beautiful baby.' He bent close to the child. 'Aren't you?' He touched a fingertip to the soft little cheek. 'Don't tell me – he's a boy.'

'A girl,' the mother said.

'I knew it. What's her name?'

'Teresa.'

'Teresa.' The mother seemed impatient. 'I'm sorry, I'm holding you up.'

'I need to get her down.'

'Of course. Goodbye for now.'

When he stepped into the surgery Dr Ryan was talking on the phone. He looked angry. 'Brian, the point is – ' He cut off, pursing his lips, nodding, 'Yes, but – ' Nodding again, 'Yes, yes... ' He brought his head down once, with finality. 'All right. I'll speak to you later.' He put down the phone and looked up. 'That man, I swear... take a seat, Father.'

'What?' Peter sat very carefully.

'Brian Quigley.'

'Oh.'

'He's been dumping organic fertilizer next to a caravan with a young family inside.'

'Organic fertilizer. Is that what I think it is?'

'It is.'

'You mean he's been dumping it deliberately?'

Dr Ryan nodded. 'It's ridiculous. I mean, we're not talking about an encampment, for heaven's sake.'

'Was that her, the woman who just left?'

The doctor nodded. 'She wonders if the odour from the fertilizer might have something to do with her child's cough.' He sighed. 'Now then Father, what can I do for you?'

Peter explained about the football match and the elbow that ramrodded his chest. 'It hurts a lot. I just wondered if you could confirm my ribs haven't been shattered.'

Dr Ryan examined him and concluded that, painful as it was, Peter's injury amounted to no more than severe intercostal bruising. He said he would prescribe painkillers to cover the first few days when the ribs would feel most tender, then the best thing was to let nature take over without further assistance. As Peter put on his shirt again the conversation swung back to Brian Quigley. Peter wanted to know how he came to be connected with the Ballykissangel football team.

'Money,' Dr Ryan said, 'The fiercest bonding material in the world. There's that, and Brian's devotion to the ethics of winning, whatever the odds.'

'So it's Quigley who turns them into a fighting machine?'

'He sponsors the team. And it's his ball.'

'So he gets to be coach.'

'They put up with him bawling at them.'

The doctor wrote out a prescription. As Peter took it he asked if Ryan would like him to have a word with Brian Quigley about the fertilizer.

'I'm sure the family would,' Ryan said.

'No problem. Where is this caravan, anyway?'

'Well it's a fair distance…'

Peter nodded, happily accepting that. Any opportunity to use the newly-acquired bike, and to break in the helmet and gloves, was welcome.

✠

Miss Clarke, the young woman who had come looking for Peter, arrived at St Joseph's shortly after 6.00 pm. Now she wore a long floral skirt and a soft, blue woollen top. At the rear of the church she genuflected, crossed herself and went to sit in the pew by the confessional.

For a time she sat with her head bowed, praying silently, then she stood up and went to the confessional. At the door she stopped, seeing the sign:

CONFESSION:
MONDAY
WEDNESDAY
SATURDAY
4 – 6

She looked at her watch. It was 6.10 pm.

She turned away from the confessional. If she was disappointed, it did not show. She left the church and walked out into the evening sunlight, taking her time, a person in no hurry to do whatever she had come to do.

SEVEN

Baby Teresa's mother was called Frances, and her father was Edso, the bearded man Peter had spoken to at the football match. They lived in a plain, clean, sparsely-furnished caravan parked by the corner of a field toward the north end of Ballykissangel. A few yards from the caravan, on the other side of the fence, was a sizeable pile of manure. The smell was impossible to ignore.

Peter called at the caravan after leaving Dr Ryan's surgery. Edso was not at home. Peter explained to Frances that he was going to speak to Brian Quigley as soon as he could track him down and that in the meantime, if there were any further problems with fertilizer, Frances or Edso should not hesitate to get in touch with Peter.

Frances persuaded Peter to wait, saying that she was sure Edso would soon be home. So Peter stayed and watched Frances put Teresa to bed. As they both looked at the child lying peacefully in the cot, her eyes closing as sleep overtook her, there was the distant rattle of a heavy-duty diesel engine. As it grew louder Frances glanced anxiously at the window. A moment later the door burst open.

'Frances!' It was Edso. He was agitated, pointing out at the field beyond the caravan. 'They're – '

'Will you shut up!' Frances hissed at him. 'I've just put her down!'

'And you think she'll hear me over that?'

The baby began to cough. Edso glared at Peter. 'What's he doing here?'

'He wants to help.'

'Why?'

'He's the curate at Saint Joseph's.'

'And he's going to help us?'

'Oh that's right, go on and insult him.'

Peter watched through the window as Donal and Liam came across the field in a dumper truck laden with steaming manure.

The baby began to howl. Edso turned and ran outside.

'No, Edso! No!' Frances shouted.

Peter went after him. When he got outside Edso was already over the fence, getting ready to square up to Donal and Liam.

'Edso! Edso, don't!' Peter jumped over the fence after him, feeling a pain like a knife being shoved between his ribs. 'Don't! Please don't!'

Instead of taking the expected swing at Liam and Donal, Edso tried to climb up on the truck. Donal started yelling at him. Liam jumped down and tried to pull Edso back on to the ground. The truck stopped and both Donal and Liam piled onto Edso. Donal got a grip on his shirt and drew back his fist, ready to deliver a punch on the ear.

'Don't you dare!' Peter roared.

Frances was leaning over the fence, clutching the baby and shouting at Donal. 'You take your hands off him!'

Donal hesitated. It was Peter who really worried him. He had never seen a priest look that mad. As he backed away, Peter lunged forwards and dragged them both away from Edso. Edso scrambled free and started swinging.

'Edso!' Peter yelled, grabbing his arm. 'Stop it!'

With a sideways snaking movement Edso shrugged Peter off. Peter spread his feet to regain his balance, stepped in the manure, slipped backwards and fell into the reeking pile.

There was a shocked silence as Peter sat up, steam rising off the back of his jacket.

'Father…' Edso came forward and helped him up. 'I'm sorry.'

'I'm sorry, too, Father,' Donal said, 'but this is private property.'

'And this is a young baby', Peter said, pointing to Teresa, 'and you're making her ill!'

Donal looked at the child crying in her mother's arms.

'She lives there,' Peter went on. 'She sleeps there. How would you like it?'

Donal was trying not to look shamefaced. He cleared his throat. 'We have no fight with you, Father.' He nudged Liam. 'Come on.'

They got back on the truck and turned it round. Peter stood with Edso and watched until they were over the brow of the hill.

The smell coming off Peter was terrible. Frances washed the worst of the stains off his windcheater while he cleaned his hands and arms at a bucket of water beside the caravan. As he scrubbed he simultaneously lectured Edso, trying to urge him to get away from the place.

'This can't be good for your daughter.'

'Do you think I'm not aware of that?' Edso said. 'Do you think I want this?'

'Yes you do,' Frances said. She was standing at the door of the caravan. 'You love it. You can't wait for them to come back and make a martyr of you.'

'I didn't start this!' Edso shouted, and inside the caravan baby Teresa started to cry again.

'There,' Frances said flatly. 'Are you proud of yourself? The pair of you?'

She went inside. Edso held up a warning finger to Peter.

'Don't start on me, Father. If I want a sermon I'll come in to you on Sunday.'

Peter sniffed his knuckles. 'You'll be the only one there if I don't get this lot cleaned.' He immersed his hands again and looked at Edso. 'How can this be worth it?'

'We have a right to be here.'

'Why would you want to be here?'

'You haven't been in Ireland long, have you, Father? I suppose you think we've a horse tied up around the back.' Edso shook his head. 'Why wouldn't you? Come to Ireland and hire yourself a lovely red and green caravan with flowers painted around the door. Live the life of a real traveller.' He looked round as his wife came to the door again. 'Ah sure, we love travellers in Ireland, don't we, Frances?'

'We are not travellers,' she said.

'We live in a caravan and we've no work.'

'We are not travellers.'

'Everyone thinks we are,' Edso squatted down beside Peter. 'Listen, Father, I've been traipsing round this country now for five years. I've tried to look for any kind of regular work that might provide a home for us. I've been abused, spat at and worse by my own countrymen. I'm sick of it.'

'I'm sorry,' Peter said.

'*You're* sorry?' Edso stood up.

'You said you had a right to be here,' Peter reminded him.

'The job is over,' Frances said from the doorway of the caravan.

'The contract isn't.' Edso looked at Peter. 'Quigley wanted an extension built. The weather's been good, we finished early.'

'Hang on...'

'We're talking about four weeks, y'know? He promised.'

'It's the principle,' Frances said sourly.

'It's the fact we've nowhere to go,' Edso said bitterly. 'Or have you forgotten that?'

Peter put up a dripping hand, beseeching peace.

'And yes,' Edso said, 'it is the principle.'

In Peter's view these were people with a genuine

grievance. It was hard to believe Edso might be fabricating the things he said, or that he was exaggerating the degree of hardship. As Edso wandered off to attend to something on the back of their lorry, Peter followed Frances inside and watched her soothe the baby.

'How come you're on the road?' he asked her.

'My father needs long-term care. We had to sell our house to pay for it.'

'There was no work at home,' Edso said, coming back. Frances explained he was a builder.

'So you got on your bike,' Peter said.

Frances nodded. 'We don't choose to live like this.'

'You won't find a speck of dirt in here,' Edso said.

Peter sniffed. 'Is that me?'

Edso told him that if he stayed long enough he would get used to it.

'What has Quigley got against you?'

'We're living in a caravan without work,' Edso said. 'We're an eyesore.'

'To whom?'

'To anyone who lives in the holiday homes he's going to build here.'

'When are the houses going up?' Peter said. 'Tonight?'

Edso said Quigley wanted a sales office at this location. 'We're not good for business.'

'And the fertilizer?'

'That's for the flowerbeds and the trees he's going to plant.'

'Oh, right,' said Peter, understanding perfectly.

✟

At dusk Niamh Quigley arrived at a small terraced house in the centre of the town. She was carrying two bags of shopping which she transferred to the crooks of her elbows as she fished out her key. This was Ambrose Egan's house and the key still looked very new.

'Hi, lover!' she called as she let herself in.

She shut the door and walked straight through to the living room, where Ambrose sat reading the paper. He got up and dropped the paper as soon as she swept in. He had taken off his jacket but he was still in uniform, which made him look cold and official in a domestic setting and emphasized his awkwardness as she threw her arms around his neck and kissed him.

She pulled back after a second and stared at him. 'What?' she said, alluding to his lack of enthusiasm.

'Nothing.' He grinned at her. 'It's good to see you.'

She stepped back from him. 'Good to see me? What am I, a distant cousin?'

'Oh, come on...' he grinned again, and the strain was more severe than the first time.

'What's going on?' Niamh said.

'Nothing's going on.' Ambrose shuffled his feet and did his best to meet her stare. 'I was talking to your father...' He watched Niamh's eyes carefully. 'He's entitled to be heard.'

Niamh's lips tightened. She was on the threshold of a silence, or a tirade. It could go either way. Ambrose couldn't take the tension. He forced a showdown.

'Niamh, I'm my own man. You know that.'

She nodded sharply. 'Will I pack now?'

'Niamh.'

'I'm sorry, have I got it wrong?'

Ambrose was wriggling, wondering what happened to his initiative.

'You know your problem, Ambrose? You don't know a good thing when you see it.'

She turned, strode to the kitchen with the shopping and dumped it on the worktop.

'Niamh...' Ambrose came after her, half-angry, half-scared to push this into the territory of a domestic row – a situation where men in his job were sometimes summoned to pull the bloodied parties off each other.

'Was he going to drop you?' she demanded. 'Was he?'

'Now you're being silly.' He stared at her, amazed at the way she could read a situation without having any of the facts. 'I worked hard for my place in that team.'

Niamh let out a sound that managed to cover despair and the thin edge of loathing.

'So what's so bad about getting married?' Ambrose asked her.

'We have been through this.'

'And decided nothing!'

At last Ambrose had control of the situation. He could feel it, he could see it in Niamh's expression. He had control because now he was arguing for something that sang in him, a righteous conviction that he felt through to his marrow.

'We're still arguing and I've had enough of it. So I'm telling you now, Niamh Quigley, either you do the decent thing, or that's it.'

✝

While Niamh was getting her composure back, her father was at home pouring dry ginger into a crystal glass of whiskey held by an unexpected caller, Father Clifford. As Quigley poured, he screwed up his nose discreetly at the smell emanating from his guest.

'Keep pouring,' Peter said as Quigley made to stop.

'Sure I'm drowning it.'

'Did you hear what I said?'

The conversation to that point had been terse and one-sided; Peter had laid down the moral law while Quigley shuffled around his sitting room and shrugged, as if fundamental morality did not apply to him or to anything he did.

'It's no life for a child,' Quigley said now. He put down the ginger ale bottle and went to an easy chair, putting a distance between himself and the odour of Peter's jacket. 'Sure it isn't, Father.' He settled into the upholstery and looked squarely at Peter. 'It's the life they chose.'

'They chose to be homeless? Do you know why they're on the road?' Peter explained about Edso and Frances having to sell their home to raise money for her father's long-term care.

'So what's this got to do with me?'

'You want to get rid of them.'

'Oh, I see.' Quigley nodded, nursing his glass. 'So it's my duty now is it to provide them with a halting site?'

'No. Four weeks. It's all they're asking.'

Quigley snorted. 'Get real, will you? Do you think he'd really leave after four weeks?'

'Well what harm are they doing you?'

'Oho! None at all.' Quigley let out a bitter little laugh. 'I mean, there'll be a great welcome there for the tourists when they turn up for the holiday homes.'

'They're not built yet.'

'I want a sales office there this week. He's in the way.' Suddenly Quigley was too impatient to argue. 'Why am I listening to this? I'm the one that gave him work, or have you forgotten?'

Peter sniffed his drink, which made a change from the miasma surrounding him. 'Brian, that stuff is damaging the baby's health.'

'Then she shouldn't be there.'

'But you said they could stay.'

'Till the end of the job.'

'Till the end of the contract.'

'Father…' Quigley sat forward, his expression on the borderline of menace. 'This is not what we pay you for.'

Peter tasted his drink. 'I don't work for you,' he said.

He had no trouble identifying stalemate when it set in. He left without finishing his drink.

At home he parked the bike and let himself in, banging through the living room, dropping the helmet and gloves, unzipping his jacket and muttering to himself. He hadn't done much good this evening, and he hated a day to end on a down note.

'Temper, temper,' a soft voice said.

He turned and saw a girl in the doorway to the kitchen, the girl who had come looking for him. His face ran through several expressions as he stood staring at her.

'Jennie…'

'You're as sloppy about security here as you were in Manchester. You left the door open.'

He found he couldn't speak. Sensations were colliding in him, a hundred shades of response he had consigned to the dead-and-gone past. Or so he had thought.

'Hi Jennie, it's nice to see you,' she said, her voice gently mocking him for his silence. 'Yeah, it's nice to see you, too.' She sighed. 'I've come a long way. Can I have a hug please?'

Peter didn't move. 'Jennie, what are you doing here?'

'What do you mean, what am I doing here? I came to see you.'

'Why?' He looked deeply uncomfortable. 'I mean…'

'Why?' She tilted her head at him, her eyes troubled, incredulous. 'You ask me why?'

Eight

The bar talk in Fitzgerald's that evening kept moving, as it always did, but on this occasion it didn't stray far from the topic of Father Peter's attractive visitor.

'I'd say she found him, then,' said Padraig.

'I'd say she did,' Assumpta agreed.

'It's a long way to come for spiritual guidance,' Brendan said.

'Ah, come on now, lads…' Padraig put up his hand; 'It's hardly her fault that Manchester's such a godless place.'

Timmy-Joe shook his head. 'Nowhere can be called completely godless that has Eric Cantona.'

Ambrose Egan, out of uniform and looking distinctly brighter since his showdown with Niamh, stepped up to the bar and asked the barmaid, Angela, for a glass of lager. As he waited he looked at Siobhan and grinned. 'Did you get home all right last night?'

Siobhan's silent affront was intensified by someone bleating like a sheep. Brendan turned to Timmy-Joe and asked him if Coach Quigley knew he was in here breaking the curfew.

'A curfew?' Timmy-Joe looked at Brendan as if he was mad. 'For a game against Cilldargan?'

'Quigley's told them all to go out and get langered,' Padraig said. 'He's so confident, he thought it'd make a nice change to celebrate before the match.'

'But to resist the sheep if they possibly could,' Brendan said, pointedly looking at Siobhan, who immediately got off her stool and walked out.

The men burst out laughing.

Ambrose remarked that, at the kick-about, Father Peter hadn't been completely useless, but he seemed to find the game a bit physical. Padraig asked Ambrose if they had given Edso a game.

'What are you talking about?' Ambrose said.

'Maybe you should have given him a game,' Padraig said. 'My young fella saw him having a kick-around after the game. Said he was brilliant.'

Ambrose looked contemptuous. 'A kick-around on his own and he looked brilliant? Have you seen my golf swing, Padraig?'

✝

At the priest's house, the shock of finding Jennie under his own roof had left Peter drained. He still hadn't taken off his jacket and so far they hadn't moved from the middle of the living room, where he had been when she first spoke.

'I think I need a drink,' he said.

'You need a bath.'

'Is it that bad?'

He sat down at the table. Jennie sat opposite and hoisted up a carrier bag from the floor. She took out a few wrapped packets of food and put them on the table. Then she pulled the last item from the bag, a bottle of wine.

She held it aloft. 'Alcohol first?'

She opened it and poured two glasses. Peter drank his faster than was wise or polite and excused himself. 'I can't relax until I've had that bath,' he said, and hurried upstairs.

The truth was that he couldn't relax, or do anything positive, until he'd had time alone to regroup his senses and get some perspective on this event.

In the bath he lay back, letting the heat soothe his bruised ribs and soak the cowshed aroma from his skin.

He closed his eyes, instantly seeing Jennie, her smiling face, her hurt face, her accusing face…

She was the reason he had been assigned to Ballykissangel. No-one, least of all Peter himself, would ever have believed such a step would be necessary. But it had been, and it was undertaken swiftly, in order, as Peter's Bishop in England had put it, 'to preserve the decencies and to rescue a good career threatened with disaster before it was properly begun'.

It had seemed ironic to Peter that he had managed to underestimate the effect that one young woman could have on him. Usually it was other people who underestimated Peter because he looked so young and ingenuous.

In fact, Peter had always been brighter than average for his age. He was the second of five children, their father a first-generation Irish general practitioner who had set up his practice in a northern mill town and stayed there. Peter had gone to a local grammar school where he preferred science to the arts, and football to cricket. He moved comfortably to Cambridge where he studied astronomy. Then, to the delight of his mother, he discovered he had a vocation for the priesthood.

He had gone from Cambridge to the seminary at Allen Hall in London, and from there to Manchester. Soon he distinguished himself as a young priest with decent instincts, a capacity for hard work and an endless, effortless gift for compassion. He was sceptical on certain points of theology, and he had his misgivings about the more inflexible aspects of Catholic doctrine. In particular, he was inclined to believe that individual conscience should have precedence over dogma.

Peter had begun to enjoy his standing in the community. If there was a problem, it was that he was becoming too sure of himself. After nearly three years of uncritical acceptance in Manchester he was ripe for emotional damage. And along it came, in the heart-wrenching shape of Jennie Clarke.

They met at a social function in the church and, because Jennie was attracted to Peter straight away, she made it her business to see that he got adequate chance to start feeling the same way about her. She turned up in his life at every opportunity and, inevitably, he began to fall in love with her.

But the priest in him was strong. So was his idealism. Nothing had yet happened between himself and Jennie, so while that remained the case he forced himself to set his feelings on one side and tell his parish priest the whole story. The matter passed into the hands of the Bishop, who decided to put as much distance between Peter and the inner city as possible. He telephoned a colleague in Ireland, another Bishop with whom he had attended the seminary. This Bishop knew of a curate's position where they'd had little luck holding on to incumbents in recent years.

So the plans were laid. Peter hadn't the time to tell Jennie what was happening before he was transferred to Ballykissangel. He arrived lacking much of his old confidence and self-esteem, but he had felt those qualities were reviving quickly in the new surroundings.

Now, lying back in the cooling bathwater, he felt his assurance begin to fade again. He sat up, telling himself this time there was no room for wavering. He had to be firm. He had to make her see there was no point in pursuing a future that included him.

He dried himself and dressed quickly in a T-shirt, plain trousers and a blue shirt open at the neck. When he went downstairs he could smell cooking. The table was laid. Jennie had even found a candle and stuck it in the neck of an empty Coke bottle.

'That's better,' she said, coming from the kitchen.

'You can tell from there?'

'Yes.'

They stood looking at each other across the room. Peter shook his head slowly. 'Jennie...'

'Peter, don't make me sorry I came.'

He didn't want to be unkind, but he didn't want to back down, either. 'This is a small town...'

'So?'

'You know what I mean.'

'Oh, right. So people don't talk in a big town, yeah?'

'Jennie – what do you want?'

'I want an explanation.'

He watched her take matches from the sideboard and light the candle in the bottle.

'What explanation? I got transferred.'

'Like a footballer.'

'No, not like a footballer.' They sat down at opposite sides of the table. 'With us there's no fee and no choice.'

Jennie poured more wine into both glasses. Peter found something accusing in her silence.

'Once the Bishop says you've got to go – '

'And you're not even allowed to say goodbye?'

'I did say goodbye.'

'From the pulpit. It's not the same thing.'

Peter nodded. 'I know.'

'Or did you have a special relationship with all your female parishioners?'

There was a knock at the door. Peter went and opened it, wincing as he moved too fast and pain stabbed across his ribs. Assumpta was standing outside, cowering under the downpour. Her hair was already soaked.

'Assumpta, come in.'

Jennie turned and stared. Assumpta didn't miss the intensity of the look, or the coldness. She stepped just inside the door.

'I won't stop, Father.' She held up the room key. 'Your friend left this behind. I'd hate her to be locked out on a night like tonight.'

Peter took the key. 'That's very thoughtful of you.'

Jennie turned away again.

'Not at all,' Assumpta said. 'Room service.'

Peter looked from one woman to the other. 'I should have said, Jennie's parents are good friends from England.'

'Is that right?' As Peter squirmed, Assumpta turned back to the door. 'I'd better go. They'll be screaming for pints.' She opened the door. 'Bye.'

Peter closed the door and looked across at Jennie.

'Problem?' she said.

'Not really. It's like I said. It's a small town.'

Jennie got up from the table and went through to the kitchen. A moment later she called to Peter and told him dinner would be ready in five minutes. Just enough time, she added, to open another bottle and let it breathe before they attacked it.

They had grilled fish with steamed green vegetables and boiled potatoes with fresh butter. It was an excellent meal, but Peter kept trying to play that down. The last thing he wanted to do was to make Jennie feel needed.

Halfway through the meal she asked him for his verdict.

'It's all right. I don't see what's wrong with hamburgers, though.'

She made a face and jokily aimed her fork at him. But the humour wasn't there. The mood between them was too solemn to carry a joke.

'Peter, we're going to have to talk about this.'

'I know. How long are you here for?'

She put down her knife and fork. 'I left home.'

'You did what?' Her words chilled Peter. 'And what do they say, your mum and dad?'

'I haven't told them yet.'

'You haven't told them? For God's sake...'

'You never told me you were leaving!'

'I'm not your father.'

'I don't want you to be – '

'And I'm not your lover.'

They looked at each other across the candlelit table. Peter saw her eyes were misty, perhaps with tears she was holding back.

'Nothing happened between us,' he said.

'It was going to,' Jennie said. 'Wasn't it?'

Peter stared at his plate.

'Look at me,' Jennie said. 'It was, wasn't it?'

She reached out and touched Peter's face. Gently, he put his hand on hers. Outside, in the rain, Kathleen Hendley was walking her dog and happened to pass Peter's house at that moment. She glanced through the window and saw the young woman at the table with her hand on Father Clifford's face. Kathleen moved closer, her plastic rainhat dripping, the lines on her face growing deeper as she frowned. She made a sharp mental picture of what she could see. When she was confident that the tableau was clearly registered in her mind, she tutted to herself, shuddered once with indignation, and moved on, the dog trotting at her heel.

Inside, Jennie nodded at the rain-battered window. 'You're not going to send me out in that, are you?'

She got up from the table, looked at Peter for a long moment, then went upstairs. At the top she opened the door to his room and looked inside. In the dim light from the landing she saw his narrow iron bedstead and the crucifix on the wall above it. She went in and sat on the bed, clasped her hands in her lap, and waited.

Downstairs, Peter stared at the congealing remains of his dinner on the plate before him. After a while he poured another glass of wine and sipped it slowly, thinking. He took another sip, and another, then put down the glass. He stood up, went to the light switch by the door and turned it off. Only the flame of the half-burned candle lit the room now, throwing wavering shadows on the walls. Peter leaned over it and blew it out.

Sitting on the bed, Jennie heard him moving. She clasped her hands tighter. There was a moment of shuffling sound, then silence. She waited, straining her ears, her breath unsteady, tremulous.

Then she heard the front door close. She got up and

looked through the window. Peter was outside, buttoning his jacket. She watched as he turned up his collar and hurried away. So much effort, she thought, so much struggle against her own sense of what was proper, and all for what? She stood there for a long time, not feeling the cold, willing herself not to cry.

✝

A few miles away, in the pouring rain, Edso was out by the side of his caravan, shovelling the pile of manure from the corner of the field onto the back of his flat-bed truck. It was hard, punishing work but he attacked it like a demon, breathing through his mouth to minimize the stink, moving to a rhythmic drumbeat in his head.

Frances came out to plead with him, not for the first time that night.

'Please, Edso! Don't do it!'

'Get away from me!' he yelled, without breaking his pace. 'Go on! Get back inside!'

She went and he carried on, spadeful by spadeful, and within half an hour he had finished the job. The reeking mound of dung was now gone from the field and was piled like a hayrick on the back of the truck.

Edso wiped his hands on a rag, shook his sopping hair from his eyes and got into the cab. He started up, seeing Frances at the window of the caravan. He waved briefly to her and drove off.

Twenty minutes later the truck freewheeled almost soundlessly down the neat winding path that led to Brian Quigley's home. Edso pulled up by the side of the house, got out of the cab, climbed up on the back of the truck and began shovelling again, transferring the manure from the truck to a spot adjacent to Quigley's curtained patio doors.

Inside, Quigley had just eaten a good meal all by himself. He was now on to the brandy, having seen off a bottle of Valpolicella with his main course and a half-bottle of Sauternes with the pudding. On the hi-fi one of his favourite albums was playing at full belt – the BeeGees' 'Saturday Night Fever'.

As Edso laboured a couple of yards beyond the windows, making the mound on the patio grow at an impressive rate, Quigley got up from the table and did a small dance step to the music. On a tricky heel-and-toe manoeuvre one foot got caught under the other. He toppled into an armchair without spilling a drop of the brandy.

He leaned back and smiled. It had not been a bad evening, if he discounted the visit from Father Peter. A couple of hours earlier his darling Niamh had returned home from her brief bout of living in sin with Ambrose. She had flounced into her room without giving an explanation. The important thing, however, was that she had come back.

And now all this. A grand dinner, fine wine, great brandy, and his very favourite music on the turntable, all of it enjoyed in the comfort of his lovely home. What more could a fella ask for?

Outside, as the rain got heavier, Edso finished transferring manure for the second time that evening. He stood for a minute on the back of his empty truck, savouring his creation, a gigantic pile of ripe muck, creatively placed slap-bang in the middle of the patio where it would achieve maximum impact.

Finally, when he had done enough savouring for one night, Edso got down off the truck, leapt into the cab and drove away, smiling for the first time in days.

✝

When Peter arrived at Fitzgerald's the late racing results were being flashed up on the television. In the 8.15 at Fairyhouse, Roxy's Cracker had romped in first at eight to one.

'That'll shut them up,' Assumpta told Peter. 'Siobhan gave them a tip and they wish they'd taken it.'

Peter remembered the tip being offered in the confessional, but at the moment it was the least of his concerns.

'What can I do for you?' Assumpta asked.

'I need a room.'

She sensed his embarrassment. 'I'm not sure we've got one.' She went to the register.

'Jennie...Miss Clarke won't be using hers,' Peter said.

'I have the key.'

As he headed for the stairs Assumpta asked him if he was all right.

He paused. 'I'm fine,' he said, and walked on up.

NINE

Early next morning, Brian Quigley, wrapped in his dressing gown and with a bowl of cereal in his hand, drew open his patio door to behold a horrifying sight which, a second later, was accompanied by a matching smell.

'Mother of Jayz…'

He staggered back inside, his cereal forgotten. He dressed in a frenzy and less than 10 minutes after leaving the house he was in town, pounding with the side of his bunched fist on Liam's front door.

A weary, sunken-eyed figure appeared at an upstairs window.

'Liam?' Quigley glared up at him. 'Get your arse down here. I've got work for you. And give Donal a ring!'

Minutes later Assumpta was on the street in front of Fitzgerald's, shouting up at the room Peter had occupied for the night. She had already tried banging on the door. Now, as she shouted his name over and over, Peter came to the window, still half-asleep.

'Message for you, Father,' she said. 'Something about a dumper truck…'

Peter was dressed and out on the street in no time. He ran all the way home, put on his helmet and was astride the Honda, revving it up, when Jennie appeared at the door.

'Peter…'

'I can't, Jennie. Not now.'

He drove off, leaving her staring at his exhaust fumes.

By the time he arrived at the caravan, Edso was standing in the field holding a baseball bat, ready to defend himself as a dumper truck laden with steaming manure was driven towards him.

Peter cut the bike engine, pulled off his helmet and leapt over the fence. By then the dumper had stopped in front of Edso. On the other side of the piled dung were Quigley, Donal and Liam, staring at him. The hydraulic jack cut in and the container began to tip towards Edso. The weight of the manure shifted ominously, threatening to spill over the front.

'Brian!' Peter shouted. 'Turn that thing off!'

Either Brian chose to ignore him, or couldn't hear for the noise of the engine. The dumper continued to angle upwards, its load sliding forward, ready to smother Edso. Peter, furious now, clambered onto the truck on the driver's side and turned off the ignition. He jumped down again and walked up close to Edso. Frances had appeared behind them, holding the baby.

'Edso,' Peter said, 'there will be no dumping here today. You have my word. Now please leave before he calls the guards. You're trespassing.'

'So are you,' Quigley snarled.

Peter ignored him. 'Edso, please.'

Edso reluctantly turned and climbed back over the fence. Peter immediately took up his place in front of the dumper.

'Come on now, Father,' Donal said, 'We don't want any trouble.'

'There'll be no trouble,' Peter told him. 'But if you're going to dump that, you're going to have to dump it on me.'

'I've no problem with that,' Quigley said. 'Start her up.'

The engine fired again and turned over, but Donal was reluctant to operate the dumper. Quigley grabbed the handle himself and started the hydraulic ram. The container tilted up sharply, then began its steady tilt forward, the manure shifting again to the front edge.

Peter stood his ground. His eyes were locked on Quigley's as the angle of the container got steeper and steeper. Donal and Liam were looking away, clearly distressed. The load began to slide as the container neared the top of its incline. Peter stared at Quigley. Quigley stared back. The load surged forward, ready to spill.

Quigley cut the hydraulic ram. It settled back again, taking the container down with it. Without a word, Donal spun the steering wheel and the truck turned around. A moment later it was trundling away again across the field.

Peter climbed back over the fence. Frances thanked him for what he did.

'I don't think I've done you any favours,' he said.

'You took a stand, Father,' Edso said. 'A lot wouldn't.'

Peter sighed. 'You still want to stay here?'

'Or go where?'

Peter shrugged. 'I don't know.'

'You think it might be different somewhere else?' Edso said.

'Well, there might be more work.'

'Mending kettles, right?'

Peter was at a loss for a suggestion. 'Surely at least renting somewhere... '

'Even renting you need a deposit,' Frances said.

Peter looked at her, sensing the hopelessness, seeing at last the brick wall she and Edso had come up against for so long.

✝

Later, as he prepared his sermon notes in the sacristy, there was a knock at the door.

'Come in.'

It was Jennie. 'This is getting to be a habit,' she said.

'What's that?'

'You just disappearing.'

'Jennie...'

'Still, at least last night it was your decision.'

'To leave?' Peter put down his notes. 'Jennie, it was my decision to leave the first time.'

'What?' She appeared to be on the verge of understanding, but was unwilling to go one step further to grasp what he was saying to her.

'It was me who asked for a transfer. I wanted to put some distance between us.'

'You wanted to?' She looked hurt. 'Like this is my fault? You told me I was special. You made me feel special. What was the point? What were you trying to do?'

'I don't know.'

She was staring at him, still wanting an answer. He thought hard, trying to see honestly what had been happening back there in Manchester.

'Have it both ways, I don't know,' he said. 'I wasn't thinking, I was feeling. These were feelings, not thoughts. Not logical or sensible, just powerful feelings.'

Jennie moved closer. 'What feelings? Feelings for me? For a woman's body?'

'Jennie, please…' Peter stepped back from her.

'I need to know.'

'Stop, please…'

'You're ashamed of them?'

He nodded. 'Yes.'

'I bet you put them into words for your confessor.'

'I tried to do the right thing.'

'You ran away,' she said angrily.

'I'd have ruined your life!'

She stared at him. 'My life?'

'Our lives.'

The telephone rang. Peter picked it up. It was Father Mac. He sounded displeased. He told Peter he wanted to see him in his house at Cilldargan straight away.

Peter hung up. 'I have to go.'

He took his jacket from the hook on the door and put it on. They looked at each other for a second. Peter tried to think of something else to say, but couldn't. He left. Jennie stood in the doorway, watching him disappear once again on his bike

Moments later, riding down the main street, he saw Assumpta washing the windows at Fitzgerald's. He stopped.

'Thank you for last night,' he said. 'What do I owe you?'

'Forget it.'

'Thank you.'

'Your friend paid up front.' Assumpta stopped rubbing the window and turned to him. 'Your boss rang here.'

'I know.'

'If I were you I'd plead the fifth.'

It was hard to say how much she knew; she had probably surmised trouble from the frost in Father Mac's tone. Peter revved the engine, swung right and drove off across the bridge to Cilldargan.

As soon as he arrived the housekeeper ushered him into the study. Father Mac was at his desk, hands resting on top, looking as solemn as a cardinal. He told Peter to take a seat, then he came directly to the point. A parishioner had reported that Father Clifford had been observed, through the window of his own house, behaving improperly with a young woman.

Peter felt himself turn cold. 'Who told you that?'

'Someone who has the Church's best interests at heart,' Father Mac said. 'Is it true?'

'No, it isn't!' Peter realized he had shouted. He paused to take a grip on himself. 'Yes, I had a visitor last night. And yes, she stayed the night. I didn't.'

One of Father Mac's eyebrows lifted in silent query.

'I went to Fitzgerald's,' Peter said.

'You spent the night in a public bar?'

'Father, my accuser can't have it both ways. An old friend turned up unexpectedly. I couldn't put her out in the pouring rain, so I turned myself out. The only woman I spent the night with was Assumpta Fitzgerald.'

Father Mac scowled at that.

'It was a joke,' Peter explained.

'Father, that kind of joke stopped being funny in this country when people realized it was actually happening.'

'Yes, Father.'

'And the sight of painted women – as it was put to me – cavorting round the curate's house at midnight...'

'What?'

'...does nothing to dispel people's prejudice.'

Peter shook his head. It would have been easy to let himself feel stunned by this. Or outraged.

'I expect high standards of my curate, Father, and there are still some of my parishioners who do, too.'

'With respect, Father...' Peter hung on to his temper, knowing there was no gain in turning blustery, '... you have a right to expect high standards of me, but a man who makes a young family's life a misery selling holiday homes does not.'

'What?'

'I presume it was Brian Quigley who came to you.'

'Brian Quigley?' Father Mac looked puzzled. 'What are you talking about? Anyway, it's not Brian Quigley who owns that field. It's Assumpta Fitzgerald.'

✝

Peter's first stop when he left Cilldargan was Fitzgerald's, where he found Assumpta in the kitchen making sandwiches for the lunchtime trade. He confronted her with what Father Mac had told him and she didn't deny it. The field was hers. Which meant, Peter said, that the tribulations of Edso, Frances and young Teresa could be justifiably blamed on Assumpta Fitzgerald.

'What are you telling me?' she said. 'That it's my doing?'

'Well it's your field, you must know about it.'

'I know about it,' she nodded. 'I hired them.'

'Liam and Donal?'

'Yeah.'

'Ah, well.' Peter folded his arms. He was almost shaking with indignation. 'You must be proud of them; they won't let a small child get in the way.'

'Now look…'

'Please go on.'

'I heard what they did,' Assumpta said, 'but I didn't ask them to do it.'

'What?'

'Nobody did. They were using their initiative.'

Peter nodded. 'That lets you off the hook, doesn't it?'

Assumpta rounded on him. 'How dare you!'

'Well who's going to stick up for these people?'

'Why should you? It's none of your business. That field is my lifeline.'

Peter followed her through to the bar. There were only two customers, old men sitting at opposite ends of the bar.

'Is this place losing money?' Peter asked.

'My finances are none of your business.' She put down plates and cutlery on the back shelf. 'Look around you. The 12 apostles would be a full house around here.'

'You wouldn't let them in, would you?'

'Out of season,' Assumpta said, 'I'd let the Pope in.'

She went back to the kitchen. Peter followed her again. The anger that had flared between them was gone. Assumpta simply looked fed up. She laid out slices of bread on the table and began buttering them.

'Quigley wants the field to build holiday homes,' she said, 'but he doesn't want it with a caravan next door.'

'So?'

'So I asked Liam and Donal to make them an offer.'

'What kind of offer?'

'I said I'd pay them to move on. They refused. The boys decided to up the ante.'

'I see.'

Assumpta stopped what she was doing and looked at

Peter. 'Understand, Father, sooner or later Quigley would have had them out anyway, with a sore head and an empty pocket.'

'They'd live in a house if they could,' Peter said.

'Not on the kind of money I was offering them.'

Siobhan came into the bar. Assumpta went through to serve her. Penance was still the order of the day with Siobhan, as much on account of her shaking hands as her loss of self-esteem, and she asked Assumpta for a mineral water.

'Congratulations,' Peter said, coming round to the front of the bar beside Siobhan.

'What for?' she said.

'Roxy's Cracker.'

'Did you back it?'

He shook his head sadly. 'I wish I had.'

'Never mind, Father.' Siobhan handed over her money and lifted her glass. 'You'll know the next time.'

'I certainly will.'

Siobhan tasted the fizzy water and made a face. She looked at Peter. 'I believe the lads are awful cocky about this afternoon.'

'They can't lose, apparently.'

The outcome of the match between Ballykissangel and Cilldargan was a foregone conclusion, according to every opinion Peter had heard or canvassed. Winning this one was simply a matter of tradition for Ballykissangel.

'Is that right?' Siobhan's tone, and her expression, suggested she might favour another point of view.

'What? Cilldargan can beat them?'

'There's only two teams playing,' Siobhan said.

'And one of them hasn't won for 20 years.'

'They weren't good enough.'

Peter was intrigued now. So was Assumpta. They both stared at Siobhan.

'And they are now?' Peter said.

Siobhan shrugged. 'Quigley doesn't think so.'

'But you do.'

'I can't see into the future, Father,' she said coyly.

'You can see far enough for me. How easy would it be to get a bet on?'

'Easy as waking up with a sheep.'

Peter looked across the bar. 'Assumpta?'

'What?' She was playing defensively dumb, even though she knew it wouldn't help her.

'The money you were going to offer…'

'I know what you meant.'

'All they need is a deposit.'

'By backing Cilldargan?' she tried to look amused.

'They'll be a big price,' Siobhan pointed out.

Assumpta nodded. 'But they can't win.'

'Your call,' Siobhan said.

She put her hands on the bar and waited. So did Peter. Assumpta looked deeply unhappy.

TEN

As the lunchtime trade began to
warm up Peter decided it was time to leave Fitzgerald's.
He was halfway to the door when the phone rang. He
waited. Assumpta picked up the receiver. It was Brian
Quigley; he asked for Father Clifford. Assumpta covered
the mouthpiece and mouthed 'Quigley' at Peter. He
shook his head.

'Sorry Brian, there's no sign of him in the bar.' She listened for a minute then put down the phone and relayed
Quigley's summons. 'He wants to see you up at his
house, whenever you can find the time.'

Peter thanked her, winked at Siobhan, and left. Sitting
outside astride the bike he considered what he should do
next. He decided it would be as well to get the visit to
Quigley over with.

At Quigley's house Niamh let him in.

'How's the bruising?' she asked as she showed him
along the hall.

'What?' he touched the side of his chest. 'Oh, I'd forgotten about that. It's terrible. How's Ambrose?'

'I think I'm going to have to marry him.'

'That'll be nice.'

'Yeah,' she said glumly, 'won't it?' She pointed to the
sitting-room door. 'Dad's inside.'

She went upstairs. Peter ran a hand across his short
hair, not sure what kind of reception to expect. He
tapped the door and went in.

'Ah, Father Clifford.' Quigley made the greeting
sound cordial. 'Thanks for coming. Can I get you a
drink?'

Peter declined. He said he could only stay a few minutes. Quigley, he noticed, was already making inroads on a large whiskey.

'That's a pity. Never mind.' Quigley paused to top up his drink, then stood in front of Peter.

'I have two things to say to you. That business up at the field…'

'Yes?'

'It's no business of yours. Understand that, it doesn't concern you. I think you'll find Father Mac would agree with me.'

Peter caught the warning and smiled. 'Uh-huh?'

'Second, my reserve goalkeeper's been injured, a pig trod on his foot. How would you like to deputize?'

'Me?'

'Well…' Quigley shrugged with one shoulder. 'You'll only be keeping the bench warm but sure, what harm? I've seen worse.'

Peter reflected that although every life was crowded with ironies, a priest experienced more than anybody else.

'What do you say, then?'

Peter nodded. 'I'll be there if I'm needed.'

When he got back home Jennie was still there, sitting in the kitchen. She made a pot of tea while Peter went upstairs and washed his hands. When he came down again she poured two cups.

They sat opposite each other at the kitchen table.

'I keep walking out on you,' Peter said.

She nodded. 'You'd think I could take a hint.'

'I'm sorry.' He drank the tea, watching her over the rim of the cup.

'I'm leaving,' she said. 'I'm going home. I made a mistake and now I know.'

'Painful way to find out.'

'No-one asked me to come here.'

'That doesn't make it your fault. When are you going?'

'The bus leaves after the match.' She picked up her cup and put it down again. 'Will you see me off?'

'You know I will.'

☩

By 2.00 pm the road to the playing field was thick with people making their way to the match. Siobhan and Assumpta walked together, wrapped up warm against the wind, Assumpta wearing a black beret pulled down across her forehead. As they neared the entrance to the field, Peter jogged up beside them looking decidedly unpriestly in his tracksuit.

'All set?' said Siobhan.

'Oh yes.'

Assumpta was amused by his athletic performance. 'Are you hoping for the call, or what?'

'Well…'

'You do realize, Father,' said Siobhan, 'it'd be very bad form for you to be seen shouting for the away side?'

'I'll try not to.'

'And I think it would look very odd if you were not to cheer on the home side's successes.'

Assumpta frowned. 'But there won't be any home success, will there, Siobhan?'

'I never forced you to have a bet,' Siobhan said.

Peter and Assumpta swapped nervous glances.

'This is for the best, isn't it?' Peter murmured.

'I'm taking advice from a priest,' Assumpta said. She sounded alarmed at herself.

The three of them stood near the Portakabin where the players changed. As the Ballykissangel team came out, Peter and Assumpta applauded politely while Siobhan roared and shouted and jumped up and down. When Brian Quigley walked past, cheering on the team, he turned to Peter and said, 'I don't think we'll be needing your prayers today, Father.'

'You won't be getting them,' Assumpta said, but quietly.

The Cilldargan team ran on to the pitch and Peter noticed straight away that one of the players was Edso. Quigley had noticed too. The only one who didn't look surprised to see him was Siobhan.

The match got under way. Ballykissangel went straight to the attack and within a minute they had scored the first point. That delighted the bulk of the crowd, including Siobhan. Assumpta and Peter remained silent.

Siobhan looked at them and laughed. 'What's the matter with you?' she said. 'It's only a point.'

'I know,' Peter said.

'And a goal is worth three points.'

'I know.' The crowd roared again. 'And they've just scored another one.'

'We, Father, we,' Siobhan shouted above the noise. 'We're the home side.'

'Right.' Peter leaned close to Siobhan. 'Did you, er, have a bet yourself?'

She stared at him. 'Against my own side? What do you take me for? But don't worry, *you're* on.'

Twenty minutes in, the tide of the game began to shift. Cilldargan were on the offensive, with Edso leading the fray. Assumpta began to get carried away.

'Go on, Cilldargan!' she yelled, then realized what she had done. She saw Quigley staring at her, amazed. 'Go on, the underdog!' she shouted, mending where she could.

Out on the field, in spite of a momentary surge from the opposing side, Ballykissangel scored another point, putting them three up. Peter and Assumpta applauded, exchanging miserable glances.

As the game progressed, with one cause for despair piling up on another, they dropped even the pretence of support. Ballykissangel scored point after point, and although Edso played a skilful game on the Cilldargan side, he didn't have the backup he needed to make a dent in the opposition.

'It's nine–nil,' Peter told Assumpta.

'I know, I know…'

Then there appeared to be a change, a serious one this time, as Edso, angry, began to jink, duck and weave, flanked by team-mates who were covering his every move and feint. All of a sudden the ball shot away from Edso at speed, whizzed past Ambrose and hit the back of the Ballykissangel net.

'A goal!' Assumpta squealed. 'That's three points!'

'I know,' Peter said, trying to look as mystified as Quigley was by her behaviour.

Then Edso scored another goal. Assumpta nearly took off. Siobhan yanked her down and muttered to her to cool it.

A few feet away Padraig was going berserk. 'Ambrose! You're thick!' he yelled. 'You might as well leave the ball in the net – it'll save you the trouble of taking it out next time!'

Niamh was standing beside him looking peeved. 'He's doing his best,' she said.

Padraig glared at her. 'Doing his best? The last time Cilldargan scored against us, Jesus Christ was a carpenter. Now he's after letting two in!' He moved closer to Niamh, frowning at her. 'Have you two had a fight?'

Niamh stomped off. Brendan sidled across and asked Padraig if he had ever thought about taking up counselling.

Assumpta meanwhile was trying to cover her joy at Edso's performance, but at that moment he sent the ball soaring over the bar and between the posts, earning Cilldargan another point.

'One more goal', Peter muttered, 'and Cilldargan are in the lead.'

Suddenly there was high drama on the field of play. Edso and Ambrose went up to punch the ball simultaneously and Ambrose came down in agony. Quigley was outraged. So was the crowd. Following a minute of confusion around the goalmouth, Ambrose was helped off the field by Quigley and Timmy-Joe Galvin.

As they trotted past, Quigley shouted. 'Father! You wanted to play, come on, you're playing.' He jerked his thumb at the goal posts.

Assumpta stared at Peter. 'What's this?'

'I'm the reserve goalkeeper.'

She nodded. 'That's handy.'

'No way. Assumpta…' Peter pulled off his tracksuit. 'This is different.'

She stared at him, horrified. 'What? This is my money we're talking about here!'

'Assumpta, I can't throw a game. What do you take me for?'

'Have you forgotten what this is about?' Assumpta pointed across the field to where Frances was standing, holding Teresa. 'Do you want that woman and her child to live in a caravan for the rest of their lives?'

Peter stared back at her.

'All right,' she said, 'I want to sell my field. What's so bad about that?'

'Are you two quite finished?' Quigley demanded. He slapped Peter on the shoulder, urging him on to the field. 'Go on, make a name for yourself.'

Peter took up his position in goal to a ripple of good-natured applause. Within a minute of the game restarting he stopped a high ball cleanly and cancelled a dangerous cross. He caught one straight shot at goal from Edso and swiped the ball out of another attacker's line of approach. Assumpta watched, getting really grumpy as the crowd around her cheered the priest's performance.

And then Peter brought down an opposing forward. The referee declared a foul and came along and pointed to the spot. Edso lined up to take the spot kick.

'I'm impressed,' Siobhan said to Assumpta.

Assumpta made a face. 'It hasn't gone in yet.'

Edso walked back for his run-up. Peter glanced at

Assumpta, who glared back. Quigley gave Peter two thumbs up. Peter squatted, facing the oncoming Edso, committing himself to a dive a split second before Edso's boot hit the ball. It came rushing for the net, perfectly aimed to land in the corner. Peter unfolded like a gazelle and sent the ball wide of the post.

The crowd went crazy, roaring and cheering. Then, quick as a shift in the wind, the roars turned to bawling outrage as the referee blew his whistle and demanded another spot kick. In the teeth of torrential complaint he stood his ground: the keeper, he said, had moved before the kick was made.

There was nothing else for it. Edso lined up to take the kick again. This time Peter remained motionless until the ball left the ground, then he sprang sideways, correctly predicting the ball's line of travel. But it scraped the tips of his fingers and landed in the back of the net.

Assumpta couldn't help herself. She was up on her feet, punching the air, squealing with ecstasy until she noticed everybody was watching her.

'Bad luck, Father,' she shouted weakly, just as the final whistle blew.

✝

Fitzgerald's was packed after the match. Ambrose accepted condolences for his twisted ankle while Peter was praised for a very brave effort. 'Just think if we'd had God on our side,' Padraig said.

Peter ordered a pint and tried to look disapproving as Assumpta, pulling the beer, gave him her warmest congratulations. 'Brilliant,' she said. 'I'm lost in admiration.'

'The ball went in,' he reminded her.

'I know. Brilliant.'

He joined the others at the top end of the bar and heard Timmy-Joe Galvin announce that the bookies had been offering odds of four-to-one for Cilldargan to win.

'And do you know something else?' Timmy-Joe said. 'That Edso only played senior football in Kerry.'

'So', Brendan said drily, 'he fell on hard times before he got here.'

Peter turned to Siobhan, who was standing next to him. 'How did you know?' he asked her quietly.

'I saw him play when I practiced in Tralee. I didn't think he was *that* good...'

Peter looked at his watch suddenly. 'Excuse me,' he said, putting down his pint on the bar. 'I'll be back in a second.'

He ran outside and across the road, where the bus was about to leave. Jennie was standing by the open door, her bags on her shoulders again.

'Well, goodbye,' she said, as Peter reached her. 'It was still nice to see you.'

'And you.' His expression was a mute apology.

'You'll know next time,' Jennie said, climbing the step into the bus.

'I'm a priest.'

'There'll be a next time,' she said, and turned away. He saw her get into her seat, then he stood back and watched the bus as it pulled away.

When it was gone he turned and walked back across the road to Fitzgerald's. Before, it had been hard to put Jennie from his mind. Now, he realized, it would be even harder to forget the last thing she had said to him.

Eleven

Brian Quigley had given Niamh a lift to St Joseph's, where she and Ambrose had an appointment with Father Peter to discuss the arrangements for their wedding the following Saturday. On the way to the church, Quigley and his daughter argued and, when they got out at St Joseph's, they were still arguing. Up on the roof, hoisting the stone effigy of a saint's head on a rope pulley, Timmy-Joe Galvin chuckled as he worked, listening to every bitter word from below.

'Are you out of your mind?' Niamh shouted as she got out of the Land Rover. 'I mean, what are you having? A mid-life crisis?'

Quigley got out the other side. 'What are you talking about?'

'That's what it looks like to me!' Niamh stamped across to the church door.

'What?' Quigley followed her 'Because I'm seeing an old friend?'

Niamh turned on him. 'An old girlfriend!'

'So it's an old girlfriend. So what?'

'You haven't seen her in 20 years.'

'Twenty-five. What's your problem?'

Niamh flounced into the church, leaving her father standing at the door.

In the sacristy, Peter was reading to Ambrose from the Wedding Book. The matter of a suitable text to provide a theme for the service had to be decided and Peter was trying out First Corinthians, 13:11. Ambrose, in police uniform with his hat on his knees, sat glumly sucking a boiled sweet.

'When I was a child,' Peter read, 'I spake as a child, I understood as a child, I thought as a child: but when I became a man – '

Niamh came in. 'Sorry I'm late, Father.' She took off her coat. 'Carry on.'

She sat beside Ambrose, who had caught her grim expression and hadn't chanced so much as a smile.

'...but when I became a man, I put away childish things.'

Niamh frowned at Ambrose. 'Are you eating a sweet?'

He looked at her, startled. 'What?'

Niamh held out her hand. 'Give it.'

'What?'

'Give it.'

Ambrose, like a scolded child, let the sweet fall from his mouth into her hand. Niamh dropped it in a bin by the table and sighed like an exasperated parent.

'Anyway...' Peter closed the big book and put it down. 'It's very beautiful and a lot of couples choose it.'

'We'll have it,' Niamh snapped.

'Er, right.' Peter forced a smile. 'Marriage, they tell me, is a bit trickier...'

The atmosphere in the room was terrible, and it was all being generated by Niamh, whose darker moods, Peter had noted, could effectively override any other. He battled on.

'...But I won't insult your intelligence by asking if you're both sure you know what you're doing – '

'That's a relief,' Niamh said. 'Are we done?'

'Um, well...' Peter looked about him for a moment. 'Yes, I suppose so.'

Niamh stood and Ambrose dutifully did the same.

'Just think,' Peter said, determined to brighten the pair of them, 'this time next Saturday, you'll be wondering why you stayed single so long. Isn't that right, Ambrose?'

'Tis a lonesome wash doesn't have a man's shirt in it,

right enough,' Ambrose said, with no discernible enthusiasm. He did an apologetic little shrug as they left.

✝

That same morning, at the highest point of the mountain closest to Ballykissangel, Donal and Liam were putting the finishing touches to a small hut. The weather was never warm at that height, so to sustain body heat and to get the job over as soon as possible, they both worked with unusual speed.

'How are you, boys?'

Liam turned and saw Eamonn, the region's oldest hill farmer, standing on the slope, leaning on his crook.

'Hello there, Eamonn. How's it going?'

'Fine, fine.'

Eamonn had the proportions and the clothing of a scarecrow. His years in the hills had dulled him and he had never been known for his sunny disposition, but that morning he was a shade more baleful than usual. Beside him was a sour-faced man in long wellingtons, carrying a clipboard. Liam guessed he was the reason for the added gloom.

'Can we help you?' Donal asked.

'We were looking for sheep,' the man with the clipboard said.

Donal nodded, catching on. 'Is that right?'

'Mr McKenna here's from the Inspectorate,' Eamonn explained.

'Well, I'll tell you, now,' Liam said, improvising, 'we must have passed around 50 or 60 of them on the way up, isn't that right, Donal?'

'Easily,' said Donal, who had caught on too.

McKenna gave them a bleak look. 'With the herd of wildebeest, were they?'

Liam looked blank. 'What?'

'Nothing.'

Eamonn and McKenna moved on. They walked

another 100 yards over uneven terrain then Eamonn stopped again, leaning on his crook, catching his breath.

'Incredible,' McKenna said, looking at the bare hill-sides around them. 'It never ceases to amaze me.'

'What?'

'How the natural camouflage of these creatures hides them entirely from view.'

Eamonn did not catch the irony. 'We're looking for sheep,' he said, refreshing the inspector's memory.

'Yes.'

They walked on for another 10 minutes. Suddenly Eamonn stopped and pointed. 'There's one.'

'We've already counted that one.'

'Ah no, look. That fella has a limp.'

McKenna sighed. 'Tired himself out, no doubt?'

'What?'

'Trying to be in so many places at once.'

'What?'

'Nothing.'

✝

Meanwhile Peter had left the church and gone for a stroll. He saw Brendan Kearney fishing on the bank of the river and went down to stand beside him. Brendan was always a good source of local intelligence and straight away he told Peter that there was an Inspectorate man in town – or, more accurately, up the local mountain – to take a tally of old Eamonn's sheep.

'And will they find his sheep?' Peter said.

'Well that very much depends on what you mean by find.' Brendan jiggled his rod, making the bright red float bob in the water. 'They'll turn up, they always do. Not necessarily on the day the inspector comes to count them, though. You know sheep – in their own time. On paper.'

'Excuse me?'

'It's one of the European Union's more civilized ideas.

To pay hill farmers like Eamonn a small consideration for each head of sheep.'

'They pay him for his sheep?'

'They pay him to keep his sheep. A small subsidy.'

'Why?'

'Because he wouldn't survive without it. Neither would many of the mountainy men.'

Peter was getting the idea. 'And the more sheep he has, the greater the subsidy?'

'Which is why it takes so long to count them.'

'Right.' Peter smiled.

With one more fish in the box on the back of his bike, Brendan decided he had enough for the time being. Peter walked back up through the town with him. As they passed Fitzgerald's, Assumpta was outside having an altercation with the brewery rep, a young man called Walter Dargan. She was trying to make Walter understand that she had only one customer who drank draught stout, and until the tourist season came around it didn't make sense for her to throw away money buying barrels of the stuff.

'You can't do this,' Dargan said.

'Why not?'

'I don't know.' He shrugged. 'Treason.'

'Walter,' Assumpta said, 'I'll tell you once more. When the tourist season comes round I'll have another think, but until then…'

She signed the delivery note on his clipboard and slapped the board against his chest. He snatched it and went off in a huff.

Peter and Brendan carried on up the hill towards the church gates where, at that moment, Ambrose was warning Padraig O'Kelly that if he didn't control his goat, which kept getting loose and running around the town, he would lock him up.

Padraig had just caught the goat by the church railings and was winding its leash around his hand.

'How often do I have to tell you?' Ambrose yelled.

'I'm sorry, Guard, it's the young fella,' said Padraig.

'You're his father. You're responsible.'

'I've tried telling him – a goat is for life, not just for Christmas.'

Padraig hurried away, scarcely in control of the animal as it pulled him across the road. Ambrose went to where his official blue-and-white police car was parked by the church. He got in and put the key in the ignition.

Two things then happened more or less simultaneously. Up on the church roof, Timmy-Joe Galvin was manoeuvring the stone saint's head towards its appointed place on the parapet. He used the pulley rope to move the heavy sculpture into position and, as he swung it towards him, he saw something out of the corner of his eye. Looking down, he saw a mouse sniffing around his sandwiches. He turned, stamped his foot and the mouse ran away. In that instant, preoccupied with the possible contamination of his lunch, Timmy-Joe slackened his grip on the pulley rope. The heavy sculpture began to drop and, when Timmy-Joe grabbed the rope, it burnt his hands. He jumped back, helpless, as the saint's head hurtled downwards, struck a maintenance catwalk, bounced once and continued to fall.

The second thing that happened was that Padraig's goat got away from him again. It cut back towards the church and ran right past the police car. Ambrose saw the goat, got out of the car and ran a couple of yards in front of it. He stopped and opened his mouth to yell at Padraig. In that instant the saint's head plummeted down and crashed through the roof of the police car. It landed in the driver's seat.

Ten yards away Peter and Brendan heard the crash and saw what had happened.

'Mother of God!'

Brendan dropped his bike and ran. Peter was right behind him. They found Ambrose staring at the car. On the roof, Timmy-Joe was calling, asking if Ambrose was all right. Peter and Brendan asked him the same thing.

'Sure he's in shock,' Brendan said. 'I'll call a doctor.'

'I don't need a doctor. I'm fine. OK?' Ambrose took a step nearer the car, looking at the impassive saint lying in his seat. 'It isn't even chipped,' he said.

Peter looked carefully at Ambrose. The young guard was smiling. Brendan looked at Peter. They both looked at Ambrose again and watched as he crossed to door of the church and went inside.

Peter went looking for Niamh. He found her in Fitzgerald's, at the far end of the bar, deep in conversation with Assumpta. Peter stood and waited until they noticed him, then he smiled brightly, so brightly that both women knew something was wrong.

'What?' Assumpta said.

'It's nothing to worry about.' He came to the bar. 'Assumpta, will you do me a sandwich?'

'What colour?'

'Fresh.'

'Oh cute.' She went to the kitchen.

Peter sat down beside Niamh. 'OK.' He clasped his hands and tried to look reassuring. 'Ambrose's car has had an accident.'

'What?'

'It's all right, he wasn't in it. No-one was hurt.' Peter tried to hold Niamh's gaze, but her expression was so aggressively querulous that his eyes kept darting away.

'What do you mean?'

'Well, something fell on it, but like I said, he wasn't in it. He's up at Saint Joseph's. Giving thanks.'

'What's he giving thanks for?'

'Well...'

Niamh frowned hard for a second and came up with her own answer. 'He just got out.'

'He's a lucky man,' Peter said.

Niamh was pensive for a while, gazing at her twined

fingers. Then she looked up. 'Father, would you do something for me?'

'Of course.'

'Will you talk to my father?'

✝

Peter called at Quigley's house that afternoon. It was a sunny day, already quite warm, and Quigley suggested they sit in the garden. When they were settled with glasses of beer, Quigley said he had no trouble guessing why his daughter had asked a priest to talk to him.

'She thinks I'm being disrespectful to her mother.'

'Has she said that?'

'No, not to me.' Quigley shrugged. He always knew what was being said about him, whoever was saying it.

'Your wife died what, five years ago?'

'Five years and six months.'

'Right. And this woman you're seeing –'

'I'm not seeing her. I haven't seen her for 25 years. I'm hoping to meet her again.'

'On the mountain,' Peter said.

'On the mountain, yes.' Quigley had even taken the trouble to get a little hut built up there. His men should have finished it by now. 'It's where we arranged to meet.'

'Twenty-five years ago,' Peter said flatly.

Quigley took a postcard from his pocket and tossed it to Peter. It was a view of Belfast city centre. There was writing on the back, a round, clear longhand: 'How could I forget? Rosarie'.

'Look…' Quigley leaned forward, gesturing with his beer glass. 'I was crazy about her. I was 18. I asked her to marry me. After she stopped laughing she kissed me.' Quigley sat back in his chair. 'We spent a lot of time up on the mountain. Even Father Mac couldn't follow us up there. Have you ever been up?'

Peter shook his head.

'There's be just you and Eamonn's sheep. Anyway, we

were up there one evening, not a breath of wind or a wisp of a cloud. We were lying on our backs and, I remember, as the sun was sinking down into Ballykay, our feet had haloes. Our toes were glowing with holiness, which was more than could be said for the rest of us. Anyway I said to her, we must never lose this, what we have here, right now, this moment.'

'What did she say?'

Quigley smiled. 'She said I was drunk. Maybe I was, but I meant it. I said to her if ever we split up – if you find someone, if all this falls apart or whatever – can we agree now to give ourselves a second chance?'

'To meet up on the mountain?'

'That's right. Same time, same place. If we split up. And she said, "Brian, the only way we're ever going to split up is if you leave me. And if you do that, you'll break my heart".'

'And obviously you did split up.'

Quigley nodded, and for once Peter saw him look vulnerable, like a man temporarily lost.

'I fell in love with Niamh's mother.'

Twelve

Niamh was leaning on the end of the bar in Fitzgerald's, explaining a portion of her family history so that Siobhan could better understand her predicament. The way she recounted it, the meeting of her father and mother was a match ordained by angels.

'And then he married her and they had me.'

Siobhan exchanged a tired look with Assumpta, then asked Niamh, 'So what happened to the other one, Rosarie?'

'She went up to uni at Belfast and never came back.'

'So what's your problem?'

'She's coming back now.'

'So what?'

Assumpta winked at Siobhan. 'She's afraid of a double wedding.'

Niamh glared at Assumpta, her mouth working behind pursed lips.

'Oh, come on,' Assumpta said, smiling, shrugging, signalling it was only a quip.

Niamh turned from the bar and walked out. Assumpta groaned. A fault of Niamh's, one of several, was her inability either to see a joke or to take one. As the door banged shut behind her, the other door opened and Brendan walked in. Assumpta groaned again, quieter this time, getting ready for trouble.

'What can I get you?'

Brendan stared at her. 'The usual, of course.'

'It's off,' she said.

He nodded patiently. 'Well, change the barrel. I can wait.'

'There is no barrel. Not of your usual.'

'What?' He stared again, this time with his mouth open.

'I don't have it,' Assumpta said. 'There's no call for it. Nobody drinks it.'

There was a tense silence now in the bar.

'I drink it,' Brendan said.

'Apart from you.' Assumpta waved her hand. 'Look around you. It's all American lager and diet cola.'

'So?'

'So that's what I have to keep in the cellar.'

Brendan put both hands flat on the bar and lowered his head for a moment. When he looked up he had the appearance of a man who had arrived, with some surprise, at the end of his tether.

'Assumpta. I don't want the beer that made Milwaukee famous, I want my usual.' He slapped the bar and his voice rose. 'I want my cultural inheritance! I want the drink that defines my country!'

'Give him a pot of tea, so,' said Siobhan.

Assumpta leaned across the bar and looked up at Brendan's angry face. 'I don't have it,' she said firmly.

Meanwhile, at the top end of the town, Peter came away from the church relieved that Ambrose had finally given up his marathon session of thanksgiving by the altar. At one point, when he had been there for more than an hour, Peter had touched him on the shoulder and told him it was enough, he should go home and rest after his ordeal. Ambrose had politely asked to be left alone. A few times after that Peter looked out of the sacristy to find Ambrose still there, on his knees, with head bowed and hands clasped at his breast.

Now at last he was gone. Peter decided to go home, make a pot of tea and perhaps catch up on his reading. As he approached the house he saw he had a visitor. Ambrose was sitting on the doorstep.

Peter drew close, cautiously. Ambrose looked as if he was suffering. 'Are you OK?'

Ambrose stood up, dusting the seat of his trousers. He took a deep breath and held it.

'Ambrose?'

'I… I can't go through with it, Father.'

'Excuse me?'

'I can't get married. The wedding's off.'

'Come with me.'

Peter took him into the house and led him to a chair at the kitchen table. Ambrose sat there saying nothing, staring at the window. Peter made a pot of tea, stirred it to hurry it along, and poured two cups.

'Come on, now…' Peter sat down opposite Ambrose. 'It can't be that bad.'

Ambrose smiled weakly.

'Look, I think I know what's behind this, but let me go through the motions anyway.'

Ambrose shrugged.

'You're already married.'

'I am not.'

'Good. You have some terrible disease.'

'I do not.'

'Right, Now we're getting down to it…'

'Father, please…' Ambrose was recoiling from this approach. 'I'm not like other men.'

'I was coming to that,' Peter said. 'You're gay.'

'What?'

'I didn't think so. Which leaves the big one. God has spared you for a purpose.'

'Don't make fun of me, Father.'

'Am I wrong?'

Ambrose shook his head. 'No.'

'And is this purpose what prevents you getting married?'

Ambrose was silent. He reached out slowly and touched the black leather cover of Peter's missal where it lay on the table.

'Ambrose.' Peter was shocked. 'You can't be serious.'

'I have a vocation, Father.'

'You want to be a priest?'

'I do.'

'You don't.'

'I do.'

'You don't. Take it from me.'

'I do. I wish I didn't, but I do.'

'You don't!'

✝

Back in Fitzgerald's, Brendan had grouchily accommo-dated Assumpta's suggestion that he try his favourite stout in bottled form. Padraig and Siobhan watched from the end of the bar as he poured the drink, picked up the glass, examined it suspiciously at eye level, then sipped. He waited a moment, sipped again.

'Assumpta, for pity's sake.' He put down the glass.

'What?'

'This.'

'What?' She came forward. 'It's your usual, isn't it?'

'It's bottled.' Brendan made it sound like a felony. 'It doesn't taste the same. I don't like it.'

The door opened and Eamonn the hill farmer came in.

'Here he is,' Padraig said. 'The Sicilian bandit.'

'Did you see him off, Eamonn?' Assumpta asked him.

The old man stepped up to the bar. 'Diet Coke please, Assumpta.'

'Doesn't he always see them off?' Siobhan muttered to Padraig. 'Back to Brussels in despair.'

Padraig said, 'Have you any idea, Eamonn, how much you're costing the European Union?'

Eamonn pulled himself to his full 5 foot 5 inches and tilted back his head, giving himself a shabby hauteur. 'The sheep are there for him to count,' he said. 'If he doesn't have eyes to see, I can't be to blame for it.'

He picked up his Diet Coke and took it to a table in the corner by the window.

'Well...' Padraig shook his head slowly, 'I wouldn't feel so confident, Eamonn. Seeing off a bureaucrat is one thing, but modern technology's another.'

'What are you talking about?' When Eamonn's curiosity was caught, which was not often, he was inclined to pursue a topic until he knew enough about it to ignore it again.

'He means a sheepdog that can count,' Assumpta said.

'I mean a satellite that can count,' Padraig said, and now Eamonn really was hooked. He stared at Padraig.

'A satellite that can count sheep?' Siobhan feigned wonderment.

'How does it stay awake?' Assumpta said.

'I mean,' Padraig said darkly, looking over his shoulder at Eamonn, 'a satellite that can count the warts on your nose.'

'Thank God he doesn't get an allowance for the warts,' Brendan muttered, still huffy about his stout. 'Otherwise the country'd be bankrupt.'

'He knows what I mean.'

Padraig went on to describe a satellite system of such intricacy and power that it could differentiate between sheep and any other creature, including man. It could, furthermore, make a tally of all the sheep it saw, complete with map references, and transmit the findings to its masters at the Commission of the European Community.

'That's fantastic,' Siobhan said. 'Are you sure you got it right?'

'I'm only saying what I read in the paper,' Padraig told her. 'Apparently the satellite's already up there.'

'But sure, what has all this got to do with Eamonn?'

'Ah, stop teasing him, would you?' Assumpta said. She picked up Brendan's nearly full glass. 'Finished?'

Eamonn was staring fixedly at Padraig. He was gripped. The miraculous concept had been planted and the worry was beginning to set in.

'And these satellites count them from the sky?' he said, getting the terrible picture fixed in his mind.

'As clear as day,' Padraig said. 'And if they can't see them, they're not there.'

Eamonn clasped his hands around his glass and considered that. Few people there had ever seen him look so alert, or so troubled.

✠

Brian Quigley strode alone up the mountain, keeping a careful pace, pausing every few minutes to look up and see how far he was from his new hut. He wore jeans, stout walking boots and a good weatherproof coat. His hat was pushed down firmly on his head and on his back he had a canvas bag with a blanket, sandwiches and a flask of coffee. The walking was tough; as the mountain got steeper it got tougher, but he strode on with vigour and more bright hope in him than he thought he would ever feel again.

When he finally reached the hut he paused outside to catch his breath. The hills were suddenly full of significance for him, they were the mute repository of memories, of long-ago passions that could, perhaps, be reborn.

He stepped into the hut. The first thing he noticed was the television set, mounted on a bracket high in the corner by the window, just as he had directed Liam to position it. The second thing he saw was Ambrose, in his guard's uniform, sitting in the opposite corner.

'What are you doing here?'

'I needed some space.'

'Glad I could be of help,' Quigley unslung the bag from his back. 'What for?'

'It's a bit personal, Mr Quigley.'

'Pre-wedding nerves, is it?'

Ambrose hesitated. 'Yeah.'

'Only natural,' Quigley unbuckled the bag. 'Don't worry about it.'

'No.'

Quigley paused with the bag half-open. He looked at Ambrose. 'Don't worry about it here, anyway.'

It took a second to sink in. Ambrose stood up. 'No,' he said. 'Right.'

Quigley waited. Ambrose went to the door, nodded an awkward farewell and left. Quigley resumed what he was doing. He unpacked his blanket, sandwiches and flask, preparing for the wait that he hoped, fervently, would not be too long.

As Ambrose half-marched, half-ran back down the mountain, intent now on making a clean breast of it with Niamh, Peter and Father Mac were nearing the top of a ladder outside St Joseph's. On the way up they discussed the novelty of Ambrose's call to the service of God.

'Well, I don't say it isn't tragic,' said Father Mac, stepping gingerly onto the walkway around the parapet. 'But better he abandons her for the Church than another woman.'

He walked along the parapet with Peter behind him, stopping by the newly positioned effigy that had precipitated the change in Ambrose.

'Father,' Peter said, 'this is not a good idea.'

'If he has a vocation, he has a vocation.'

'He doesn't have a vocation. He just thinks he does.'

They studied the vacuous expression on the saint's face. Father Mac turned to Peter.

'You can read his mind, can you?'

'Father, he *thinks* he has a vocation because he was nearly pulverized by the stone head of Saint John the Evangelist, the patron saint of priests.'

Father Mac nodded. 'So you think that he should carry on as if nothing ever happened.'

'I think four hours on his knees is probably sufficient.'

'And he doesn't.'

'No.'

'So what it comes down to is this: that you know his mind better than he does.'

'No.' Peter said it doubtfully; then, more certainly, 'Yes.'

'Did you know that we have a shortage of priests in Ireland? Can you imagine a thing like that? A vocation needs to be tested. Put under pressure.'

Peter gazed out over Ballykissangel, spread like a picture below them. 'Niamh won't take this lying down,' he said.

It was not a remark that called for great powers of prophesy. Niamh did take the news badly. She couldn't have been more incensed if Ambrose had told her he was going off with the lady traffic warden from Cilldargan. She stood in her father's sitting room absorbing the news, her eyes darting from side to side, making Ambrose afraid she was looking for something expensive to smash.

Finally her narrowed eyes settled on him. 'You're dumping me for God?'

'I'm alive because of him.'

'You're alive because a piece of concrete didn't hit you.'

'Niamh…' Ambrose stepped closer to her. 'I know this isn't easy. It isn't easy for me.'

'What? You're asking me to feel sorry for you?'

'No. Just…try and understand.'

'Understand?' She looked at him aghast. 'I might have understood if the bloody thing had struck you, but it missed!'

'And it was no accident!'

'Ambrose.' Niamh's voice struck a note of serious warning. 'Don't do this.'

'I have no choice.'

'Look at me, Ambrose. You have a choice.'

He seemed to cower under the pressure of his own conviction. 'Do you think I don't…' He reached out a hand to her. 'Niamh, please…'

'Don't.' She moved aside from his touch. 'All of a sudden, Ambrose, you make my father look mature.'

✞

Up on the mountain, the evening faded by purple stages into night. In his hut, Brian Quigley sat wrapped in his blanket, staring at the half-eaten remains of his last sandwich. He had stopped rising to look out of the window every 10 minutes when at last all he could see was his own pallid reflection in the lamplight.

He sighed and chucked the sandwich in its crumpled foil wrapper into the corner. Getting out his portable telephone, he tapped in Liam's home number and put the phone to his ear. 'Liam? Brian Quigley. I'm in the hut. Could you get up here?' He frowned, listening. 'Now,' he snapped, and switched it off.

THIRTEEN

Late that same evening when Peter let himself into the back kitchen at Fitzgerald's, Assumpta was comforting the sobbing Niamh, rocking her in her arms like a baby.

'It's all right, it's all right,' Assumpta crooned, 'I know, I know…'

'Niamh,' Peter hovered by the door. 'I'm so sorry.'

She ignored him. Assumpta looked at him with open distaste.

He spread his arms helplessly. 'You don't think this was my idea?'

'You, your stupid church,' she hissed. 'What's the difference?'

Peter went back to the bar. He was in time to catch a surge of merriment that centred on Ambrose feeling the call to holy orders.

'Ambrose! A priest!' Siobhan howled, tears of laughter glistening.

'And him already an ayatollah!' Padraig said, setting off a fresh wave of hilarity.

'It's not funny, Padraig,' Peter said, because he felt he should.

'Indeed it isn't,' Siobhan nodded, laughing all the same. 'The state of poor Niamh…'

Peter made for the door. Eamonn shuffled after him and touched his arm. 'Father, could I have a word?'

'Sure.'

'Am I right, you're an educated man?'

'Well, yeah…'

'All right.' Eamonn stepped closer. 'Is it true then that

satellites can see the warts on your nose – if they have a mind to?'

'Well, I don't know about the warts on your nose, but something the size of, oh, a sheep, maybe...'

'Thank you, Father,' Eamonn said, suddenly preoccupied. He walked out ahead of Peter.

'You're welcome,' Peter said, baffled.

In the meantime, Brian Quigley had arrived back home, leaving Liam in the hut with instructions to call him the moment a woman by the name of Rosarie appeared on the scene.

In the sitting room Quigley poured himself a stiff whiskey. He swallowed a mouthful to counteract the cold he believed had seeped into his bones. Then he tip-toed upstairs, humming cautiously as he went, hoping his daughter might condescend to talk to him now that she'd had time to accommodate the idea of him having feelings for a woman other than her mother.

'Niamh?' He tapped the bedroom door. 'Niamh?'

He put his ear to the door, then opened it a fraction. He looked in. She wasn't there. He registered the tidi-ness of the room, the bed undisturbed even though the clock showed it was nearly midnight. He turned and closed the door sharply.

He went back downstairs, stood for a moment to gulp more whiskey, and stared at the black rectangle of the window. His mind was racing, darkening. A thought occurred. He slammed down his glass, even though there was still plenty of whiskey in it, and got his coat.

At Fitzgerald's, Niamh was at a table in the corner of the bar, being watched over by Assumpta and Siobhan.

'I don't care any more,' Niamh was saying, her elbow on the table, hand supporting her chin. She had taken a lot to drink and her speech was slurred. 'I don't care if he becomes a priest or a publican, I want nothing to do with him.'

'Nothing wrong with being a publican,' Assumpta said.

Niamh looked at her unsteadily. 'I didn't mean – '

'Ah, shuddup.'

'Shame about the reception,' Siobhan observed.

Niamh blinked slowly, taking that in. 'There'll be a reception,' she announced.

Assumpta and Siobhan looked at each other.

'I want my reception.' Niamh's voice had climbed suddenly, almost to a shout.

Assumpta tried to be soothing. 'Niamh…'

'I want my reception! I want to be able to say thank you to my friends who gave us presents, then give them back…'

'Niamh…'

'And then I'd like to dance, and get drunk, and fall over.'

'Hardly a wedding reception,' Assumpta said.

The remark appeared to inspire Niamh. 'That's what it'll be called. Hardly a Wedding Reception.'

'Come on.' Assumpta stood up. 'We'll talk about it tomorrow. Up to bed.'

'What?'

'You're not going home to an empty house.'

'I haven't finished my drink.'

Before Niamh could reach for her glass Siobhan had picked it up and swallowed the contents. Niamh glared at her, her head wobbling.

'That's not very nice,' she muttered. 'I don't think I'll be inviting you to my reception.'

'Come on.'

Niamh allowed herself to be led away to bed. When Assumpta came down the stairs 10 minutes later, Peter was waiting.

'Is she all right?' he asked.

'She's asleep, anyway.'

Peter nodded, smiling. They stood awkwardly, a couple of yards apart.

'What I said to you before,' Assumpta said, 'I…I was out of line.'

'No problem.'

'You know what this is all about, don't you?'

'What?'

'With Ambrose.'

'Well,' Peter said, 'I know what he's told me.'

'Yeah. That's what he's made himself believe, but it's not the real reason.'

'No?'

'He's lost his bottle,' Assumpta said. 'He's been pushing like mad to get Niamh to the altar, and now she's agreed, suddenly he's thinking, hang on, I'm getting married.'

Peter shook his head. He couldn't buy that.

'Bet I'm right,' Assumpta said.

There was some kind of disturbance outside. Peter and Assumpta went through to the bar. Voices were being raised in the street and there was the sound of feet running. Peter made to go to the door.

'Let the guard sort it out,' Assumpta told him. 'He's not a priest yet.'

The door opened and Siobhan came in. 'Father,' she said, jerking a thumb over her shoulder, 'if you wouldn't mind...'

Assumpta tutted. 'Let Ambrose deal with it.'

Siobhan spread her arms. 'It's Ambrose that's being throttled.'

Peter went out, looked along the street and ran to Ambrose's house. Quigley had Ambrose out through the a ground-floor window in his pyjamas. His head was through the railings and Quigley was choking him. The onlookers were telling Quigley to stop, but they looked amused.

'Brian, Brian...stop!' Peter pulled at Quigley's shoulders, trying to prize his grunting bulk away from the gagging and spluttering Ambrose. 'Get off him! You'll kill him!'

With the help of some of the men from the pub Peter managed to get Brian separated from his prey.

'It's all right,' Ambrose said, as soon as he could speak again. 'It's all right, he has every right.'

'Oh, Ambrose...' Peter glared at him.

Quigley was snarling, held fast in an armlock by two of the pub regulars. 'When I'm finished with him,' he warned Peter, 'I'm coming for you.'

'No you're not,' Peter told him. 'You're going home to bed. And keep the noise down before you wake up your daughter.'

'Where is she?'

'Assumpta's looking after her.'

The fight went out of Quigley. 'All right,' he muttered as the lads released him. 'All right.'

He did a full slow turn, making placating gestures with his hands. He stood and watched as Ambrose was helped back through the window into his house.

'Come on, Brian.' Peter slapped Quigley on the shoulder. 'I'll walk you home.'

✟

Shortly after 9.00 am the following morning a red saloon car drew up outside Fitzgerald's. It was driven by the brewery rep, Walter Dargan. He got out and went straight to the bar. Assumpta's expression, the second she saw him, transmitted the fact that she knew he was here to raise the matter of the cancelled stout order; he could also tell she had not shifted her stance.

'I'm asking you to change your mind,' Dargan said.

'Why?'

'Because I think you're acting precipitously.'

'Precipitously.' Assumpta looked at him carefully, taking in his smooth suit and his geometrically tidy hair, performing the appraisal slowly enough to make him feel uncomfortable. 'So you think I should wait until I have no customers who want the stuff instead of just one – has Brendan Kearney been on to you?'

'Please,' Dargan said, 'I understand how you feel.'

'Oh, good.'

'The thing is, there's a public relations problem here.'

'Well let him drink bottled, I still have that.'

'For us,' Dargan said, his voice rising. 'A problem for us, not for him. If it ever got out that an Irish pub had stopped taking draught – ' He stopped sharply, getting hold of himself. 'So I have a proposition for you. We'll give you the stuff.'

'What?' Assumpta was astounded.

'Only until the tourist season starts. After that it's back to normal, OK?'

Assumpta did a slow shrug. 'OK.'

The deal was done. Dargan relaxed visibly.

'Can I get you something?'

He nodded. 'Give me a Bud.'

✝

Later, as Assumpta worked through her paperwork at the reception desk, Niamh came down the stairs slowly, hanging on to the banister. She looked as if she had been beaten up.

'Did you sleep all right?'

'I don't know. I was unconscious.' She came and leaned on the desk. 'Did I have a lot to drink?'

'Oh, yes,' Assumpta whispered. 'Will I make you a sandwich?'

Niamh shuddered. 'No thanks.' She ran her tongue across her teeth and palate, trying to dampen her mouth and stop the clicking when she spoke. 'About the reception...'

'No, no,' Assumpta said, putting up a hand. 'Forget it.'

'I don't want to forget it,' Niamh said. 'I meant it. I want it.'

She clasped her hands across her stomach suddenly and groaned.

'Not on the carpet,' Assumpta warned. She took a

careful look at her friend and decided that hungover
and ill as Niamh was, she had definitely made up her
mind.

FOURTEEN

The day wore on towards the time when Niamh and Ambrose would have been wed, and for a few local people this was turning out to be a distinctly unusual Saturday. For Liam, still in the hut up on the mountain and doing press-ups on the wooden floor to retain warmth and sanity, it was a day when his need for a sighting of the mysterious Rosarie had become as intense as Brian Quigley's.

For Eamonn, the hill farmer, it was a day of unbroken toil, out in his crude workshop, sawing and hammering hour after hour. Since talking to young Father Clifford in the bar, Eamonn had decided there was no time to waste; his project was top priority. The work must be seen through to its end, fatigue or no fatigue, before he allowed himself the luxury of standing on a hillside and staring into space, which was one of his chief recreations.

For Brian Quigley it was a day of coming to terms. Father Peter had explained about Ambrose's sudden access to grace, and Quigley accepted that Niamh would not now be getting married. He also accepted, though with less equanimity, that his long-lost Rosarie might not appear after all. He would not abandon hope, though, nor vigilance. Not as long as Liam was able to look out of a window across a mountainside.

For Ambrose, because he had cancelled his wedding leave, it was a day of duty as usual, but he couldn't help but see this day as one more strangeness to complicate his view of life. Just walking along the main street was rather unnerving. From being an accepted part of the background of everyday life in Ballykissangel, he was suddenly the object of special attention, a curiosity, a man apart who had changed considerably in the eyes of his neighbours. From being Ambrose the self-important functionary, Ambrose the strictly-by-the-book policeman, Ambrose the uncomplicated young man, he had become variously Ambrose the deep one, Ambrose the breacher of promise and Ambrose the eejit.

Outside Fitzgerald's he saw a transit van with bright lettering on the side:

IRELAND'S HIT FACTORY
U3
ONE UP ON THE REST

A number of young musicians were hauling their equipment out of the van and taking it into the bar.

It was impossible for Ambrose to miss the signs, puzzling as they were: preparations for the reception – an event slated to be financed by Brian Quigley – appeared to be going ahead. Through the windows of the bar he could see streamers being put up, and the caterers were parked behind the band's vehicle, unloading trays of cakes and sausage rolls, and one man was carrying what was unmistakably a wedding cake.

Guests were coming to town, too, carloads of them, dressed up and wearing flowers. Many of them Ambrose recognized from photographs he had seen in Niamh's family albums and in her packets of holiday snapshots. A festive rhythm was building up around him and Ambrose couldn't ignore the certainty of what was happening. A wedding reception was set to roll and wedding guests were turning up to attend it, even though there was no longer going to be a wedding. A strange, queer day.

From across the road Peter saw Ambrose walking slowly along, his uniform well-pressed and his buttons shiny as ever, looking as if he had recently emerged from anaesthesia. Peter had never seen him look so stunned, so obviously detached from people and what they did. It was a toss-up whether to go after Ambrose with a dose of moral uplift, or to leave him and let his turmoil grind on to its outcome. Peter opted for leaving him alone. He went into Fitzgerald's instead.

The band was setting up under a big banner that said 'HARDLY A WEDDING RECEPTION'. Women were laying out trestle tables and Assumpta was on a stepladder, attaching crepe-paper garlands to a light fitting. Peter stood and watched her for a while. Finally she acknowledged him and asked why he looked so dismal. He told her he did not think this was a good idea.

'You know, Father, the days are gone when a priest could just think something and it would happen.'

'You're over-reacting,' he told her.

'You're over-reaching.'

'All I said was, I didn't think this was a good idea.'

Niamh appeared from the kitchen. She wore jeans and a loose denim shirt. She looked fresh and completely recovered.

'What's going on?' she asked, getting up on a chair to tie more garlands by the door.

'Niamh…' Peter put a touch of pleading in his voice.

'Are you coming tonight, Father?' she asked lightly, a laugh away from hysteria.

'Is this really what you want?' he said.

'Why not?'

'A reception without a wedding?'

Niamh used two thumbs to push in a drawing pin. She glanced at Peter. 'Where am I going to get a husband at this notice?'

'I don't want you to get hurt,' Peter said. 'I don't want Ambrose to be hurt.'

Assumpta glared at him. 'Ambrose?'

Peter glared back. 'He's very confused.'

✝

By late afternoon, the bar was beginning to fill up.

Padraig and Siobhan were at their usual places. When Brendan came in they listened carefully to hear what he would ask for, but as he stepped up to the bar Assumpta pulled him a cream-headed pint of his usual.

He smiled at her, and at the pint sitting on the bar before him. 'Would you look at that...'

He picked up the glass, took one deep swallow and sighed. As he took the second Brian Quigley came in.

'A pint of the same please, Assumpta.' He nodded at Brendan's drink. 'Last time I had a pint of that stuff,' he said, turning briefly to make a public announcement of it, 'was the day my daughter was born.' As Assumpta pulled the stout Quigley slapped the bar. 'Right!' he said. 'The tab starts now.'

Assumpta opened her till book. At the top of the left page she wrote 'BRIAN'S TAB' and at the top of the opposite page she put 'STOUT'.

Day wore into night. People drank, talked, laughed a great deal, sang, danced and drank some more. There was food on the tables and plenty of women on hand to make sure nobody drank more than a few mouthfuls without putting some padding in them to absorb it. At the head of the longest table stood the three-tiered wedding cake; the sugar bride and groom were in their traditional place on top, except that the groom was upside-down with his head buried in the icing.

Brian Quigley tried hard to join in and look cheerful, but his daughter's predicament was breaking his heart, and there didn't seem much prospect of Rosarie showing up to lighten his gloom. Peter got himself into a corner where he could talk and keep an eye on Niamh. She sat at a table at the back of the room with other women, looking her prettiest in a new dress, talking, steadily drinking, noticeably subdued.

Out in the darkness, up in the chill air of the mountains, Liam kept his vigil, numb with cold, beginning to wonder if he was hallucinating. For several hours he had been hearing sawing and hammering, clear and faint according to the direction and strength of the wind. It was a frenetic, persistent series of sounds like the echoes of a ghostly carpenter. Now and then, to take his mind off the cold and the tedium and the creepy sounds, Liam closed his eyes and added details to a colourful mental scenario where Brian Quigley got his violent and bloody comeuppance.

At 10.00 pm, as the band left the platform for a break, Assumpta took the microphone and called for quiet. The crowd immediately applauded and whistled.

'Ladies and gentlemen… ladies and gents, please, a bit of hush…'

She waited until they were silent.

'OK. Well, there's no point in pretending this is the joyful occasion it was supposed to be. On the other hand, some of us do have a living to make…'

She let the renewed cheering die away before she continued, '…and this is still a reception, even if it isn't what Brian had in mind.'

People turned and looked at Quigley where he sat at the end of the bar, shielding his eyes with his hand.

'Anyway, this being a reception, Niamh would like to say a few words. Come on, Niamh, all yours.'

Niamh made her way shyly on to the little platform. She took the mike from Assumpta and looked nervously around the bar.

'This seemed like a good idea at the time,' she said. 'Hardly a Wedding Reception. Although I don't think Father Clifford agrees. I know my father doesn't.'

For appearances, Quigley made an easy-going shrug.

'Thank you all for coming…' Niamh's voice shook. She paused to let the flutter of emotion die away. 'Thank you for all your presents – I don't know who gave what exactly, but they're here when you want to collect them…'

For a moment it looked as though she would break

down in tears. Peter, standing near the platform, exchanged a worried look with Assumpta.

'It's OK, it's fine,' Niamh said, 'I'll be all right.' She sniffed. 'I wanted to say something. A lot of you have been immensely supportive, and I know what most of you think about Ambrose. I've heard some of it and I've said the rest myself. But give him a chance, would you? He's not a bad man, he's not a cruel man, he's just... confused. Take it easy on him, OK? Just let him work it out. Thank you.'

She left the stage in silence and hurried away upstairs. Assumpta jerked her head at Peter, indicating he follow her to the kitchen. When they were there she shut the door.

'You've got to do something,' she said.

'Why me?'

'Because he listens to you.'

'I wish you had,' Peter said.

'This reception wasn't my idea.'

'What am I supposed to do?'

Well...' Assumpta propped her knuckles on her hips. 'You could try disabusing him of this stupid priest idea for a start.'

Peter felt a sting of annoyance. 'You know it is just possible that his vocation might be genuine.'

Assumpta made an exasperated noise.

'All right,' Peter said, calming down. 'I agree with you.'

'I'm not trying to ridicule the priesthood.'

'Today.'

Assumpta started again. 'Can we agree that someone has to do something?'

'You mean me.'

'Look, this statue...'

'Saint John. You can say it.'

'Are you sure it's him?'

Peter nodded. 'With the name "Saint John" chiselled beneath his feet, I'm sure.'

'Then lie.'

'What?'

'Be economical with the truth. It's an English tradition, isn't it?'

'It's a sin to tell a lie,' Peter pointed out.

'Oh, please – says who?'

'I can't remember.'

'That's more like it.'

Peter sat down, looking troubled. Assumpta went to the door. She turned.

'He'll never get to heaven if he breaks her heart.'

Peter looked up. 'Dionne Warwick, right?'

Assumpta went back to the bar. Peter sat thinking for a minute, then he went to the bar too and eased his way through the guests to the door. Out on the street he looked around and saw Ambrose sitting on the bridge with his police cap in his lap, gazing over his shoulder at the river.

Peter went across and sat up on the bridge beside him. He nodded in the direction of the music. 'Good band,' he said.

'Hmm?' Ambrose looked preoccupied.

'At Fitzgerald's.'

'Ah.'

'And Assumpta was worried they might be a bit noisy.'

'You only get married once,' Ambrose said.

Peter smiled.

'Do you think I'm mad, Father?'

'No.'

'You think I'm wrong, though.'

'Yep.'

'Easy to say.'

'Yeah. And if I was you, and that had been the stone head of, oh, I don't know, Saint Francis of Assisi, then I'd probably want to chuck my job in too and become a vet.'

Peter saw Ambrose's neck stiffen, the defensive recoil. 'I'm not trying to mock you, Ambrose. I don't think you're right, but it didn't happen to me. I'm not feeling what you're feeling.'

Peter smiled again, looking reflective, acting but hoping it didn't show.

Ambrose looked at him. 'What?'

'You saved me a speech, anyway.'

'Did I?'

'Well, more of a pep-talk, really,' Peter said. 'You would not believe the amount of people going to get married who suddenly get cold feet. It's not that they don't want to go through with it, they just get these terrible feelings of doubt – you know, "There goes my freedom, am I ready for this…".'

Ambrose was trying not to look too interested.

'You probably felt the same thing yourself before…was it really only yesterday?'

Ambrose started to say something. Peter saw it coming and breezed straight on. 'You know,' he said, 'I once read somewhere that a man who fears love fears life. And I thought, that's it, that's exactly what it is. A man who fears love fears life. And once you know that, suddenly commitment doesn't seem so frightening any more. I mean, why would anyone cut themselves off from the one of the richest experiences life has to offer?'

Ambrose did not look preoccupied any more. He was hanging on to every word Peter said.

'Anyway…' Peter jumped down from the parapet and turned up the collar of his jacket. He made to walk away. 'Oh,' he said, and turned back to Ambrose. 'You were wrong about the patron saint of priests.'

'What?'

'The patron saint of priests is John the Evangelist.'

'I know.'

'The statue that nearly hit you was John the Baptist.'

Peter watched the bombshell land. He shivered. 'I'm getting cold.' He turned and walked back to Fitzgerald's.

When he got inside the place was even noisier than

before. People were still dancing, and all the women who were sitting now appeared to be drinking draught stout, which had been the hit drink of the evening. Behind the bar Assumpta was serving as fast as she could, communicating with elaborate mouth movements to compensate for the noise from the band.

Two minutes after Peter got back, the door opened and Ambrose stepped in. He looked very sure of himself. He stood scanning the room and, as the crowd saw him, the music died and they all stopped dancing. The place fell silent.

A moment later Niamh came down the stairs, bewildered by the quiet. She saw Ambrose. She got to the foot of the stairs and stood there. He walked slowly across and looked straight into her eyes.

'Will you marry me?'

She made the smallest nod. 'Probably.'

'Can I kiss you?'

''kay.'

They kissed and a cheer tore through the bar.

When the noise died Ambrose said, 'Would you like a drink?'

She nodded. 'Glass of stout.'

All at once people were slapping Ambrose on the back and lining up to shake his hand. Niamh crossed to where her father was sitting by the bar. He stood and put his arms around her, holding her close.

Peter and Assumpta looked at each other across the room. They smiled.

✝

The telephone on Brian Quigley's bedside table rang early the next morning, jangling him out of his sleep. As soon as he sat up pain sliced across his skull. He groaned and reached for the phone.

'Yeah?'

It was Liam. 'Mr Quigley, she's here. Your one.'

The hangover magically lifted. In a very short time Quigley was dressed and out of the house and striding up the mountain. His heart was hammering against his ribs but he was confident it would hold up. The closer he got to the hut, the more excited he became.

At the foot of the slope leading to the tiny building he looked up and saw her, in a long grey skirt and sheepskin coat, older but still the girl he remembered. He held his arms wide to her. She held out hers.

They ran towards each other, arms outstretched. As the space between them narrowed, Quigley ran faster. So did Rosarie. He spread his arms wider, ready to clasp them around her. His face lit with ecstasy as she came close and he caught the scent of her. Then she punched him in the mouth.

He landed on his back, clutching his jaw. When he looked up, Rosarie was hopping from the pain in her fist. Gingerly he touched his lip. It felt as thick as a brick.

'What was that for?'

She turned, eyes blazing. 'For dumping me, you faithless bastard!'

He sat up. 'That was 25 years ago.'

'It still happened!'

'Ah, Rosarie, come on…'

She came and stood over him. 'How could you?'

'You went away.'

'For the weekend.'

Quigley stood up, frowning at her reddened hand. 'Let me look at that…'

'Don't touch it.'

He looked concerned. 'Is it sore?'

'Yes. Your mouth is bleeding.'

'Yeah, well…' He shrugged gallantly. 'I had it coming.'

'You'd far worse than that coming.'

He sighed. 'You went away to Queens.'

'That was after.'

'No, you were always going to go.'

She stared at him. 'I would have come back.'

Quigley stepped away a few paces and stared huffily down into the valley.

'Sorry about your wife,' Rosarie said.

'Yeah.'

Liam, standing in the doorway of the hut, cleared his throat loudly. 'Will there be anything else, Mr Quigley?'

Quigley turned, startled. 'Are you still here?'

'Apparently,' Liam said, pinching his wrist.

'Go on,' Quigley told him.

As Liam trotted off down the mountain he passed Eamonn, who was unloading the product of his labours from the back of his lorry.

'You all right there, Eamonn?'

'Grand, thanks.'

Liam paused, doing a double-take on the objects under Eamonn's arms. They were four-legged and boxy, and others were already distributed over two slopes and up by the crest of a third. They were sheep, artificial lash-ups of wood and fragments of wool, crude but realistic enough at a distance.

Liam laughed. 'Good man,' he shouted, moving on.

By the side of the hut, Quigley had spread the blanket on the ground. He and Rosarie lay on it side by side. They were comfortable with each other now, but as they lay there they were careful not to touch.

'I'm not staying, Brian.'

'No?'

'My husband might wonder where I'd got to.'

'Ah.'

She glanced at him. 'What did you think, I'd joined the nuns?'

'I suppose not. Do you have a family?'

'Yes.' Rosarie pushed herself up on her elbows. Quigley did the same. 'Three young men,' she said.

'That's great. Full-time job, I'd say.'

'No.' She smiled. 'I manage to have a career as well.'

It was too cold to lie there for long. Finally they got up and strolled together to a point where the ground dipped to the gentler slopes that marked the northern boundary of Ballykissangel.

'Well, professor,' Quigley said, 'is there a lesson in all this?'

She shook her head. 'Too late for the learning, wouldn't you say?'

He nodded.

'Anyway,' she added, 'I don't teach these days.'

He asked her what she did and she told him that, at present, she was heading up a research project for the European Union.

'Go away.'

'Oh yeah, riveting. Still, we can use the money.'

'And what is it?'

'Oh. just monitoring the output from a satellite. You'd probably call it counting sheep…'

Her voice tailed off as she spotted Eamonn's wooden flock, too far away to look like fakes. She had come up that way, yet she hadn't notice one sheep then.

Quigley saw her frown. 'What?'

'Nothing.' Her smile was a little sad now. 'It's just exactly as I remember it. Peaceful, still.'

They stood there a while longer, company for each other's silence.

Back in Ballykissangel, Peter had spotted Ambrose on the main street, standing beside Assumpta's van.

'Morning, Father,' Ambrose said brightly. 'Beautiful day.'

Peter realized Ambrose had been writing out a parking ticket. 'I think that's Assumpta's van,' he said.

Ambrose nodded, still smiling. 'I believe so.'

'She was a great comfort to Niamh when she needed it.'

Ambrose folded the ticket and stuck it under the wiper. 'There's good in everyone, isn't that right, Father?'

Peter watched him move briskly on, full of dedication and energy.

Later, as Peter sat at home putting his parish paper-work in order, Father Mac arrived. He marched into the living room and demanded to know what had been done in the way of support and guidance for Ambrose's vocation. Peter said he had managed to get Ambrose to see his situation in a clearer light, and as a result he had abandoned the idea of becoming a priest.

Father Mac was angry. 'Have you any idea how rare vocations are these days?' he said.

'Father, Ambrose isn't a priest, he's a policeman. Nat-ural-born, cold-hearted, ruthless.'

'There's good in him,' Father Mac insisted.

'I'm not saying there isn't. I'm just saying that at his job, he's a zealot. Better out there on the street than in the confessional.'

Peter looked through the net curtain. Ambrose was on the opposite pavement, supervising the shackling of a car prior to it being towed away. The car looked familiar.

'How did you get here?' Peter said.

'I drove, of course.'

Father Mac came to the window. Together he and Peter watched the hatchback being towed away. On the windscreen a little printed sign that read 'PRIEST ON CALL' was clearly visible.

Father Mac said nothing, although his cheeks turned an unaccustomed pink. When the car had gone one way and Ambrose the other, Father Mac muttered something about additional business in the town and left without another word.

Later, Peter dropped in at Fitzgerald's, where he bought a coffee and took it out to one of the bench seats at the front. As he sat there, sipping and staring, Assumpta came out of the bar, rolling an empty metal barrel. He watched her roll it past his feet and set it on its end beside the far end of the bench.

'Keeps you fit,' he said.

'Yeah.' Assumpta nodded. 'I can see you're rushed off your feet.'

'Listen, I can be called out any time of the day or night.'

'I know. You'd wake me up to tell me.'

Peter smiled. 'How's Niamh?'

'Getting back her self-respect. Giving Ambrose a hard time.' Assumpta watched Peter's smile turn uneasy. 'Father, when two people are meant to be together, there's no force on this earth that'll keep them apart.'

Peter opened his mouth to say something, but she carried on.

'I mean, you can delay the inevitable like Ambrose did, or you can help speed it up like you did.'

'We did.'

'Well, if it's meant to happen, it'll happen.'

She stepped inside the doorway to fetch another barrel.

'That's a bit homespun for you,' Peter said.

She reappeared. 'I was trying to make you feel better about losing a live one. Oh, before I forget –' She took an envelope from the hip pocket of her corduroys and handed it to him. 'For the church roof.'

Peter looked inside. 'What?' There was a thick wad of banknotes. He looked at Assumpta. 'Thank you.' He glanced at the money again. 'I don't know what to say.'

'Don't say anything. We got through an awful lot of stout last night.'

He didn't entirely understand.

'Another coffee?' Assumpta offered.

Peter looked across the road and saw Father Mac get on the Cilldargan bus. He didn't look happy.

Peter smiled. 'Why not?' he said, and held out his cup.

Fifteen

In recent days the engine of Peter's motorbike had developed an intermittent, scratchy noise whenever he engaged third gear. He had also noticed that it was reluctant to start if he left it standing for more than four or five hours. In the mornings, the run-and-jump-on start was the only one that offered quick results and, this morning, even that hadn't worked.

He decided to go back to the conventional method. He sat astride the machine and operated the kick-start, twisting the throttle sharply each time his foot went down. Nothing happened the first three times. On the fourth shot it coughed, but on the fifth and sixth it remained lifeless. He was about to try for the seventh time when he heard music behind him, loud and clear and getting louder.

He turned. It was Siobhan in her Land Rover. She pulled up and shouted to him over the music from her radio.

'Happy birthday, Father!'

He got off the bike and stepped over to the Land Rover. 'How did you know?'

'Angel FM,' Siobhan said.

'Angel what?'

She pointed at the dash. 'The new radio station.'

Peter nodded, too preoccupied with his inert bike to take much notice.

Siobhan waved and drove off. He went back to the bike, kicked the starter a few more times, then gave up. He looked at his watch, zipped up his jacket, grabbed his Bible and started running.

Fifty yards down the road he saw another Land Rover, Quigley's, parked by the verge. A trailer was attached to the back and, standing upright on the trailer and held in place by ropes, was a huge hoarding. It was a picture of smart new houses, with a twice life-size colour photograph of Brian Quigley smiling alongside. The sign read: 'VALE VIEW MANOR – LUXURY DETACHED 3-BEDROOM HOUSES'. At the bottom, below the telephone and fax details, it said 'ANOTHER QUIGLEY DEVELOPMENT'. Quigley, Liam and Donal were standing beside the trailer, appraising the effect.

'Happy birthday, Father,' Quigley said as Peter clattered to a halt by the trailer.

'Don't tell me,' he panted. 'You heard it on the radio.'

Quigley nodded. 'One-oh-six-point-five FM. The medium is the message.'

'Well look,' Peter said, 'if you're around later this evening for a drink – '

'Ah, sorry.' Quigley made a fleeting show of regret. 'Too busy.' He turned to his men. 'Right lads…' He motioned for Liam and Donal to get in the Land Rover, then he turned to Peter again. 'What do you think of it?'

'It's, er… it's very big.'

'Well, you know yourself, Father, you've got to spread the good word.'

Quigley got in the vehicle and Peter ran on, down to the bus stop. Across the road at Fitzgerald's, Assumpta was washing the windows. She saw him as he joined the queue.

'Is your bike broken again?' she called.

Peter came across. 'I think I've just given it the last rites.'

'You need a car.'

'Tell me about it. Father Mac's been on at me to take driving lessons and buy one. He didn't say what with, exactly.'

Assumpta wrung out her cloth into the bucket. 'You'll have to start charging for confession.'

The bus approached over the bridge and Peter started to move off. 'Are you going to be around at all this evening?' he said.

'No,' Assumpta said, 'I'm going out with Niamh. Why?'

'I was just going to suggest maybe having a drink.'

'Sorry. Some other time.'

'Yes, of course...'

Peter ran across the road and got on the bus. The driver's radio was blaring the same kind of lively music Siobhan had been playing. As Peter stepped forward with his fare ready, the passengers called out in unison: 'Happy birthday, Father.'

✝

Kathleen stood at her shop window, watching the bus pull away. The music playing in her general store that morning was the more sedate kind provided by RTE Radio 2. Kathleen kept the radio switched on because, as she had told her customers over the years, it was congenial company when she was there on her own. It had been observed by Brendan Kearney that the congenial company had never produced any noticeable brightening effect on Kathleen, who would still sooner think badly of people than look for the good in them.

Kathleen had just turned up the volume a fraction to counteract the rattle from a refrigerator when Padraig came in and asked for 20 cigarettes.

She put them on the counter. 'That's £2.75, please,' she said.

'Jayz, Kathleen...' He gave her a fiver. 'You could be arrested for that.'

'Don't blame me for your vices, Padraig O'Kelly.'

Kathleen got his change. She came back from the till with a censorious frown. Padraig followed her line of vision and saw Kathleen's 17-year-old nephew, Daniel, packing cartons into the cool display.

'Will you hurry up and get that milk in there before the sell-by date.'

'Yes, Auntie.'

'Don't you know sloth is a sin?'

Daniel had an expressive, instantly likable face. He looked at Padraig with only a trace of a smile. 'I thought it was a hairy mammal.'

Siobhan opened the door, kicking mud from her rubber boots before she came in. 'Have you heard about the Angel?' she said, hurrying over to the counter.

'Siobhan,' Padraig said, 'those drugs you carry around with you, they're for the animals.'

'Shush!'

She leaned over the counter and turned the tuning knob on the radio.

'What are you doing?' Kathleen demanded.

'Listen...'

'And for those of you who don't already know,' a mid-Atlantic male voice said, 'it's Father Clifford's birthday today.' He then sang 'Happy Birthday' with electronic organ accompaniment.

'Who's that?' Kathleen asked.

'I've no idea.' Siobhan smiled. 'Isn't it wonderful?'

Padraig said it sounded like a pirate radio station.

The song finished and the DJ made another announcement. 'Reports are coming in of several bargain offers in Kathleen Hendley's shop. Pigs have also been seen flying in the area.'

Padraig and Siobhan smothered their amusement. Kathleen, red and affronted, switched the radio off.

Later, when there was no-one else in the shop, Kathleen switched on the radio again, curious to learn who might be behind this latest offence to propriety. The music was jangly and not at all to her taste, and when the American-sounding announcer came on again he had the temerity to make another cheap joke about the shop – not only was this a day for the priest to celebrate, he said, but two of the pork pies in Hendley's fridge were having a birthday as well.

That did it for Kathleen. She went round to Ambrose's house and found him in the kitchen having his elevenses. When he said he didn't know, until that minute, that there was a new radio station, Kathleen took the liberty of tuning in his set. Again the raucous music poured out.

Ambrose listened for a minute. 'Sure, what's the harm in it?'

'The harm, Guard Egan,' Kathleen said indignantly, 'is that this pirate is spreading vicious rumours over the airwaves.'

Ambrose doubted that. 'Come on, Kathleen, you know what this place is like.'

Shh!' She turned up the volume. 'Listen.'

'We interrupt the programme with a very important newsflash. There has been a robbery in Ballykay. A man was seen running out of O'Reilly's hardware with tins of red and blue paint.'

Ambrose stiffened for a second, then he jolted into action. He slammed down his coffee mug and pulled his uniform jacket off the back of a chair. As it swung clear of the chair it hit a box on the table, knocking it over. Dozens of jigsaw pieces scattered across the tiled floor. Ambrose made for the door, struggling to get the jacket on.

'The local Gardaí advise no-one to approach him,' the announcer said, 'I repeat, no one should approach him, as he may be violet.' He finished the announcement with a silly laugh and the music came back.

Ambrose switched off the radio, trying not to see Kathleen's smug expression.

✝

Peter had conducted the weekly Mass for ambulant patients in the chapel at the local hospital, St Columcille's. When it was over, he walked along the main corridor to the front door with the senior sister.

'Thank you, Father. Everyone appreciates your visits.'

'It's all part of the service.'

Peter noticed a tall, distinguished-looking man go past, tightening the belt of his dressing gown.

'He's new, isn't he?'

'Yes. That's Mr Bradley. He used to be the judge in Cilldargan. He was admitted yesterday. Demanded a private room.'

Peter had sensed something in the man's bearing, a tension he had sometimes found in seriously ill people who, for various reasons, found it hard to unburden themselves or discuss their illness. They had an air of isolation that he found especially sad.

'Has he no family or friends?'

'His wife died a few years back,' the sister said. 'He doesn't have any children. As for friends, somehow I doubt it.'

Peter decided to have a word before he left. He waited until the patient had been back in his room for a couple of minutes, then he knocked on the door and opened it.

'Mr Bradley, isn't it?'

The man was in bed, lying back on the pillows, staring out of the window. His iron-grey hair was swept back in wings on either side of his forehead; when he turned his head and looked at Peter his eyes appeared sunken. There was no warmth in his expression.

'Is that what it says above my bed?'

'Er, yes.'

'Well then, that's who I am.'

He looked away again, staring out at the hills beyond the window.

'Would you rather I left?' Peter said.

'Please yourself. The Church owns the place.'

'It's not quite as simple as that…'

'Well they act like they do.' Bradley looked at Peter again. 'And you're a priest, aren't you?'

'Is that what it says round my neck?'

There was a moment of silence. Bradley's eyes softened a fraction, acknowledging Peter's small thrust.

'Save your prayers for someone who needs them. I may be dying but I don't need you, Father MacAnally or the Church to make my peace with God.'

'I see.'

'So there's no chance of you lot getting any of my money.'

Peter smiled. 'I don't want your money.'

Bradley widened his eyes. 'Don't let the Vatican hear you saying that.'

They fell silent again. Peter turned to the door.

'I'll see you another time, maybe.'

'I'm not going anywhere.'

Later in the day Peter sat with Father Mac in the study of his house at Cilldargan, working out the monthly rota. On such occasions Father Mac dressed informally, in a cardigan and an open-collared shirt. Nevertheless he was all business. When Peter told him he had met a new patient at the hospital that morning, he did no more than acknowledge the remark.

'Is that a fact?' He stared at his schedule. 'Now if you do Tuesday evening's Mass, I'll do the following Thursday.'

'Fine.' Peter waited, then he tried again. 'His name's Michael Bradley.'

Now Father Mac looked up. 'Mickey Bradley? The judge?'

'That's him. He was admitted yesterday. It's his heart.'

'Never knew he had one.'

'Did you know him well?'

'I haven't seen him since his wife died, must be nearly 10 years ago. She was ill for a very long time, God rest her. I hear he hasn't been the same since.' Father Mac looked thoughtful. 'He used to be a demon chess player.'

'He's suspicious of the Church. Thinks we're after his money.'

Father Mac laughed. 'Sure, the man is paranoid. Mickey and I never saw eye-to-eye. Mind you, he might be different with a newcomer like you.'

Peter shrugged.

'By the way,' Father Mac said, 'I hear your transport failed you again today.'

'Yeah, well…'

'It's not good enough, you know. You'll have to learn to drive.'

'I can drive, sort of. My dad taught me the basics before he died. I just didn't pass my test.'

'Well you must,' Father Mac said firmly. 'Ballykay needs a four-wheeled priest.'

'Easier said than done. I don't have the money.'

Father Mac was unmoved. 'You'd better start saving. It's either that, or we may have to reconsider your posting.'

That remark shook Peter. It made him realize, sharply, how much he wanted to stay in Ballykissangel.

The circular problem of raising the cash for a car plagued him as he waited for the bus back to Ballykissangel. The worry got him nowhere, he knew that, but it was hard to get his mind off the subject. When he got on the bus he saw a young man with a familiar face and deliberately sat down beside him, hoping for distraction.

'Mind if I join you?' He sat down and held out his hand. 'Peter Clifford.'

The young man shook his hand. 'Daniel Goggin. I work in Kathleen Hendley's shop.'

'Yes, I know. She's your aunt, isn't she?'

'Yeah. The aunt from hell – oh, pardon the expression, Father.'

The bus radio was tuned to Angel FM. The DJ's voice came over the air crisp and clear as the music was momentarily muted for a weather report: 'While the rain in Spain stays mainly on the plain, it's a sunny day for May in Ballykay.'

Peter grinned and asked, 'How long have you lived in sunny Ballykay?'

'I don't live there,' Daniel said. 'I just work there, Father. There aren't that many jobs around here. If there were, I wouldn't want to work for my aunt.'

'And do you want to stay in the area?'

'Sure it's my home, Father. Anyway, why would anyone want to leave here?'

So there was no distraction after all. Peter was back at the same roundabout pattern of thought – how could he raise the wherewithal to buy a car and stay on in Ballykissangel?

That evening he got out of uniform and walked down to Fitzgerald's wearing jeans and a checked shirt, much as he had been the day he arrived. He pushed open the door and was met with a loud chorus of 'Happy Birthday, Father!'

Behind the bar a banner said the same thing. All the regulars were there – Siobhan, Padraig, Brendan, Liam, Donal, Quigley, Niamh and Ambrose. Assumpta was behind the bar. She raised a glass to him as a pint was put into his hand. He could tell from looking at her that she was behind this surprise.

Music played from the radio and the mood was festive. Ambrose and Niamh brought Peter a wrapped present. He tore off the paper. It was two slender books – *Rules of the Road* and *A Guide for the Irish Learner Driver*.

'We thought you might need them,' Niamh said.

'Someone's been talking to Father Mac,' Peter said. 'Thanks anyway.'

Assumpta sidled up. 'They go with this,' she said, and handed him an envelope.

'Assumpta, you shouldn't...'

'I know. It's against my religion to give presents to priests.'

Peter opened the envelope and read aloud: '"This card entitles you to six free driving lessons." Great. With who?'

Assumpta held up two L-plates and grinned. 'Me.'

At the end of the bar, meanwhile, Quigley was asking Ambrose if he had heard any more about the whereabouts of the new radio station.

'He wants to close it down,' Niamh said.

Padraig looked shocked. 'What for? It's not doing any harm.'

'I have to uphold the law,' Ambrose said.

Siobhan snorted. 'Kathleen just wants to keep Ballykay's gossip to herself.'

'Look,' said Ambrose, 'it's illegal to broadcast without a licence.' He cast a serious look around the little group at the end of the bar. 'If anyone knows anything, they'd better tell me.'

Sixteen

Young Daniel Goggin positioned a brightly coloured 'SPECIAL OFFERS' sign in the window of his aunt's shop, angling it carefully for dynamic effect.

'Don't use much tape,' Kathleen called to him as she came out. 'It's not staying up for long.'

At the foot of the steps she found Siobhan staring at the sign and wearing a theatrical look of wonderment.

'Is anything the matter?'

Siobhan looked at her and asked, 'Are you feeling all right, Kathleen?'

'I'm feeling fine,' Kathleen said huffily. She walked on.

Not many yards away Peter was in the van with Assumpta, having his first free lesson. In the short time since they had driven away from his house, he had been barked at and badgered as he made all the mistakes of a man who only ever gained a few driving skills, and had had time to lose most of them.

As they came jerking down the main street Assumpta said, 'When I hit the dashboard I want you to make an emergency stop.'

Peter groaned. 'That's what I failed on the first time I took my test.'

'How many times have you taken it?'

'Only twice.'

'Now he tells me.' Assumpta rolled her eyes. 'What did you fail on the second time?'

'Observation.'

At that moment Kathleen Hendley stepped out in front of the van.

'Look out!' Assumpta yelled.

Peter slammed on the brakes. The van squealed to a stop. Kathleen stood in the middle of the road, glaring at them both. They smiled at her before she marched on up the street.

'How was that?' Peter asked.

'Better luck next time.'

He gave Assumpta his admonishing look. She grinned back and told him to drive on.

Half an hour of steady driving made him feel much more sure of himself. As his confidence increased, so did the speed.

'Y'know, I'm getting back into the swing of this. I hope my father's watching me.'

'He'll be seeing us in person if you don't slow down.'

He took the warning and dropped the speed. They drove at a steady pace along near-deserted country roads flanked by fields and bordered with wild flowers. Back in England, he thought, they hadn't seen roads this free of traffic since the 50s.

'I'm visiting a patient in the hospital this morning,' he said. 'Michael Bradley. Do you know him?'

'Everyone knows Judge Mickey. Some more than others.'

'He reminds me of my dad a bit.'

Assumpta made a face. 'I bet your dad never fined you 50 quid for something that was no fault of your own.'

'Michael Bradley fined you? For what?'

'Dangerous driving.'

Five minutes later they arrived at St Columcille's hospital. Peter swung the van into the car park and stopped.

'What are you visiting him for?' Assumpta said. 'I thought he was another lost cause like me.'

'There's always hope.'

Assumpta opened her door. 'Well, I suppose it's different for him. He has two things that always interest the Church – money and no next of kin.'

They got out and Assumpta went round to the driver's side.

'It is easier for a camel to pass through the eye of a needle', Peter intoned, 'than for a rich man to enter the Kingdom of Heaven. Matthew, chapter 19.'

Assumpta gave him a withering look. 'Money, so they say, is the root of all evil today. Pink Floyd, "Dark Side of the Moon".'

She got in the van and drove away.

Peter found Mr Bradley sitting at a table by the window in his room. A chessboard and pieces were set out in front of him. He looked more ill than the last time.

'You don't give up, do you?' he said as Peter came in.

'I have my orders.' Peter sat on the side of the bed.

Bradley nodded at the car park. 'Who's the girl? I recognize her face.'

'She's a friend. She's teaching me to drive.'

'You call that driving?'

Peter was aware he might be imagining it, but Bradley seemed less aloof today, and less defensive. A moment ago he had almost smiled.

'I'm a little rusty,' Peter said, 'But I have to pass my test somehow.'

'You see that?' Bradley pointed to a framed picture on the bedside locker.

Peter picked it up. It was a black-and-white picture of a woman standing by a shiny Jowett Javelin saloon.

'I've been driving that car since before you were born and I never took a test.'

Peter pointed to the woman. 'Is this your wife?'

'Yes.'

'What was her name?'

'Emily.'

The pose had a demure quality which alone would have dated the picture. Emily's hands were clasped lightly, one foot was a fraction behind the other, one shoulder was turned away from the camera. Her smile was tentative and shy, her eyes looking at the lens but giving the impression they would dart aside at any moment.

'She was very pretty,' Peter said.

'She was beautiful.'

Peter went across and sat in the chair opposite Bradley. He looked at the chessboard. 'I believe you're good.'

Now Bradley did smile, thinly. 'Father MacAnally has been briefing you.'

'Well…' Peter rubbed his hands. 'I can't say I'll give you a great game, but I promise to try.'

Bradley nodded, accepting that. 'What's your name, Father?'

'Peter Clifford.'

'Well, Peter Clifford, let me warn you. I enjoy sacrificing bishops.'

They played in silence for 10 minutes. The game moved evenly between them, neither one gaining a significant advantage. Bradley was first to break the silence, while Peter sat pondering his next move.

'Tell me, Father, what did your mother say when you told her you wanted to be a priest?'

'She was pleased. She always said I'd go far in the Church – and you can't get much farther than Ballykissangel.'

In spite of himself Bradley smiled. 'And your father?'

'Well let's just say that he had more faith in professions than vocations.'

'"Listen my children to a father's instruction".'

'I did listen to him,' Peter said, 'but he didn't return the favour.'

'Sensible man.'

Peter shrugged, realizing that self-pity wouldn't stand a chance around this individual.

'I once considered being a priest,' Bradley said. 'Many young men do in this country.'

'What stopped you?'

Bradley drew his fingers thoughtfully along the edge of the table. 'I wanted to marry someone other than the Church.'

Peter made his move and Bradley made his almost at once.

Peter looked at him. 'You must miss Emily a lot.'

'Every day she is my first thought and my last. You'd understand if you had ever loved someone as I love her.' Bradley looked at the board, then at Peter. 'Have you?'

In this territory it was Peter's habit to be politely evasive. 'I don't know anyone who hasn't been in love at one time or another.'

He made his move quickly, trying to get Bradley's attention back on the game. Bradley tutted the moment the move was made.

'You're not concentrating, Father.' He leaned forward and made his move. 'Check.'

'Sorry,' Peter sighed. 'I told you I wasn't very good at this game.'

'Which game do you mean?' Bradley sat back in his chair, staring at Peter. 'Chess, or priest?'

Peter smiled, shaking his head. 'You know sometimes, Mr Bradley, you sound like the devil himself.'

Bradley started to laugh. 'You're all right, Father.'

The laughter was full and hearty and it infected Peter, who began to laugh too. Then something changed. Bradley's laugh became a deep rattling cough. His body jerked and his arm flew out, knocking the chessboard off the table. He hunched forward, his shoulders heaving as he coughed soundlessly. Peter went round behind him and held him by the arms.

'Sister!'

Bradley began to struggle against Peter, pushing his hands away, panting as if he had just run a mile.

'I'm all right,' he gasped. 'Just leave me in peace...'

Sister came in, moving fast without bustling. 'Let's have a look at you, Mr Bradley.'

He stared up at her, wide-eyed, struggling for air. 'Get that priest out of here!'

Sister looked at Peter, her eyes apologetic. 'I think you'd better go, Father.'

✝

Brian Quigley was standing in front of a microphone in a cedar-walled, soundproofed recording studio. Liam stood beside him. They both held scripts. At a signal from an engineer on the other side of a window Quigley began to read aloud: 'Howdy folks, my name is Brian Quigley. I'm here to talk to you about my new homes for beautiful Ballykay.'

He paused for a second to swallow. Donal watched him and did the same.

'Each one is individually designed and comes with the Quigley quality guarantee. Here's one lucky customer who's already decided to move in.'

Liam leaned closer to the microphone, making the engineer cover his eyes.

'Er, yes,' Liam said, his voice stilted and a shade higher than usual. 'I spent a long time looking for the right place, but now my search is over, thanks to you, Mr Quigley.'

'My pleasure,' Quigley said. 'Remember folks, Quigley homes means quality homes. So don't delay, move up now to Ballykay.'

He paused, then looked through at the engineer. 'How was that?'

The engineer looked dubious. 'One more time,' he said.

After the third take Quigley was told they probably had enough to put together a tape of reasonable quality. He stood with Liam and waited. Fifteen minutes later the engineer brought the tape out to him.

'There you are. All ready for broadcast.'

Quigley took it and thanked him. He looked around the place, at the shelves crammed with electronic equipment, the clusters of tape decks and the editing console in the engineer's booth.

'You've everything you need here, haven't you? All the necessary.'

'Necessary for what?' the engineer said.

'Oh, say, setting up a radio station.'

The engineer grinned. 'Thinking of competing with Angel FM, are you?'

'Do you know it?'

'Should do. I fixed the fella up.'

Quigley's face remained impassive, but he couldn't keep the glint of curiosity from his eyes. 'What fella was that?'

'He was, er, a very secretive sort,' the engineer said. 'If you get my meaning.'

Quigley took out his wallet and flipped it open. 'How secretive, exactly?' he said, easing out a few banknotes.

A short timer later he was back in Ballykissangel. He parked the Land Rover on a quiet road and got out, carrying the big rectangular box with his recording tape. He walked along carefully, making sure he wasn't being watched. At the corner he was so busy looking over his shoulder he walked right into Ambrose Egan.

'Jaysus, Ambrose! You near frightened the life out of me.'

'I'm sorry Mr Quigley.' Ambrose touched the peak of his cap. 'Didn't mean to startle you.'

'What are you doing, skulking there?'

Ambrose put his hands behind his back, as he did instinctively every time he stated his business. 'I have orders to find this radio station.'

'But you haven't found it yet, have you?'

'Not yet. But I soon will.'

Quigley found the certainty in Ambrose's tone unsettling. 'How?'

'Can't say.' Ambrose smiled awkwardly. 'Top secret.' Then he noticed the tape box. 'What's that you have there, Mr Quigley?'

Quigley thought fast. 'Oh please, Ambrose, call me Brian.'

'Really?' Ambrose was suddenly overwhelmed.

'Yes...' Quigley let the box slide to his side and round behind him, sure now that Ambrose had forgotten it. 'You'll soon be one of the family.' He stepped around Ambrose and moved on. 'God help us,' he added under his breath.

Later that afternoon, Kathleen Hendley went into the storeroom at the back of her shop looking for her nephew. As she stepped into the section where old and broken shop equipment was kept – Kathleen believed in getting rid of nothing – jangling music came at her from Daniel's radio. It was tuned, she had no doubt, to the abominable Angel FM.

She called to Daniel again over the din of the music. There was no reply. The music faded and was replaced by a man's voice.

'Howdy, folks, my name is Brian Quigley. I'm here to talk to you about my new homes for beautiful Bal-lykay...'

Kathleen stared at the radio as if it had used bad language to her. She listened to the rest of Quigley's spiel, then switched the radio off.

✟

As soon as Assumpta was in a position to take another hour off, she and Peter went out in the van again. She told him to drive over to Cilldargan and back, just to get used to the handling of the vehicle on hilly, winding roads. Since that morning, Peter's confidence seemed to have grown. He relaxed as he drove along the country roads, sitting back and calm enough to enjoy the view.

'This is easy,' he said.

'Pride before a fall.'

'You've no faith, Assumpta.'

'So you keep telling me. I suppose you're still working on restoring Mr Bradley's faith?'

'I am not working on him, I'm talking to him. I don't think he's actually talked to anyone since his wife died.'

'Oh.' Assumpta looked at Peter. 'So it's pure coincidence that you're showing an interest in him now just when he's about to pop his clogs?'

'Why do you always suspect the Church is up to no good?'

He waited for an answer with his eyes on her. Assumpta glanced at the road again. A lorry was coming straight towards them.

'Oh, God…'

'Yeah, he's in on it, too…'

No, no, no – ' Assumpta pointed. 'Oh, God!'

Peter looked ahead and saw the lorry. He twisted the wheel and pulled the van off the road, missing a collision by inches and running into a thick stretch of bracken. The wheels sank into the damp ground and the van came to a sudden stop.

Assumpta jumped out. 'I don't believe this!' She slammed the door shut. 'I just don't believe this!'

Peter got out and went round to the front.

'Sorry,' he said.

'Sorry?' She glared at him, hands on hips. 'You nearly killed us.'

'Well it was your fault.'

'My fault? How do you work that one out?'

'You put me off, making those ridiculous accusations about Mr Bradley.'

'Ridiculous?' Assumpta was shouting and looking mad enough to hit him. 'You don't know the half of it!'

Peter stared. 'What's that supposed to mean?'

'Look…' She put up her hand, calming herself as

much as Peter. 'We're both wasting our time here. You don't need driving lessons.'

'How am I supposed to pass my test?'

'No priest round here has ever failed his test.'

Peter groaned. 'What is this? Another of your little conspiracy theories?'

'No!' Assumpta was in danger of getting furious again. 'It's fixed! A priest's perk!'

'Yeah?' Peter couldn't believe that. 'Well, if it's fixed, why are you bothering to give me driving lessons?'

'Because, strange as it may seem, I didn't want to see you kill yourself behind the driving wheel.' Assumpta stumped round to the driver's side and opened the door. 'Now will you push?'

She got in and Peter put one hand on the bonnet and grasped the bumper with the other.

'I don't believe you,' he said.

Assumpta stuck her head through the open window. 'I'm not asking you to believe me.' She was almost crying with temper. 'I'm asking you to push!'

She put the engine in reverse and Peter threw his weight against bonnet. The wheels spun and threw up a stream of mud that splattered Peter. Seeing the mess it made, Assumpta revved the engine harder. Peter hung on grimly, spluttering, shutting his eyes against the onslaught and pushing until the van was back on the road.

They drove back to town in silence. Peter was so dirty he had to travel in the back. When Assumpta drew up in front of Fitzgerald's she got out, threw open the back doors of the van and flounced away into the bar.

Peter scrambled out, shut the doors and began walking slowly away. Assumpta reappeared at the door of the bar.

'And where do you think you're going?'

He looked at her sheepishly, his face blotched with dried mud. 'To clean up,' he said.

'Hah!' Assumpta pointed to the muddy van. 'Not until you've cleaned up this.'

She threw him a sopping sponge. He caught it, gripping it so tightly the water squirted down the front of his shirt. Assumpta went back indoors.

Peter shuffled to the front of the van, not sure where to start. He got on his knees and began wiping, trying not to guess how many people were watching him.

SEVENTEEN

Ambrose Egan walked up to the front door at Brian Quigley's house and knocked. Lurking inside, Brian peered through the side of the curtain and saw who it was. He went into the hall and stood in the kitchen doorway. Ambrose knocked again just as Niamh came down the stairs.

'Dad – '

'Shush!' Brian put a finger to his lips and whispered. 'I'm not in.'

'Who is it?'

Quigley said nothing. He sidled into the kitchen. Niamh looked at the frosted panel in the front door and saw the shape of Ambrose, unmistakable in his police hat. He moved away and walked round the side of the house, glancing at the kitchen as he passed, making Quigley press himself flat against the wall.

Niamh could see where Ambrose was headed. She went to the back and crossed to the patio doors as he arrived.

She pulled open the door and smiled at him. 'Hi, Ambrose.'

'Niamh.' He made to move past her into the house, but she blocked him. He frowned. 'Is your father in?'

'What do you want him for?'

'Police business.'

'What's he done now?'

'He's been advertizing on this illegal radio station.'

In the kitchen Quigley leaned through the hatch, listening.

'So?' Niamh could make a small word sound like a serious challenge.

'So…' Ambrose pulled himself to his full height, hands behind his back. 'He knows who's behind it.'

Niamh narrowed her eyes. 'You mean you don't?'

'Is he in or isn't he?' Ambrose demanded crossly.

'No,' Niamh snapped.

'Fine. Well, it doesn't matter anyway. By this time tomorrow I'll have all the means necessary to find out where the radio transmitter is.'

'How?'

Ambrose almost smirked. 'My lips are sealed.' He walked off.

Niamh watched him go. In the kitchen, Quigley leaned back against the worktop. He looked as puzzled as Niamh, and just a shade concerned.

Meanwhile, over at the hospital, Peter had arrived in Michael Bradley's private room and found the bed stripped. There was no sign of the patient. Peter stared at the bed, gripped with a sense of foreboding. He thought back to Tommy Hassett and his late arrival at the little house on the mountain.

He turned at a sound behind him. Bradley came in from the corridor. He was gaunt and seemed thinner and his dressing gown looked too large for him. In spite of looking so ill, he appeared to be smiling.

'There you are,' Peter said, relieved.

'Thought I'd gone without you, eh?'

'It's good to see you up.'

Bradley sat at the table by the window. The chessboard was set up again, the pieces ready for a fresh game. Peter sat in the chair opposite.

'Fifty pounds,' Bradley said.

Peter looked at him. 'Sorry?'

'Your girlfriend. I remembered I once fined her £50…' Bradley laughed, '…for dangerous driving.'

'She's not my girlfriend.'

'Oh? Fallen out, have you?'

'We just see things differently.'

They began to play. As before, the early part of the game was conducted in silence. Bradley had a fiercely logical style of attack and it took all Peter's concentration to predict even half his moves and counter-strategies.

Again, Bradley began talking unprompted. 'Emily was a terrible back-seat driver,' he said, and smiled at the recollection. 'We had some great arguments.'

'I can imagine.'

'We often used to drive down to the coast and walk along the sands, filling our lungs with the air. Even when she was quite ill, she still insisted I take her there.'

Peter saw Bradley's smile fade.

'Towards the end, though, we never got out of the car. We'd just park and sit and watch the sea in silence. Then I'd drive us home. We hardly spoke a word.'

Peter asked if she knew she was dying.

'Yes. They wanted to bring her in here, but she refused. I nursed her at home those last few months.'

The game was all but forgotten.

'It must have been very difficult for you.'

Bradley took a slow, deep breath and let it out on a sigh. 'You can't imagine what it's like, watching someone you love more than your own life waste away before your eyes in such pain.'

'I imagine I'd be very angry.'

'Anger,' Bradley nodded, 'hate, despair. I didn't know what to do. But Emily did. She made me promise.'

Peter's sense of foreboding stirred again. 'Promise?'

Bradley hesitated, then he said, 'The hospital had given me a supply of morphine for her pain. She was in such agony. She kept pleading, "Please, Michael, please…"'

Peter understood. He listened with growing distress.

'In the end I couldn't refuse her. I made up a dose with the remaining morphine. She drank it, and I held her quietly in my arms until it was over.'

There it was. He'd killed her. Played God. Dimly Peter

recalled the Church had a line on that sort of thing but it didn't seem to make a lot of sense right now. Bradley's pain filled the room and Peter said nothing, swallowing the platitudes that sprang uselessly to mind.

Bradley fixed him with a glare, misinterpreting the silence. 'Spare me the party line. I don't expect absolution for something I don't regret.' He paused, looking out of the window for a moment. 'All my life I've passed judgment on others. Now it's my turn to be judged.'

✝

Ambrose was in his living room, studying a set of printed instructions. On the coffee table beside him was a grey electronic box with a meter in the front; attached to the box were a complex-looking antenna and a set of headphones. He looked up as the front door opened and closed again.

'Ambrose?' Niamh appeared from the hallway, frowning already. 'What are you doing?'

'Nothing.' He put the instructions behind his back.

'You're hiding something.'

'No I'm not.'

'Ambrose…' She moved close, making him feel insecure.

'OK.' He sighed and brought the instructions into view. 'But you must promise not to breathe a word, especially to your dad.'

'Cross my heart and hope to die.' She made a tiny cross with her fingertip over her left breast, then bent down and peered at the device on the table. 'What is it?'

'It detects radio transmissions,' Ambrose said, rather proudly. 'I'm about to discover the whereabouts of one Angel FM.' He waved the instructions. 'Once I find out how it works.'

'Here, show me.' Niamh snatched the instructions from him.

'Oh no you don't.' Ambrose grabbed them back. 'It's secret.'

'It's also secret that you tuck your shirt into your underpants.'

Niamh took the instructions again and started reading.

✝

'Ah, Father Clifford.' Father Mac smiled with only a trace of cordiality as Peter came into the study, looking rather subdued.

'I wondered if I could have a word. I need some advice about... about a parishioner.'

'Certainly.' Father Mac pointed to the chair in front of his desk. 'Sit down. In fact, I'm glad you called. I have a date for your diary.'

Peter was preoccupied, absorbed with his dilemma. 'It's Mr Bradley.'

'Oh, yes.' Father Mac leafed through a notebook.

'It's just that... I had a very difficult conversation with him.'

'Well he's always been very difficult. I did warn you.' Father Mac seemed to dismiss the matter. He consulted his notebook. 'Now, on Thursday morning at 11 o'clock you are taking your driving test.'

Peter blinked at him. 'What?'

'I rang the test centre. They gave me a cancellation.' Now Peter looked alarmed. 'But I can't. I'm not ready.'

'Fear not, Father. I'm sure you'll pass with flying colours.'

'So it's true.'

'What?'

'It's a fix.'

'What is?'

'Priests don't ever fail their tests around here, do they?'

'Oh, I wouldn't say that.' Father Mac looked thoughtful. 'There was a curate once who failed, but he was unlucky. He crashed into the police station. He passed the second time, though.'

Peter shut his eyes for a moment with almost a wince of pain as he recalled how he had called Assumpta a liar. 'It's an abuse of our position,' he said. It's cheating.'

'In this town,' Father Mac said, 'we call it tradition.'

'Well.' Peter stood up. 'I for one don't want any part of it.' He went to the door.

'Father, I did tell you that I wanted you mobile if you were to stay on in Ballykay.' The signal in the domineering tone was already familiar to Peter: Father Mac was about to issue an edict. 'I see you're down to say Mass in the hospital on Thursday. I'll cover for you. Who knows, I may even be able to persuade our difficult Mr Bradley to receive communion.' His face hardened. 'In the meantime, I do advise you to be at the test centre, on Thursday, at eleven.'

Peter opened the door.

'And Father...' The note of warning was clear. 'Wearing your collar.'

As Peter travelled back to Ballykissangel in the bus, with Angel FM playing full blast, Brian Quigley was stealthily entering the home of Ambrose Egan, which he believed at that moment to be empty. Quigley was accompanied by his employee, Donal, who had been brought along in case anything needed forcing or breaking open.

Donal had been reluctant to do this. He had only agreed after Quigley made two points: one, he wasn't intending to break any laws or commit a felony because his only purpose was to find out what Guard Egan possessed that made him sure he could track down the pirate radio station, and two, Donal had better go along or first thing Monday he would be looking for alternative employment.

A few minutes before Quigley and Donal entered by the front door – which they found unlocked – Ambrose had been making a tour of the house with his newly-acquired signal detector slung round his neck, the headphones on his head and the antenna held out in front of him. Meanwhile Niamh, who was hiding, was seductively reciting a love poem into a walkie-talkie while Ambrose monitored the signal and tried to home in on her hiding place.

The equipment was very good. Ambrose quickly narrowed his search to the big fitted wardrobe in his bedroom. He opened the door to squeals of delight from Niamh, who promptly pulled him inside and shut the door.

As Quigley and Donal began creeping through the house they heard a tinny reproduction of Niamh's voice, giggling and muttering, alternating with the equally tinny but unmistakable voice of Ambrose, who sounded more anxious than amused.

As Quigley crept nearer the bedroom the reproduction got louder. Donal, a yard behind, was inclined to grin, but he was too nervous. Quigley pushed open the bedroom door and stepped in. A walkie-talkie receiver stood on a low table, its light blinking as Niamh's voice, issuing from the small speaker, told Ambrose to relax and give her a kiss. Ambrose began to giggle.

Quigley stared down at the walkie-talkie, his face a study in outraged parenthood. He snatched up the instrument, pressed the 'transmit' button, and put it close to his mouth.

'Good evening, Guard Egan,' he said.

There was a crash from the wardrobe.

✝

When Peter stepped into Fitzgerald's Donal was there, sitting at the top end of the bar, regaling Siobhan and Padraig with the tale of what happened at Ambrose's house. Peter went to the other end of the bar. Assumpta watched him. He eased down onto a stool and looked at her.

'Assumpta, can I ask a favour?'

'What?'

'Father Mac has arranged my test for Thursday at eleven.'

'What's it got to do with me?'

'I was wondering… I've sort of got used to driving your van… '

She stared at him coldly. 'You don't deserve it.'

He nodded. 'I know.'

Assumpta wiped a glass and put it on the shelf behind the bar. 'I'll pick you up at ten,' she said.

'Thanks.'

'And don't try to look so worried. You don't fool me.'

'It's not you I'm fooling.' He got up off the stool again. 'It's myself. Good night.'

When he had gone Siobhan called to Assumpta. 'Did you ever hear of a priest from around here that failed his driving test?'

'There's always a first time,' Assumpta said.

Donal shook his head. 'He'll pass.'

'How much?' Siobhan said.

Donal considered it. 'A fiver.'

'Include me in,' said Padraig.

Siobhan nodded. 'You're on.'

Eighteen

A penitent entered the other side of the confessional. Peter sat forward, ready to listen.

'Howdy, Father.'

Peter sighed. 'It's usually, "Bless me, Father, for I have sinned".'

'But I haven't sinned,' the quasi-American voice said. 'Well – at least I don't think I have.'

Peter recognized the accent. 'You're the DJ, aren't you?'

'The voice of Angel FM. Of course you realize I have to remain incognito. There's a load of people looking for me.'

'Well what do you want?'

'Support.'

'Why?'

'The way I see it, Angel is a kind of a community service for the people of Ballykay.'

'You may be right, but you are breaking the law.'

'But surely there are times when you should break the law for a greater good?'

Peter reflected on that.

'Father?'

'I'm sorry.'

'Have I done wrong?'

'I think perhaps if you truly believe that what you are doing is right, and for the best of intentions, then perhaps you should follow your conscience.'

'Thank you, Father. Oh, one other thing – would you be interested at all in doing a kind of God slot on Angel FM? You know, sort of soul for soul, that kind of thing?'

'I'll bear it in mind,' Peter said. 'If I fail my driving test tomorrow, I may need all the breaks I can get.'

That night before turning in, Peter sat with his Bible and read again the passages that dealt with charity. It was easy, given the automatic authority of the job, for a priest to forget that humility and a proper compassion for his parishioners was paramount to his work. To know something was simple, but it was less simple to find the flexibility within the knowledge.

He thought of what the voice of Angel FM had said: surely there were times when you should break the law for a greater good?

And then Peter thought of Michael Bradley. God's statutes were clear enough, but it would have to be a savage God that took no account of Bradley's good intentions when he breached the moral law.

'Charity as important as knowledge,' Peter scribbled in the margin of his diary. He opened the Bible and looked at First Corinthians, chapter eight, and committed a line of the first verse to memory: 'Knowledge puffeth up, but charity edifieth'.

Next morning he made sure he was ready on time. He had put on his clerical collar as instructed, but stopped short of wearing the black jacket. Instead he put on his fawn windcheater, zipped it up and waited for Assumpta to sound her horn.

She arrived on time. Peter got behind the wheel and pulled away smoothly. They took the road to Cilldargan without speaking, the silence filled with the sound of Angel FM. Eventually Peter tried to crack the ice.

'Got a nice day for it,' he said.

Assumpta glanced at him. 'Did you fix that, too?'

The silence came down again. After another minute Peter said, 'Do you mind if we make a quick stop before we get there?'

'You're driving.'

At that moment the DJ cut into the music. 'Now, on

behalf of Angel FM and all our listeners, I'd like to dedicate this next record to Father Clifford, who takes his driving test this morning. Good luck, Father, and give 'em hell. By the way, all betting is now closed.'

Peter looked at Assumpta, who was doing her best to suppress a smile. Fifty yards further along he took a right turn on to the road that led up to the hospital.

When he entered the private room Bradley was lying in bed, gazing at the window. He looked very weak. He turned his head slowly as the door opened and looked at Peter standing there.

'I didn't expect to see you again.' His voice had become frail, too.

I can't stay. I'm taking my driving test this morning. But...' Peter went to the table and picked up the chessboard. The pieces were still laid out as they had been when he abandoned their last game. He brought the board and laid it on the bed table. 'I promised you this game, remember? And I think we should try and keep our promises, if we can.'

Bradley took a careful breath before he spoke. 'What changed your mind?'

'Let's just say I heard the voice of an angel.' Peter reached down to the chessboard and made his move. 'Check.'

They looked at each other.

'You know,' Bradley said, 'I agree with your mother. You will go far.'

✝

When they drew up in the car park outside the test centre, Assumpta told Peter she would wait for him in the coffee shop across the road. He nodded absently. He looked troubled.

'Assumpta...'

He pulled off the white strip of clerical collar and opened the neck of his shirt. 'Hold on to this for me.'

Assumpta stared at him for a moment, then she took the collar and put it in her pocket.

Two minutes later, Peter presented himself for the test. Five minutes after that he made his first mistake as he hit the kerb with his rear wheel during a turn-around.

A few minutes later, stopped at a traffic intersection, he saw Father Mac cross the road. Peter waved. Father Mac glared back, noticing that Peter was not wearing his dog collar. Peter looked away, trying to appear unconcerned, drumming his fingers on the wheel. This test, he felt, could easily turn into the most stressful episode of his life, so far.

Meanwhile, back in Ballykissangel, Ambrose Egan was walking the streets in his uniform minus the cap, with headphones on and the signal detector slung around his neck. As he walked he kept his right arm extended in front of him, holding the antenna, which was now repaired in a couple of places with insulating tape. He kept his eye on the meter and continually adjusted the fine-tuning, looking up from time to time to see where the reading was taking him.

Outside Fitzgerald's the needle swung violently. Ambrose turned to face the bar and the signal dropped; he turned the other way, facing Kathleen Hendley's shop, and the needle leapt up the scale.

Keeping his eye fixed on the reading and the antenna well out in front of him, Ambrose crossed the road to the shop, narrowly missing cars coming in both directions.

Inside Kathleen's, the signal got stronger still. Ambrose marched past the counter and into the back. Kathleen came after him, complaining, demanding to know what was going on.

Ambrose went down the stairs to the cellar. Outside the room where all the junk was kept he stared at his meter and could hardly believe it: the needle was right at the high end of the scale, indicating that he was practically on top of the transmitter. He opened the door and went in. The place was a dismal, dispiriting mess of boxes and broken equipment. Ambrose took off his headphones. There was a solitary battered radio lying on a box and it was playing Angel FM.

He couldn't believe the meter had been so easily fooled. He stepped towards a stack of empty cardboard boxes and looked over the top. His eyes widened. There, against the far wall, a large reel-to-reel tape machine was playing. Ambrose pushed the boxes aside, reached out and switched off the machine. Immediately, the radio transmission stopped.

There was a bump as something was knocked over. Ambrose crossed the room and pulled aside one more carton. Daniel Goggin, Kathleen's nephew, was standing there. He shrugged. Kathleen let out a little whimper of shock.

✝

Back at Cilldargan, Peter's test was over. As Assumpta waited by the van he emerged from the test centre accompanied by the examiner.

'Sorry about the mix-up, Mr Clifford,' the man said, handing Peter a sheet of paper.

Peter shrugged. 'Don't worry about it.'

'Your wife'll find it amusing.'

The examiner went back inside. Peter looked at Assumpta, forcing himself to smile.

At the hospital, Father Mac had finished giving Mass and was approaching his car when the senior sister called after him.

'Excuse me, Father MacAnally, before you go…'

'Yes, Sister?'

'It's Mr Bradley. He said he wanted to speak to the priest.'

Father Mac smiled. 'I was hoping he might.'

'Actually, Father, he said he wanted to speak to the young priest.'

Father Mac's smile slipped a fraction. 'Sure,' he said, moving off in the direction of the private wing. 'I hardly look a day over 50.'

✝

In Fitzgerald's, Niamh served behind the bar while Siobhan, Liam and Donal listened to Ambrose having a heated argument with Brian Quigley.

'What did I do?' Quigley demanded.

Ambrose counted on his fingers. 'Conspiracy to pervert the course of justice, breaking and entering – '

'I didn't break anything,' Quigley snarled, pushing his face close to Ambrose's. 'Unlike someone I could mention, damaging government property.'

'In the course of my duty,' Ambrose insisted.

'I wouldn't exactly call being in a wardrobe with my daughter your duty.'

'Dad!' Niamh was blushing.

'What?'

'Can I have a little word?'

Quigley still didn't catch on. 'What?'

She was about to explain to him that his line of defence caused her excruciating embarrassment, when the door opened. Padraig stuck his head inside and shouted, 'They're back!'

'Who's driving?' Siobhan said.

'I've no idea! Come on!'

They all went outside and watched as the van drew up with Assumpta at the wheel. The L-plates were still in place.

Siobhan whooped with delight. 'Thank you, gentlemen,' she cooed as Padraig and Donal handed over their fivers.

Assumpta got out. Peter stayed where he was. The onlookers crowded round, generous with their condolences.

'Never mind, Father.'

'Better luck next time, Father.'

Assumpta was smiling broadly. 'He passed,' she announced.

Siobhan's jaw dropped.

'He was too shocked to drive back.'

Siobhan dug in her pocket for her purse. 'Thank you very much, Father,' she grunted as Peter got out of the van and went into the bar. He saw Ambrose at the far end of the room and listened while Siobhan issued Assumpta with an update.

'Well done, Father,' Ambrose called.

'You too. I hear you found the angel.'

Ambrose waved the praise aside. 'Sure it was nothing. All in a day's work.'

'What'll happen to Daniel?' Peter said.

'Well there was no real harm done. He'll probably get away with a fine.'

'I just wondered,' Peter said, 'if there might not be another way.'

Assumpta called to Peter and pointed to the other end of the bar, where it was more private.

'What?' he said, following her. 'What have I done now?'

'Nothing.' She picked up her jacket and took his clerical collar from the pocket. 'I just wanted to give you this.'

He took it and thanked her.

'We wouldn't want anybody getting the wrong idea, would we, Peter?'

He grinned. 'No, Assumpta.'

He tucked the collar into his shirt pocket just as the door opened and Father Mac walked in.

Peter smiled. 'Have you heard the good news, Father?'

'Indeed,' Father Mac said. 'Mr Bradley asked me to find out so I called the test centre. Congratulations, *Mister* Clifford.'

'Thanks,' Peter nodded sheepishly. 'I must call Mr Bradley.'

'I'm afraid he passed away earlier this afternoon.'

Peter was shocked.

'I'm very sorry,' Assumpta murmured.

'Of course,' Father Mac said, 'he refused to take the last rites from me. Just like the old bugger, God rest his soul. I never could understand the man.'

✞

A few days later, on a scheduled visit to the hospital, Sister took Peter to a small storeroom where young Daniel Goggin sat at a tape console with a turntable on one side and a CD player on the other. In the centre was a microphone and Daniel was addressing it in the authentic tones of the voice of Angel FM.

'There you go now, Mrs Moloney on Ward C, that was Gerry and the Pacemakers, and I hope yours is ticking along nicely, yuk, yuk, yuk...Now on Angel Radio, we have a very special disc for a slipped disc. This one is for Mrs Young in Ward A...'

Cliff Richard struck up with 'Livin' Doll'. Daniel turned and winked at Peter.

Peter went back with Sister to Michael Bradley's room. The chess pieces were still set up on the table.

'I thought I'd leave that until you'd seen it,' Sister said. 'Who was winning?'

'He was. But he resigned.'

'So you won?'

'It was more of a draw.'

'Never mind, Father. He left you a consolation prize.' She held up a bunch of keys. 'He asked me to give you these.' She dropped them into Peter's hand. 'He said something about you going places.'

Peter stared at the keys.

An hour later, he stood in front of a garage door adjacent to Michael Bradley's house in Cilldargan. He put a well-worn Yale key into the lock and turned it. The lock opened smoothly. Peter grasped the handles of both doors and pulled them open.

He heard himself gasp as he looked inside. Facing

him, spotless, shiny, looking as good as it did in the old photograph, was Bradley's sleek black Jowett Javelin saloon.

Peter's heart swelled as he reached out and touched the chrome and enamel of the nameplate. Never in his life had he owned anything so beautiful. It was a car fit for a bishop.

Nineteen

On the morning when many other residents of Ballykissangel were attending the funeral of Bartholomew 'Big Bertie' O'Doyle, Liam and Donal were preparing ditches for the laying of sewage pipes at Quigley's holiday homes site. It was dirty work, made all the muddier by the wetness of the soil and the fact that it turned to clay 2 feet down. The men took turns at operating the JCB – one worked the big digger and the other came behind with a shovel, clearing out the dirt that fell back in as the digger's bucket swung out of the narrow ditch.

After 10 minutes of solid work, Donal took a break. He leaned on his shovel and watched the JCB gouge out huge lumps of earth and clay, making a 3-foot hole at one bite. It was a fascinating thing to watch, but Donal began to realize a lot of loose dirt had piled up in the ditch. He had just picked up his shovel ready to start clearing again when he saw something in the bucket of the digger.

'Stop!' he yelled.

Liam braked the bucket, locked the jib and cut the engine. He jumped down from the cab and came round to where Donal stood.

'What is it?'

Donal pointed. Something that looked like a bone was sticking up out of the dirt. Liam leaned forward, grasped it and pulled it free. It was definitely a bone, a long one. Donal let out a howl at the sight of it and promptly crossed himself. Liam dropped the bone.

There was a moment's indecision, then Liam pointed

up to the road. Donal understood the sign language. He nodded and stepped well back from the bone as Liam started running.

✝

At the cemetery, half a mile down the road, Father Mac was officiating at the burial of Big Bertie O'Doyle. Peter stood alongside Father Mac, assisting.

O'Doyle had been the politician representing the Cill-dargan constituency for nearly 30 years. The importance of the deceased was clear not only from the presence of two priests at the graveside but from the large turnout, which included many of the local great and good who rarely condescended to attend public functions or cere-monies. Brian Quigley was to the fore, as was another local man of conspicuous ambition, Sean Dooley. Ambrose was there too, in his best uniform, watched proudly by Niamh, who winked and smiled every time he glanced in her direction.

'We commend to Almighty God our brother Bartholomew,' Father Mac intoned, his voice carrying clearly down the hillside. He reached for a handful of earth from a spade held by a gravedigger; '...and we commit his body to the ground...' He tossed the earth onto the coffin. '...Earth to earth, ashes to ashes, dust to dust. The Lord bless him and keep him, the Lord make his face to shine upon him and be gracious to him, the Lord lift up his countenance upon him and give him peace.'

When the service was over, Peter stood beside Father Mac at the cemetery gates, saying goodbye to mourners as they left.

'That was a grand send-off,' Brian Quigley said, shak-ing hands with Father Mac and Peter. 'I trust you'll do the same for me one day.'

'Only if you get yourself elected to the Dáil,' Father Mac said, smiling broadly.

Peter asked Quigley if he was tempted to stand in the by-election.

'No, no, no, the council takes up enough of my time.'

Father Mac looked up the hill at a black-coated figure coming towards them. 'We need someone to save us from that scoundrel, Brian.'

'Who is he?' Peter asked.

'Sean Dooley,' Father Mac said. 'Plumber, councillor and Antichrist.'

'That's some CV.'

'He was Big Bertie's favourite to take over from him,' Quigley said.

Dooley came forward, flanked by his lieutenants. He was a vigorous man in his 40s, with neatly cut fair hair and the kind of pink, pampered skin that was not common among plumbers. He had a politician's steady eye and a mouth always ready to issue a retort. When he smiled, he managed to make it look like an opinion.

'Father MacAnally,' he said, pumping hands. 'Brian.'

'Sean.' Quigley kept it cold.

Dooley looked at Peter. 'I don't believe I've had the pleasure.'

'Peter Clifford. I'm the new curate.'

'Sean Dooley. Very pleased to meet you, Peter. Pity it's on such a sad day.'

'I can see your heart bleeding from here,' Quigley said.

Dooley forced a laugh, but his eyes remained serious. 'Always the joker, eh Brian?' He turned to Father Mac. 'Of course, I'd prefer to be cremated myself. It's far more hygienic than this medieval custom of yours.'

Father Mac frowned. 'Burning is for witches.'

'What's your rush, Sean?' Quigley said. 'You'll have enough flames to cope with in the next life.'

This time Dooley didn't laugh. He didn't even smile. He nodded to Father Mac and to Peter, then walked away, followed by his aides.

On a hillock nearby, Niamh and Ambrose were talking.

'I mean it Niamh,' Ambrose said. 'The next time we meet at Saint Joe's, I want you to be wearing white.'

'I want to get married as much as you do, but Dad will never agree so soon after the last fiasco. And I want a proper reception.'

'You had one!'

'I'd like the groom to be there this time.'

Ambrose grinned. He still found it hard to believe that he had actually thought he wanted to be a priest.

'So we'll have to wait and catch Dad at the right moment.'

'Well look at him,' Ambrose said. Quigley was a few yards away, walking with Father Mac to where the cars were parked. 'No time like the present.'

Ambrose went down the little slope and stepped up to Quigley. 'Ah, Brian – '

At that moment Liam appeared, breathless and apparently distressed. 'Sorry, Father...' He collared Quigley, taking him aside. 'Mr Quigley, you have to come quick.'

'What is it?' Quigley pulled his arm free. 'I've a wake to go to.'

'I can't tell you here. Just come and look...'

Quigley resisted, but finally they got in the Land Rover and drove to the building site. Quigley picked his way over the churned ground carefully, trying to keep the mud off his polished shoes. He stopped by the digger's bucket. Donal, pale and worried, pointed to the bone lying on top. Quigley picked it up and stared at it.

'It's a sheep,' he announced.

Donal shook his head anxiously. 'I've never seen a sheep that size.'

Liam was staring at Quigley. 'Are you sure?'

'No doubt about it.' Quigley held out the bone to Donal.

'Oh, no...' Donal backed away. 'I'm not touching it.'

'He thinks it's human,' Liam said.

Quigley snorted. 'What are you, a doctor? Here.' He handed the bone to Liam. 'Keep it safe and for heaven's sake say nothing. We don't want folk getting upset for no reason now, do we?'

Back at Fitzgerald's a fiddler was playing his way through his repertoire of dirges and laments, while those gathered for the wake tucked into free food and drink. The place hadn't been so busy since the height of the previous summer season.

In the kitchen, Niamh and Siobhan were sitting at the big table, which was laden with cakes and sandwiches. Assumpta transferred another tray of sausage rolls from the worktop to the table and helped herself to a cake.

'Tuck in,' she told the girls. 'Big Bertie's paying.'

Niamh shook her head. 'No more. I want to be able to get into my wedding dress.'

Assumpta looked dubious. She finished the cake and picked up another. 'Do you really think your dad's going to cough up a second time?'

'Sure the dust has barely settled on his wallet,' Siobhan said.

'It'll happen,' Niamh promised. 'You'll see.' She took the cake from Assumpta's fingers and put it back on the plate. 'So no more for you, either. We can't afford another bridesmaid's dress.'

'Always the bridesmaid,' Assumpta sighed dramatically, 'never the bride.'

Through in the bar Peter was talking to Dr Ryan. They had been discussing the unpleasant sound the bell of St Joseph's made that morning at the service. Peter called across the room to Father Mac, who was at a table by the window.

'We're going to have to do something about the church bell, Father. It sounds dreadful.'

Father Mac didn't agree. He said it sounded fine to him.

The truth was that the bell had sounded terrible for a long time. A crack in the rim meant that it no longer resonated properly when it was struck; the result was a dull clank rather than a ring.

Peter turned to Dr Ryan. 'What's your diagnosis?'

'I think we're talking intensive care.'

'I think we're talking dead and buried,' Assumpta said as she put down a tray of sandwiches and cakes.

'Thank you for that, Assumpta,' Father Mac said drily. 'But it makes no difference. We don't have the money for such luxuries.'

'Well why don't we start a restoration fund?' Peter said. 'I mean, that could really bring the community together.'

'That'll be a first,' Assumpta muttered.

A hand slid over Assumpta's shoulder and took a sandwich. As she tried to see who it was a voice complained in her ear, 'You know I like mustard on my sandwiches.'

She turned, and immediately she blushed. The young man grinned at her. 'Leo!' she gasped. 'What the hell are you doing here?'

He looked at the priests and frowned. 'Assumpta, please. Language.'

They embraced, holding each other tightly. When they separated Assumpta introduced the stranger. 'Leo McGarvey. We were at college together.'

Peter made a swift assessment. Leo was young, probably not yet 30, he was good-looking, smartly dressed and he seemed familiar. Suddenly it dawned on Peter that he had seen Leo earlier, holding a microphone and talking to a television camera outside the church immediately after the service for Bertie O'Doyle.

'Assumpta was the smart one at college,' Leo was saying. 'She always had a crease in her jeans.'

'Tell us more,' Peter said.

'On pain of death,' Assumpta warned.

Leo turned out to be a good talker. Within 10 minutes he had endeared himself, not simply by relating one good yarn after another, but by leaving space for other people to put in their contributions. Inevitably, the talk got around to the forthcoming election triggered by the death of Bertie O'Doyle.

'This is just a by-election,' Father Mac said, 'but mark my words, if that heathen has his way we'll be the first up against the wall. He should stick to plumbing.'

Padraig, who was sitting at the same table, said, 'I'd certainly never trust a man with a ballot box in one hand and a toilet plunger in the other.'

Leo was leaning on the bar, listening. He turned to Peter. 'What do you think, Father?'

'I think the Church should keep out of party politics.'

Father Mac looked shocked. 'Who's side are you on?'

'It's not a question of sides.'

'This is Ireland,' Assumpta said quietly. 'There are always sides.'

'Well then,' Peter said, 'maybe Mr Dooley has a point. Church and State should remain separate.'

'Absolutely right,' Leo said.

'What?' Father Mac was wide-eyed. 'You can't do that!'

'Why not?' Peter said. 'Everyone else does.'

'We are not everyone else!'

Quigley came in, late for the start of the wake and anxious to catch up.

'Ah! Here's the man for the job,' said Father Mac. 'Local councillor, business man, churchgoer.'

'What are you on about?' Quigley said.

'Brian Quigley, TD,' Padraig said, teasing. 'Member for Cilldargan. What do you say?'

Quigley made no response. 'Can I get anyone another drink?'

Several hands went up.

'Looks like he's canvassing already,' Assumpta said.

Quigley looked at the silent, expectant faces around

him. 'Now why in heaven's name,' he said, 'would I want to go into politics?'

✝

Within the week Quigley was canvassing in direct opposition to Dooley. They travelled from town to town in their poster-covered vehicles with loudspeakers mounted on top, coaxing the voters to do the right thing when the big day came.

The central message in Quigley's campaign patter, repeated over and over, was 'Vote for Quigley, your local independent candidate – you know it makes sense, because when it comes to Ballykay, Brian means business.'

Dooley's main message, delivered with more gusto, was, 'If you vote for Dooley you're voting for the future – the spirit of Big Bertie lives on.'

For days on end the opposing messages rang out across the constituency, and then, one morning, Quigley's Land Rover came round the corner from Ballykissangel's main street, Liam steering while Quigley delivered his exhortation, and as they crossed the bridge Dooley's Mercedes appeared right in front of them, coming into town. The two vehicles stopped, nose to nose.

'What are you doing here?' Quigley demanded through the loudspeaker.

'I've just as much right to be here as you,' Dooley announced over his own sound system.

'Clear off,' Quigley snapped. 'You're not wanted in this town.'

'Face it Quigley, your days are over.'

The words rang out across the town as Quigley took a fresh grip on his microphone.

'What do you know about politics?' he boomed. 'You're just a plumber.'

Dooley stood up, still clutching the microphone, his

head appearing through the opening in the sunroof. 'I'm not a plumber. I'm a sanitary engineer. There's a difference.'

'You wouldn't know the difference between a U-turn and a U-bend.'

'But I know a cowboy when I see one!'

'Vote Quigley, a man you can trust!'

'For a new beginning send Dooley to Dublin!'

Their noise swelled to a roar as they turned up the volume and shouted as loud as they could. Then Quigley's system suddenly gave out and began squealing. He banged the microphone on the dashboard, trying to kill the howl. Dooley laughed uproariously into his mike and signalled his driver to pass on into the town.

'Onward!' his speaker blared as he crossed the bridge and turned into the main street. 'Vote Dooley for reliability!'

TWENTY

One week to the day after installing a bell fund collection box in Kathleen Hendley's shop, Peter dropped by to check on the take. When he opened the box a handful of coppers fell out. Kathleen watched solicitously.

'Looks like I'll have to find some other way of raising money for the bell.'

'It's a disgrace,' Kathleen said. 'Folk round here should be ashamed of themselves.'

Peter picked up a copy of the local newspaper and looked at the front page. 'If only we had some of the coverage Sean Dooley's getting, we'd have no problem. He hasn't been off the front page in the last couple of days.'

'What do you expect?' Kathleen said archly. 'He plays golf with the editor.'

Brian Quigley came in with a batch of campaign posters rolled up under his arm.

'Ah, Brian,' Peter said amiably. 'Campaign going well?'

'For Dooley,' Kathleen said, edging the newspaper into Quigley's line of view.

Quigley glanced at it. 'The cheek of that man,' he grunted. 'I was helping this town while he was still in nappies.'

Kathleen made a sour face. 'You've only ever helped yourself, Brian Quigley.'

'I've no time to argue with you now.' Quigley unrolled a poster. 'Put one of these up in your window.'

'I'll do no such thing. As far as the election goes, I'm strictly non-partisan.'

Quigley stared. 'What are you talking about?'

'If I put yours up, then Mr Dooley's supporters might boycott the shop. I could scare off half my customers.'

'Well why break the habit of a lifetime?' Quigley turned to Peter. 'Here Father – you'll put one up in the church?'

'Sorry,' Peter said. 'I'm afraid I'm with Kathleen on this one.'

Quigley sighed. 'How about if I were to make a donation to your bell fund?'

'Well...' Peter nodded and brought forward the collection box. 'We do need all the help we can get.'

'Now you're talking.' Quigley took a tenner from his wallet and pushed it into the box. 'We'll make a parish priest of you yet.'

'Thank you, Brian.'

Peter walked out of the shop before Quigley could give him a poster.

'Just a minute, what about my...'

The door closed.

Quigley sighed and pocketed his wallet. 'I've just been robbed by a priest.'

Peter crossed the road to Fitzgerald's. In a corner by the fireplace Siobhan was examining a long bone Donal had brought along in a carrier bag for her to evaluate. He said his dog had dug it up, though he had no idea where.

Siobhan had studied the bone carefully and assured Donal it was not a sheep, as he had suggested. She didn't know what it was, she admitted. It could be anything – it could even be human.

She dropped the bone back in the bag as Peter entered the bar. Donal tucked it down by his side and did his best to look nonchalant. This was almost impossible, because now he was really distressed about the degree of peril in which he might have placed his mortal soul – and besides, Donal had never looked nonchalant in his life.

'Donal,' Peter said.

'Father.' Donal turned on his heel and left.

'Coffee or something stronger?' Assumpta asked Peter.

'Strong coffee.' As Assumpta poured it he said, 'You were right. No-one's interested in the bell.'

'Never mind, Father. Next time there's a funeral, you can use this.' Assumpta picked up the handbell behind the bar and rang it.

'Last orders already?'

Peter looked round and saw Leo McGarvey.

'Leo. I didn't know you were staying in town.'

'Ah, well, I've got to cover the election campaign, so I thought, who better to stay with than my old segotia.'

'He's renting a room,' Assumpta said, clarifying the point at once.

'Yeah. I'm hoping for a discount for old time's sake.'

'He should be so lucky,' Assumpta told Peter.

'Don't let her fool you, Father. She wasn't always this hard-headed.'

Again Assumpta addressed Peter: 'She wasn't always trying to run a business.'

Peter resisted the impulse to register this situation for what it was; he resisted, but it did no good. Leo was clearly smitten and had taken the first excuse available to come back. Assumpta, for her own part, was confused. Peter knew all this and believed Assumpta knew that he knew it. That created discomfort, but Peter didn't think he should try to change that. In his view it was never wise to undermine situations that could, if they were weathered, move towards some kind of resolution.

Assumpta shifted the talk to safer ground. 'Maybe Leo could help you get some publicity.'

'That's a thought,' Peter said.

'Leo was mystified. 'What about?'

'The bell of Ballykay,' Assumpta said.

Leo smiled. 'I know who that is.'

Assumpta coloured slightly. 'Wrong sort.'

'We're trying to raise money to restore the church bell,' Peter said. 'Do you think you could do a piece?'

'Er, well...' Leo appeared less than enthusiastic. 'I'll think about it.'

Peter nodded. 'I imagine that's your way of saying no.'

Quigley pushed open the door and waved to Peter. 'Father, could you come outside for a minute, please.'

As Peter went out Niamh walked in. Leo followed Peter outside, telling Quigley he needed an interview as soon as possible.

On the pavement in front of Fitzgerald's Quigley put a finger to his lips and pointed in the direction of St Joseph's. The three men listened. The Angelus bell began to ring. Quigley put on a pained face. The dull clank was even worse at this distance.

'I know it sounds awful, Brian,' Peter said, 'but I'm still hoping that the parishioners will raise the money.'

Quigley told him he would have more luck raising the dead. 'It's no use waiting,' he said. 'I'm paying for the restoration myself.'

Leo raised his eyebrows at Peter. 'An answer to your prayers.'

Peter was puzzled. 'That's very generous of you, Brian, but – '

'No buts. We can't go on with this noise.'

'Well...' Peter shrugged. 'I'll have to check with Father Mac first.'

'I already have,' Quigley said. 'He agrees. The bell's coming down tomorrow afternoon.'

In the bar Assumpta poured a glass of mineral water.

'There you go.' She put it in front of Niamh. 'So. How much have you lost now?'

'Three pounds four ounces. Not that Ambrose has noticed. What about you?'

'Nearly five.'

Niamh was impressed. 'You've lost five pounds?'

'Lost and found them again. Now I think they're breeding.'

'Well there's no hurry. Every time I mention the wedding to Dad he just pleads poverty. He's more interested in that blasted election.'

'Poor Leo's struggling to find even a half-decent story in it.'

Niamh smiled coyly. 'Of all the gin joints in all the world, he had to walk into yours.'

'Look, we had some good times together, that's all. It's a long time ago.'

'It's never too late.'

'You behave,' Assumpta said. 'We're just good friends now, OK?'

Niamh wrinkled her nose. 'Where have I heard that before?'

Peter came in, grinning. 'Great news,' he told Niamh. 'Your dad's paying for the bell restoration.'

'Oops,' Assumpta said.

Peter looked at her. 'What?'

Niamh got off her stool. 'He said he can't afford my wedding because he's broke.'

Peter groaned. 'I'm sorry. I'd no idea.'

'It's a publicity stunt,' Assumpta said. 'He's only doing it to get votes.'

'You're too cynical,' Peter told her. 'I really think it's a genuine offer.'

Niamh marched to the door and pulled it open. 'Bless me, Father, for I am about to sin.'

She found her father down a side street, cutting down Dooley campaign posters from lamp posts and tying up his own in their place. Niamh challenged him about the money he was prepared to spend on an old, cracked bell but not on his only daughter's wedding.

'I've told you already,' he said, 'this election is costing me a fortune. There are no prizes for coming second.'

'And where do I come?' Niamh demanded. 'After a bell?'

'We'll discuss it after I'm elected. It'll be worth it in the end. You'll see.'

'And what if you lose? What then?'

Quigley stared at Niamh. 'Dooley in the Dáil? Doomsday.'

✝

Next morning, preparing himself for the day, Peter put on the television for the early news. As he got out the cornflakes and put a bowl on the table the announcer read a story about disgruntled investors in Dublin being refused a chance of a takeover bid in a lucrative plastic goods factory because 30 per cent of existing sharehold- ers said they opposed the move. The ins and outs of the story were probably interesting, Peter thought, and he had no doubt he would have a better understanding of the business mind if he paid attention to such reports, but he simply didn't want to. Far too many people, he feared, had a tendency to value life's trimmings and attachments – things like share portfolios – more highly than they valued life itself. He shut out the sound as he took the milk from the fridge and hunted in a drawer for a spoon.

Then a word got through to him: 'Cilldargan.'

He went through to the living room. The announcer had moved on to a story about the by-election. 'A poll this morning suggests that the two main candidates are running neck and neck, with only a week left before polling day.'

Peter thought that was it, until the announcer said they were now going over live to Leo McGarvey on the campaign trail with candidate Brian Quigley.

Leo's face appeared. 'I'm here in Brian Quigley's home town of Ballykissangel, where the candidate is supervising the restoration of the chapel bell. With me is Father Frank MacAnally, parish priest for the area.'

Peter was motionless in front of the TV. He couldn't

believe what he was seeing. In the background, the church bell was being loaded onto a trailer, Quigley conspicuously overseeing the operation. The shot widened to include Father Mac in the foreground.

'You must be delighted about what's happening this morning, Father.'

Father Mac smiled hammily and said, 'It's an answer to all our prayers. I've been waiting years for this to happen, and now, thanks to Brian Quigley, we really can ring the changes.' Father Mac smiled to camera again, pleased with his little play on words.

Peter didn't wait for any more. He turned and ran out of the house. He arrived at the church doors just as Leo and the television crew were packing up.

Father Mac looked enormously pleased with himself.

'Ah, Father,' he cried, 'There you are. I'm afraid you've missed the show.'

'I saw it on the TV,' Peter said, panting. 'Father, this is – '

'How did I look? Could you see my chins?'

'What is going on? I was told that the bell would be coming out this afternoon.'

'Well it was,' Father Mac said, 'but when Brian spoke to the TV fella, he suggested doing it for the breakfast news. Did no-one tell you?'

'Strangely enough, no.' Peter looked up at a sound from the belfry. Two unsightly conical speakers were being lashed into place. 'What's he doing up there?'

At that moment Sean Dooley drew up in his car. He got out and came running along the path to the front of the church.

'This is some stunt!' he shouted.

Quigley appeared from the church. 'Ah, Father Peter, just in time,' he said brightly, 'and Sean!'

'OK, Mr Quigley?' Liam shouted from the belfry.

Quigley turned and gave him a thumbs up. 'OK, Liam.'

Liam waved back and disappeared inside the belfry.

'Using your church like this!' Dooley yelled, addressing Peter. 'You ought to be ashamed of yourself!'

'But I didn't – '

'You leave him out of this!' Father Mac warned Dooley.

'It's all right, Father,' Peter said, ready to explain himself, but then he found he couldn't get a word in.

'You're just as bad,' Dooley told Father Mac.

'You can't speak to me like that! I'm a parish priest!'

'And I'm a councillor! Who elected you?'

The threat of physical violence was averted suddenly as the deafening noise of multiple church bells poured out of the speakers in the belfry. For the moment everyone was struck dumb.

'The bells of Galway Cathedral,' Quigley announced, coming forward again and shouting to make himself heard. 'I thought we needed something in the meantime.' He smirked. 'It's fully automatic.'

Quigley and Father Mac both looked very pleased. Peter was dumbstruck. Dooley was furious.

'Two can play at this game, Quigley!' he shouted, and stamped back to his car.

✝

At 11.00 am Peter dropped in at Fitzgerald's for a cup of coffee. Niamh, not in the brightest of spirits, was dissipating some of her annoyance by polishing the bar. Assumpta looked gloomy, too. She looked at Peter as she put his coffee in front of him.

'What was it you were saying about the Church keeping out of politics?'

'Not you too,' he groaned, 'Please…'

'Dad will stop at nothing to win this election,' Niamh said, rubbing furiously.

Leo came in and strode up to the bar. He grinned at Peter. 'Not a bad story, eh?' He patted Peter on the back.

'Thanks for suggesting it in the first place.'

'My pleasure.' Peter forced a smile, then took his coffee and his newspaper to a table by the window.

'This calls for a celebration,' Leo said to Assumpta. 'How about we hit the bright lights of Ballykay tonight?'

Her smile was evasive. 'The only bright lights round here are used for directing traffic.'

Leo was not deterred. 'There must be somewhere we can go for dinner.'

Niamh had already taken an interest. 'There's the Castle Court in Cilldargan,' she suggested. 'It's where Ambrose proposed.'

She gave Assumpta a winsome, knowing look, and got a withering scowl in return.

'I'll book a table right away,' Leo said.

'Hold on!' Assumpta looked peeved. 'I haven't arranged anyone to cover for me here.'

'It's OK,' Niamh said, 'I'm not doing anything.'

'Great, that's settled,' Leo said brightly. He went to the door. 'Thanks, Niamh.' He waved and left.

Assumpta turned to Niamh. 'Having a fancy meal is hardly going to get me into a bridesmaid's dress.'

'I doubt you'll ever need to,' Niamh said, looking glum again and rather sorry for herself.

Assumpta stood by the pumps and seethed in silence. She tried not to look at Peter, who pretended to be absorbed in his crossword.

TWENTY-ONE

$\mathbf{S}$hortly after 6.00 pm Liam arrived at
the building-site caravan to give Donal a lift home. The
caravan, which served as office, rest room and tool store,
was plastered on the outside with Quigley's campaign
posters. Seeing them, Liam remembered that he was
required to wear a campaign rosette at all times, and he
checked to see that it was in place on his overalls.

When he went inside Donal was not lounging at the
table, as was his wont by this hour. He was standing over
by the window, looking pale and fidgety.

'What's the matter with you?'

Donal nodded at the table. Sitting there, muddy but
unmistakable, was a human skull.

Liam stared at it for a long time. Then he turned to
Donal. 'Before we do anything else,' he said, 'I think we
should have a drink.'

At Fitzgerald's, Leo McGarvey had arrived to take
Assumpta to dinner. He sat near the end of the bar with
Siobhan and Padraig. Niamh was serving.

'Assumpta doesn't get out much these days,' Padraig
said. 'Does she, Siobhan?'

Siobhan shook her head.

'You surprise me,' Leo said. 'When we were students,
fellas were falling over themselves to take her out.'

'In here,' Padraig said, 'they just fall over.'

'There are only two eligible men in this town,' Siobhan told Leo. 'One's a policeman, one's a priest.' She
pointed at Niamh. 'She's marrying one and the other
doesn't count.'

Liam and Donal came in.

'Talking of eligible men,' Niamh said.

They came up to the bar. 'Two large whiskeys,' Liam said.

'How's the rag-and-bone business these days?' Siobhan called.

'Don't know what you're talking about.' Donal said it too quickly and got a dirty look from Liam.

Leo asked if they worked for Brian Quigley. Liam said yes and Donal said no. Padraig explained they were in two minds about it.

'What do you want to know for?' Liam asked.

'Anything about Mr Quigley interests me,' Leo said. 'How's the new building project coming along?'

'There's nothing going on up there,' Donal snapped.

'What he means is,' Liam said, 'it's not finished yet.'

'There you are.' Niamh put the whiskeys on the bar. 'Six-twenty.'

'Here…' Leo reached for his wallet. 'Allow me.'

'No,' Liam snapped, then added, 'thank you.' He paid for the drinks, picked them up and led Donal away to a corner table.

Leo watched them, intrigued by their odd behaviour, but was suddenly distracted by the sight of Assumpta. As she walked towards him the light was behind her, making her hair a dark coppery nimbus, full and buoyant, touching her shoulders. She wore black high heels and black stockings, a short silky black coat over a short black dress, and her make-up was immaculate. Several men whistled as she walked across the bar.

'Cut it out,' Assumpta growled.

Niamh looked at Leo. 'What do you think?'

For a moment he was speechless. 'I think she looks fantastic,' he said.

Niamh grinned.

Assumpta stood there smiling awkwardly. Finally she flapped her arms, nodded at the door and said, 'Let's go.'

A moment after they left Donal finished his drink in two deep gulps. Liam watched him and then did the same. They had hardly spoken to each other, and now Donal was anxious to be off and moving, doing something, making the weight of worry and fear sufferable.

They left the bar and stood outside looking up and down the street.

'I think maybe we should go back up there, after,' Liam said.

Donal nodded. 'I'll come and knock your door, when it's darker.'

They walked off in opposite directions. The whiskey in Donal's blood, combined with the cool, fresh air, made him feel more decisive. He started to walk faster, heading for the church, determined to know how his immortal soul stood.

At the gates of St Joseph's he waited while a straggle of parishioners came out. When he saw Father Peter he stepped away from the shadow of the gate post.

'Father, can I have a word?'

Peter nodded. 'Of course.'

'I wanted to ask you...' Donal looked over his shoulder. 'Is body snatching a sin?'

'I'm sorry?'

At that moment someone called out, 'Father!' Both Peter and Donal turned. It was Ambrose, in uniform. He walked towards them.

'Never mind,' Donal said. 'Good evening, Father.' He moved off.

Ambrose stopped beside Peter and watched Donal hurry away. 'What's up with him?'

Peter shook his head. 'I'm not sure.' He turned to Ambrose. 'Was there something you wanted to ask me?'

'I wanted to tell you I've made a decision, Father.'

'What's that?'

'Niamh and I are going to elope.'

'Elope?'

'I can't be waiting for Brian Quigley any longer. What do you think?'

'What does Niamh think?'

'I haven't told her yet.'

'Well,' Peter said, 'I'd speak to her first.'

Ambrose considered that. 'You're right. Thank you, Father.'

Peter watched him walk away, full of purpose.

✝

It was after midnight when a taxi brought Assumpta and Leo back from the Castle Court at Cilldargan. Leo paid off the driver and they tiptoed into the darkened bar. Assumpta went to reception and switched on the desk lamp.

Leo stood examining his empty wallet. 'Where have we just come from?' he said. 'Timbuktu?'

'I live in the middle of nowhere, remember?' Assumpta lowered her voice to a conspirator's mutter. 'Do you fancy a nightcap?'

Leo waved the wallet. 'As long as it's on the house.'

In spite of all her misgivings, Assumpta had enjoyed her night out and now, mellow with wine and enjoying the company of an old friend, she gave way to a small irresponsible impulse.

'Do you remember that cocktail we invented during finals?' she said.

Leo stood thinking.

'The Terminator,' Assumpta remembered.

'The Terminator,' Leo said, recalling it too. 'A very wild drink. You don't know how to make that, do you?'

'Watch me.'

Five minutes later, having used seven ingredients, a shaker and a sieve, Assumpta filled two cocktail glasses with the scarlet drink and put them on the bar. She and Leo sat on stools and set the surfaces of the drinks alight. When the liquor had burned for a slow count of 10 the flames were extinguished, the glasses were clinked and they each took a good swallow.

Leo put down his glass at once and sat gasping.

'Wow! That's a blast from the past.'

Assumpta nodded, said 'Yeah,' in a strangled voice, then gave way to a coughing spasm.

Leo smiled. He sat watching her. His expression changed and became almost sad. 'Don't you miss it?' he said.

'Miss what?'

'The past?'

She held his melancholy gaze. 'The past was a long time ago, Leo.'

They were silent for a while, sipping their drinks, getting used to the burn.

'I don't know how you manage living here,' Leo said eventually.

'You get used to it.'

'No wonder you've been driven to drink.'

Assumpta smiled, then appeared to shake herself. 'Look, I really enjoyed this evening, I haven't had so much fun in ages, but – '

'I miss you, you know,' he said, interrupting.

She said nothing.

'I mean, I've been out with other people since us, but...'

'Yes, well...' Assumpta got off the stool. 'I'd better go. I have to be up early. Breakfasts start at 7.30 and – '

'Assumpta...'

'I got muesli in for you specially, seeing as you always used to eat mine.' She headed for the stairs.

'I still love you,' he said.

She turned and looked at him.

'I'm serious.'

'Good night, Leo.'

'Assumpta.'

'What?'

'I hate muesli. It must have been someone else.'

He smiled.

She smiled back, then she went upstairs.

Leo sat staring at the bar. He picked up his glass and swallowed the remains of his Terminator. He put down the glass gently, then sat there silently gasping for air.

✝

At roughly the time Leo was deciding to turn in, Liam and Donal were up at the building site, working the JCB by artificial light. They had decided that neither one of them would rest easy until they knew what else was waiting to be unearthed, if anything.

At 7.30 am Liam called Quigley on his mobile phone. He talked across a barrage of complaints and said bluntly that he believed there was something up here at the caravan that would justify Mr Quigley taking some time away from his precious campaign.

Quigley argued a while longer, pleading the tightness of time and the impossibility of deviating from his schedule.

'We'll be waiting for you at the caravan,' Liam said, and switched off the phone. He told Donal to stop moping and boil up the kettle.

When Quigley arrived he strode into the caravan looking appropriately stern, his rosette ribbons flapping.

'This had better be good,' he said. 'I'm supposed to be canvassing.'

'Sorry Mr Quigley,' Liam said, starting to raise the corner of a tea cloth that had been draped over something on the table. He pulled the cloth aside. 'We thought you should see this.'

It was the skull.

Quigley stared at it. 'Jaysus…'

'It goes with these,' Liam said. He flipped back the lid of an old leather suitcase. It was full of bones.

Donal shuddered. 'No-one will live in a house built on the bones of the dead.'

'Yes, thank you, Donal,' Quigley snapped. 'It had crossed my mind.'

'We think we know who it is,' Liam said.

'You do?'

Liam held up the skull so that it faced Quigley. 'Think back. Who does it remind you of?'

'Of course,' Quigley said sarcastically, 'How could I forget those eyes?'

'Not the eyes,' Liam said. He pointed to the solitary protuberance on the upper jaw. 'The tooth.'

Quigley took the skull and held it close to his face, peering at it hard. 'One-Tooth Tommy?'

'We'll rot in hell for this,' Donal whined.

Quigley told him to shut up.

'This used to be his land, didn't it?' Liam said.

There was a knock at the caravan door. Quigley threw the skull to Liam. Liam threw it to Donal. Donal caught it and stood there looking doomed.

Quigley pushed open the caravan door a crack. Leo was standing there. 'Mr McGarvey,' Quigley said, all business. 'What can we do for you?'

Leo tried to look past Quigley but he moved, blocking the view.

'I was hoping I could have that interview with you now.'

'Far too busy, I'm afraid,' Quigley said breezily. 'I have to get back on the campaign trail.'

Quigley turned his head and shouted as if Liam were several yards away, instead of standing just out of sight beyond the door.

'Liam? Bring those er, rosettes with you.'

Behind Quigley Donal threw the skull into the suitcase among the bones and shut the lid.

'Here…' Quigley, improvising, plucked the rosette from his lapel and stuck it in Leo's. 'You can have mine for now.'

✝

Ambrose was standing on the vast lawn at Brian Quigley's house, pleading with Niamh to see reason, while she travelled back and forward on a motorized lawnmower.

'Go on, Niamh, just think about it!' he shouted over the noise of the motor.

'I am not eloping with you!'

'Why not?'

'I'm not arguing with you, Ambrose. When I say no, I mean no. You'd better get used to it.'

'We don't need all this fussing around,' Ambrose cried, looking desperate now. 'I say we just run away together and get married on our own terms.'

Niamh stopped the mower and glared at him. 'My terms are, I want to get married in Ballykay.'

'But sure, eloping would be very romantic, don't you think?'

'Obviously we have very different ideas of what is romantic. I don't regard driving away to some registry office in your patrol car to be one of them.'

'So what do you want?'

'I want a real wedding with all the trimmings.'

Ambrose shook his head. 'You make it sound like Christmas dinner, you know?'

'I'm obviously not making myself very clear. It's really very simple. If you don't marry me properly, Ambrose Egan, you don't marry me at all.'

With that, Niamh put the motor in gear again and drove off in a flurry of grass clippings.

TWENTY-TWO

Peter was in the sacristy at St Joseph's, robing for Mass. Leo McGarvey was with him.

'I can't say I've heard of this One-Tooth Tommy,' Peter said. 'But then I'm new around here. Try Michael Ryan, the doctor. He's lived here all his life. He took over the practice from his father.'

'Thanks,' Leo said. 'I will.'

Peter paused, holding a coat hanger. 'How did you hear about him, anyway?

'Ah, Father, you understand, I have to protect my sources.'

Peter smiled politely, although he was sure some of his amusement showed. He watched Leo go to the door and pause.

'There was something else I wanted to ask you. About Assumpta.'

'Oh?'

'You see, when we were at college,' – Leo gestured awkwardly – 'we were very close.'

'You were in love,' Peter said, hoping Leo would follow his example and speak plainly.

'Very much so. But then right after we graduated her mother died. She'd been widowed a few years, so Assumpta came back to look after the family business. I wanted to be a journalist, so I was going to move down here and start on the local rag just so I could be near her.'

Peter found himself being drawn into the story. 'So what happened?'

'I got offered a trainee job on Fleet Street.'

'Difficult choice.'

'No,' Leo said, 'not for me. I was all ready to come here. It was Assumpta who persuaded me to go. She said if I didn't, I'd regret it for the rest of my life. So I went. And that was the end of us.'

'Only you still love her.'

'I don't think I've ever really loved anyone else,' Leo sighed. 'Trouble is, I don't know about her. She seems distant.' He paused. 'It's as if she's thinking about some-one else.'

Peter didn't know if a response was expected. Leo had gone silent.

'Has she said something?'

'No,' Leo said, 'and that's unlike her. She's very straight.'

'Yes.'

Leo shrugged. 'I just have my doubts. They go with the job, unfortunately. What do you think?'

'Well.' Peter wasn't sure how much he could rely on his objectivity which, he felt, was not working as well as it might. 'Perhaps instead of treating her with suspicion, you should treat her as a friend. Talk to her. Tell her how you really feel.'

'Yeah, you're right.' Leo grinned. 'Like Assumpta says, you're not just a pretty face.'

Peter hoped he wasn't blushing. Up in the tower, the recording of the Galway bells rang out, giving him an opportunity to change the subject.

'At least they're accurate,' he said.

Twenty seconds into the peal, Quigley's recorded voice joined in the racket from the belfry: 'These bells are brought to you by Brian Quigley, your independent candidate.'

Peter stared at Leo. Leo stared back. Neither one of them could quite believe what they were hearing. As the message was repeated Peter turned and ran out of the sacristy. Leo ran out behind him.

Peter got to the tower door and turned the handle. It was locked. The voice from the belfry boomed out across the town: 'Vote for Quigley. Brian means business for Ballykay.'

'I don't believe it.' Peter wrenched at the door again as Leo ran up. 'He's still got the key.'

'Turn off the mains,' Leo suggested.

Peter tapped the door with his knuckles. 'The mains are behind here.'

Assumpta's van pulled up outside the railings. She got out and waved at Peter and Leo. 'What's going on?'

'It's our independent candidate,' Peter said. 'He's acting independently. I'll phone Father Mac, he has a spare key.' Peter dashed off to the sacristy, pulling off the ceremonial robes as he went. Leo crossed to the railings.

'I need to talk to you,' he told Assumpta.

'What about?'

'About us. I don't want to make the same mistake twice.'

'We didn't make a mistake,' Assumpta said firmly. 'We did the right thing at the time.'

'And what about now?'

She sighed. 'I don't know, Leo…'

'Well, Peter thought we ought to talk.'

Assumpta stared at him in disbelief. 'You spoke to Peter about us?'

Peter came haring back, wearing his black shirt and trousers. 'Father Mac's out,' he shouted. 'There's only one other way.' He looked at Assumpta. 'I need your help, when you have a minute.'

He went and stood by the church doors, looking up at the belfry as the promotional messages continued to pour out over the sound of pealing bells.

Assumpta looked at Leo. 'I don't want you talking to him about us again, OK? Ever.'

She shut the van door and strode off to see what Peter wanted. Leo stood there, looking puzzled.

Ten minutes later, Peter leaned Assumpta's aluminium ladder against the belfry wall and pushed up the extension until it reached the window in the tower.

Assumpta held the ladder as Peter climbed up. A small crowd had formed to watch, some of them parishioners waiting to go in to Mass.

'Do you think this is a good idea?' Padraig called.

Siobhan asked if Peter would be down in time for Mass.

Peter looked down from two-thirds the way up the ladder. 'I'm not risking that tape going off again during it.'

He climbed to the top and steadied himself. Quigley's political message and the peal of Galway Cathedral were still pouring forth. Peter held on to the ladder with one hand and reached out with the other. He pulled open the narrow window. A pigeon flew out right in his face.

He jerked back, lost his footing and nearly fell off the ladder. At that moment Michael Ryan appeared. Ambrose, with no sense of irony, called up and told Peter it was all right, the doctor had just arrived. As soon as Leo learned who the newcomer was, he sidled over to Ryan and asked if he might have a word.

Niamh crossed to the ladder and spoke quietly to Assumpta. 'How was last night?'

'Complicated.'

Peter was trying to step through the open window into the belfry, but the gap was too narrow.

'I can't get through,' he called.

'You're too fat,' Assumpta shouted back.

As Peter descended, Assumpta looked questioningly at Padraig. He shook his head and patted his stomach: 'I had a big breakfast.'

Ambrose came forward, taking off his hat. 'I'll go.'

'You will not.' Niamh shoved him back. 'I don't want a bridegroom with a broken neck.'

Ambrose rejoined the onlookers, readjusting his hat. 'I didn't think you wanted a bridegroom at all,' he muttered.

Leo reappeared. 'What about you?' Niamh said.

'Sorry,' he said, 'can't stop.' He looked at Assumpta. 'I'll see you later.'

Peter reached the ground. Assumpta shoved past him and put her foot on the ladder. 'If you want something doing round here,' she said, 'you do it yourself.'

Peter was flustered. 'What are you doing? You can't go up there.'

She was already climbing. 'It's my ladder.'

'It's not safe! I'll go and get Quigley...'

'Ah, you should be happy, Father,' Assumpta said, getting higher and higher. 'This is the nearest I've been to God in years.'

At the top she put her foot on the stone ledge, turned sideways, and slid into the tower through the narrow window. A few seconds later the sound from the speakers stopped. The crowd cheered. Assumpta reappeared, holding the cassette tape aloft. They cheered again.

When she reached the ground Peter thanked her.

She looked at him coldly. 'I want a word with you.'

✝

Later that morning, as Brian Quigley canvassed in the streets of Cilldargan, assisted by Liam handing out leaflets, Leo McGarvey approached, accompanied by a camera operator and a sound engineer. The cameraman swiftly lined up on Quigley and Leo stepped forward, brandishing his microphone. At the sight of the camera, Quigley switched on a campaigner's smile.

'Mr Quigley,' Leo said, 'how's the campaign going?'

'Well, the polls are looking good, so I'm quietly confident.'

Leo nodded. 'Is there anything else you're being quiet about?'

Quigley's smile wilted. 'How do you mean?'

'No skeletons in your cupboard, then?'

'I don't really know what you have in mind...'

'One-Tooth Tommy, for instance?'

Quigley's eyes widened dramatically for a split second, then he forced a laugh, aiming it at the small crowd that had formed to watch. 'Excuse, me, folks, it's the fella from *This is Your Life*.'

Quigley grabbed Leo by the arm and dragged him down a side street, away from the camera. 'So. What's this all about?'

'OK,' Leo said. 'Off the record. Tommy McIvor. He had a smallholding near Ballykay back in the 50s. Lived like a hermit.'

'So?' Quigley managed to look baffled. 'Anyone could tell you that.'

'Do you remember what became of him?'

Now Quigley tried some serious acting. He made a show of scouring his memory. 'Yes... he, er... he disappeared.'

'Vanished,' Leo said. He clicked his fingers in Quigley's face. 'Just like that. No-one ever had sight or sound of him again. It's been a mystery ever since.'

'What's this got to do with me?'

'Well, you're building on his old land. I think you've found something out about him.'

Quigley snorted and made an effort to look pitying.

'You're trying to cover it up,' Leo said, 'in case they make you stop building.'

'You, sir,' Quigley said, 'are whistling in the wind.'

'I can't whistle, Mr Quigley. But I can sing. Loud.'

Leo departed with his cameraman and sound engineer. Quigley was worried. For once he didn't try to hide it.

☩

Back in Ballykissangel, Peter and Assumpta carried the ladder through the bar, Assumpta in front, aiming it at the door to the back yard.

'I just want to know what you've been saying to Leo,' she said.

'He asked my advice, that's all. I couldn't really refuse.'

'I bet you couldn't.'

Peter sighed. 'I'm a priest. It's my business.'

'Well, in future, I would be grateful if you kept your mouth out of my business. OK?'

The day was hardly underway, but already Peter had the feeling it would be one to forget. When he got back to the house he made a cup of tea. He had taken one sip when Father Mac appeared at the door. Peter showed him into the living room.

'Is something wrong?'

'You could say that.'

'Look, if it's about the bells, I can explain everything.'

'Oh never mind your blasted bells!' Father Mac held up a newspaper. 'Have you seen this?'

'What is it?'

'Your friend Dooley, up to no good.'

Peter took the paper. 'I wouldn't go as far as calling him a friend.'

He read the headline:

BY-ELECTION CANDIDATE PROPOSES NEW CREMATORIUM.

'He's raising it at the next council meeting,' Father Mac said. 'I must tell Brian. Do you know where he is?'

'I imagine he's out canvassing,' Peter said.

'Well if you see him, tell him I want to see him. Urgently.'

'I'd quite like to have a word with him myself.'

Father Mac went back to the door. 'We must nip this in the bud. It's just a gimmick. Next thing we know, they'll be proposing drive-in Masses.'

'All the same, though,' Peter said, 'he does have a point. It's bound to happen eventually.'

Father Mac looked at Peter as if had blasphemed. 'I beg your pardon?'

'Well, it's no longer a sin to be cremated, is it?'

'So you agree with him?'

'It's not as simple as that. All I'm saying is, there's no denying that cremation's becoming a lot more popular in Ireland.'

'Popular?' Father Mac's eyes were wide. 'Father, it is no part of our apostolate to be popular!'

He walked out and slammed the door behind him.

✝

From a car half-hidden by trees on a road overlooking the building site, Leo, the cameraman and the sound engineer watched as Brian Quigley came out of the caravan, wearing a long and rather bulky raincoat. He looked to right and left, then walked past the Land Rover and headed off towards the town on foot.

A moment later the caravan door opened again and Donal and Liam came out. Donal was carrying an old suitcase. Just as Quigley had done, they looked right and left, then Liam walked off in one direction and Donal went in another.

This wasn't anything Leo hadn't seen before. It was an old decoy tactic and it could be effective. But he was ready for it. He turned to the cameraman and soundman. 'You follow those two,' he said. 'I'll take Quigley.'

Close to town, Donal began to panic when he realized he was being followed. He kept looking over his shoulder and at one point walked into the path of an oncoming car.

Liam, approaching town from another tangent, was also aware that he was being followed, but he took it in his stride. He walked fast and deliberately detoured a couple of times, giving the pursuing soundman more exercise than he had taken in a year.

Quigley's progress into town, by the most direct route, was relatively slow and stately. Leo stayed well back, watching as Quigley ambled along, hugging the bulky coat about him, walking as if his legs had turned stiff.

Eventually Donal got so nervous about being followed that he walked a straight 5 yards without looking in front of him and barged into Kathleen Hendley as she came up the street. She let out a cry as Donal staggered away from her and dropped his case. It burst open. Dozens of leaflets flew out and scattered along the street in the breeze.

The cameraman shadowing Donal picked up a leaflet. It was a Quigley campaign flyer. He looked at the suitcase where it lay open on the road. It had contained nothing but the leaflets. He was clearly following the wrong man. He abandoned Donal, who was frantically trying to gather up the fluttering and flying paper, and headed for the rendezvous point.

At the top of the hill leading down to Ballykissangel's main street, Leo stopped by a tree and watched Quigley cross the road, look behind him a couple of times, then enter the grounds of St Joseph's by the rear gate. Still hugging his big coat about him, Quigley walked close to the church wall and finally disappeared through a side door. Leo stayed where he was, wondering what he should do next.

Further down the road, opposite Fitzgerald's, Liam had finally stopped walking. He stood and looked up and down the main street. After a minute he seemed to reach a decision. He strode across the road and walked into the bar.

The soundman, hiding at the side of Kathleen Hendley's shop, watched the bar door close behind Liam and wearily abandoned his cover. He too walked slowly back up the hill towards the rendezvous point.

Twenty-three

Peter sat in the confessional, reading the Psalms. Uppermost in his thoughts had been the arrogance of certain men who pushed their advantage to extravagant limits, regardless of morality or the feelings of others. He had chosen to soothe himself with an appropriate passage: 'I have seen the wicked in great power, and spreading himself like a green bay tree. Yet he passed away, and lo, he was not: yea, I sought him, but he could not be found.'

If Scripture was to be believed, the end of vaunting ambition and commercial sprawl was oblivion, nothingness. It was comforting to read, if difficult to swallow. 'Mark the perfect man and behold the upright: for the end of that man is peace. But the transgressors shall be destroyed together, the end of the wicked shall be cut off.'

'Cut off.' Peter mouthed the words. That was the thing about biblical retribution, there was no shilly-shallying. Direct action was the way. It got things sorted, and fast.

A throat was cleared on the other side of the confessional. Peter slid back the partition.

'Bless me Father, for I need your help.'

Peter looked through the gap. Brian Quigley's face was there, doing its best to look put-upon.

'Brian! I've got a bone to pick with you.'

'Funny you should say that...'

'You can't just go around using the church for your electioneering – '

'Do you want Dooley to win?'

'That's not the point,' Peter said.

'The point is, Father, I'm in trouble.'

Leo McGarvey, meanwhile, had decided to follow Quigley into St Joseph's. After tiptoeing past the door he realized the main part of the church was empty. He crept along the aisle and edged up to the confessional, neck craned, listening for voices.

'What do you think you're playing at?'

Leo spun round, startled. Kathleen Hendley was staring at him, her face stiff with outrage.

'I was, er, just seeing if it was free.'

'I know you...' The wide eyes narrowed. 'You're the man on the television, aren't you?'

Leo smiled modestly. 'Yes, actually, I am.'

Kathleen spoke in a harsh whisper, deferring to her surroundings. 'You lot are always sticking your nose in where you shouldn't.'

'But I was only – '

'You should be ashamed of yourself!'

'I'm sorry,' Leo said, 'I – '

'There's no use apologizing now the harm's done,' Kathleen said, advancing on him. 'No wonder this country's in such a mess.'

Leo turned, still telling her he was sorry, and made his way out of the church.

In the confessional, Quigley had explained his problem, and had expressed the hope that Peter would feel it a part of his Christian duty to give the bones of One-Tooth Tommy a decent burial.

'I can't just bury any old bones,' Peter told him. 'There are certain procedures.'

'Father, if this gets out I could be ruined – and Dooley will have seen to it.'

'Where are these bones now?'

Quigley thrust a bundle of them through the gap. After the initial shock Peter took them, and the others Quigley passed through, and put them on the floor at his feet.

'And this is the last of the poor fella, Father.' Quigley handed over the skull.

Peter put it on the floor with the rest. 'Well, I'll do what I can, Brian, but I'll have to go through the proper channels.'

Quigley did not look happy about that, but he said no more. He left the church the way he had come in and was walking round to the front when he saw Leo and his two colleagues standing outside the railings.

Before they had a chance to see him, he crossed the path to the rear of the church, climbed a small wall and made off through the trees beyond.

After confession Peter took the bones to the sacristy and put them in a cardboard box, which he then locked in a cupboard under the window. As he left and was locking the side door, Leo approached him.

'Ah, Leo. I'm afraid you've just missed last orders.'

Leo looked puzzled. 'Is there no-one else inside?'

'Only the good Lord.'

'Damn!'

'What's wrong?'

'Be honest, Father. Has anyone asked you to bury some bones?'

'It's possible. Why?'

'I knew it!' Leo said. 'Who?'

Peter smiled. 'I'd love to tell you, Leo. But you know how it is. I have to protect my sources.'

Peter walked away, still smiling. Leo cursed under his breath.

That evening, after surgery, Dr Ryan went through the records stored in the cabinets in his filing room. Peter stood by, watching as Ryan leafed through the old folders and the stapled bundles of paper.

'Some of these must go back years.'

'My father kept records of all his patients even after they'd died.' Ryan pulled out a folder tied with thin yellowing ribbon. 'Aha! Here we are. One-Tooth Tommy McIvor.' He blew the dust off.

Peter saw the name on the cover. 'Filed under O,' he said.

Ryan nodded, as if that was the obvious thing to do. Peter felt the Twilight Zone coming on again.

Ryan handed the record to Peter. 'What are you going to tell Quigley?'

'Let him sweat. I think it's time we called in the future son-in-law.'

Ryan grinned and shut the cabinet drawer with a bang.

Less than an hour later, Peter and Dr Ryan sat behind the desk in the surgery, confronting Quigley and Ambrose at the other side. On the end of the desk the remains of One-Tooth Tommy sat in their cardboard box.

'According to my father's notes,' Ryan said, 'Tommy came to the surgery during the winter of 47.'

'Yeah, that was the year of the big snow,' Quigley said. 'I remember my brother talking about it. The whole town was cut off.'

Ryan consulted the notes for a moment. 'Tommy was complaining of chest pains, and on examining him my father discovered he was suffering from bronchial pneumonia. He told Tommy he'd have to be admitted to hospital, but Tommy was a stubborn old man and he was having none of it. He just got up and left.'

'And that was the last anyone saw of him,' Peter said.

'A few days later,' the doctor continued, 'my father went to visit him, but when he got to the cottage it was deserted. There was no sign of Tommy. A search was mounted but the snow had covered any traces.'

'It appears the cold finally got him,' Peter said. 'He must have laid down in a ditch and died. And his body was finally reclaimed by the bog.'

Peter and Dr Ryan both looked at Ambrose, waiting to hear a policeman's evaluation of the case.

'Well...' Ambrose pursed his lips judicially. 'It seems fairly straightforward...'

'Good.' Quigley stood up. 'I'm glad that's all cleared up, then.'

'But there is the matter of your role in all of this,' Ambrose added.

Quigley scowled. 'Now hold on a minute – '

'The unlawful removal of a body – '

'Bones!'

' – is a very serious offence.'

Quigley stared at the unsmiling faces around him. He began to look sick.

'Perhaps, Ambrose,' Peter said smoothly, 'you might consider mitigating circumstances.'

Ambrose frowned. 'Such as?'

'Well, Brian's had a lot on his mind recently with the election...'

'Yeah,' Quigley nodded.

'...and of course your wedding coming up.'

Quigley's face went stiff. 'Wedding?'

Peter transmitted a look to Brian that advised him to go along with this.

'Ah, yes,' Quigley said. 'The wedding.'

'In fact,' Peter concluded, 'there seems little point in delaying it any longer.'

'No point at all,' Ambrose said, smiling now.

Peter looked at Quigley. 'So, Brian, what do you think?'

'I think, Father, it's you should be in politics.'

✝

A little after 10.00 am the following morning, in a leafy corner of the cemetery above Ballykissangel, Peter performed a burial service for the bones of One-Tooth Tommy. Also attending the service were Brian Quigley, Liam and Donal.

'Eternal rest grant unto him, O Lord, and let perpetual light shine upon him. May he rest in peace.'

They said 'Amen' in unison, and the service was over.

'Thank you, Father,' Quigley said as they walked away from the grave.

Peter nodded. 'Tommy can rest in peace now.'

They walked together down the sloping grassy bank to the gates.

'All set for election day?' Peter said, making conversation.

Quigley shook his head. 'All this has taken its toll. I haven't been able to focus my campaign. Dooley's taken a big lead in the polls.'

'Surely there's still time to catch up.'

'One thing you learn in this game is when to cut your losses. The time has come. I'm withdrawing from the election.'

'Father Mac'll be disappointed,' Peter said. 'Especially now that Dooley's set to win.'

'Oh, he'll win all right,' Quigley agreed. 'But he won't *beat* me.'

Peter would have liked to pursue that, but he could see Quigley had said enough, for the time being.

✞

A few days later, during a moderately busy lunchtime, Assumpta entered the bar from upstairs and stopped for a moment to watch. At times like this, Fitzgerald's could be the most cheering place for miles. Father Peter was in conversation with Niamh and Ambrose, who sat on the bench seat by the window and looked very happy together. Father Mac, Brian Quigley and Dr Ryan stood beside the regulars at the corner of the bar. The wedding of Niamh and Ambrose had just been announced, and everyone seemed brightened by the news. Even Quigley looked pleased.

'You're a generous man, Brian Quigley,' Siobhan said, 'making your daughter a happy woman for the second time.'

'So my invitation's in the post, Brian, is it?' Dr Ryan said, making Quigley smile through gritted teeth.

'If it's any consolation,' Padraig said, 'Dooley didn't get my vote.'

'Well, he got mine,' Father Mac said.

Quigley nodded. 'And mine.'

The others looked surprised.

'I don't understand,' Peter said.

'We had to be sure he'd be shipped off to Dublin,' Quigley said.

'But what about the crematorium?'

Quigley and Father Mac smiled at each other.

'I wouldn't worry your head,' Father Mac said.

Quigley took a newspaper from his pocket and unfolded it. He handed it to Peter. The headline read: 'DEFEAT FOR NEW TD DOOLEY: COUNCIL VOTES AGAINST CREMATORIUM'.

'He may have power,' Quigley said, 'but it's influence that counts.'

Peter took up his pint from the table. 'A toast,' he said, raising the glass. 'To Niamh and Ambrose.'

'Niamh and Ambrose,' the others echoed.

Everybody drank.

'Congratulations, at last,' Peter said.

There was scattered applause, then the rumble of bar talk set in again.

Leo McGarvey came down the stairs carrying his cases. He stopped beside Assumpta where she stood near the door.

'Don't leave it so long next time,' she said.

Leo didn't look happy. 'Next time I'd like you to come back with me.'

Assumpta smiled faintly.

'What do you say? We could try again.'

'No, Leo. Not now.'

'Sure there's nothing keeping you here.' He sighed. 'Or maybe I'm wrong.'

Assumpta saw he was looking across the room at Peter. She put up her arms and they embraced.

Peter turned and saw Leo pick up his bags and leave. He watched how sadly Assumpta stared at the door as it closed. It was the first time he had seen her close to tears.

Twenty-four

Peter and Father Mac walked slowly down the main street, oblivious to the fine warm day and the activity around them. The Ballykissangel three-day festival was almost upon them; bunting and banners were being hung from buildings, between lamp posts and across the streets. Like Christmas, the event had affected people and there was an unmistakable air of excitement, although Father Mac remained untouched by the bustle and Peter was too preoccupied to notice.

'It doesn't mean you haven't made an impact,' Father Mac was saying.

'Obviously.'

'You know what I mean.'

'Father, "Thanks for dropping in, now goodbye" speaks for itself.'

'No-one's saying that. It's not your fault they need more men in the trenches.'

'Yes,' Peter said, 'but why me?'

As the numbing shock of the news wore off, Peter had begun to smart. For weeks he had known that he liked it in Ballykissangel, but now that he had been told he was leaving it dawned on him, like a terrible pain, just how close he felt to the people and the place.

'I've only just got here.'

Patiently, Father Mac told Peter he was going back to Manchester because that was where he came from. He used the tone of a mother explaining to a child why oatmeal, vile as it seemed, was good for him. 'And the feeling is that whatever problems you had, you should be over.'

They stopped in front of Fitzgerald's where, unknown to anyone outside, an emergency was in progress. Water from a ruptured pipe or tank – Assumpta wasn't sure which – poured through the ceiling at various points into the bar. Assumpta and Niamh ran round with pans and bowls, dumping them at strategic points to catch the worst of the downpour and running back to the kitchen to empty them as they overflowed.

Niamh had already called a plumber, who promised he was on his way. That had been 10 minutes ago. The flow appeared to be stronger now and their ability to cope was diminishing by the second.

'On his way,' Assumpta howled, holding up two bowls and gasping as water poured on her head. 'On his way from where?'

'On his way from home,' Niamh shouted, moving books and ornaments and vulnerable electrical fittings.

'Where's home?'

'How do I know?' Niamh dodged a new column of water and grabbed two pans that were about to spill over. 'It just says plumber!'

More water landed on Assumpta's head. It was all about to become too much. She tried to pick up a bowl and two pans at once and ended up having to put them down again before she dropped them. As she bent over water poured onto her back.

'These are no use!' she screamed. 'We need a bucket! Not even a bucket! A bin!'

'All right!' Niamh cried, starting to panic. 'All right!'

Outside, Peter still resisted the idea that his removal from the office of curate was inevitable.

'Is there nothing I can do? Is this definite?'

Father Mac did his best to look powerless. 'It's not my decision, Father. I thought you'd be pleased to go home.'

'I like it here.'

'And the people of Ballykay? How do they feel?'

Peter hesitated. 'I don't know.'

'Would they fight to keep you?'

Peter couldn't answer.

Father Mac spoke softly: 'Do they care for you that much?'

Peter lowered his head. Assumpta, enraged, stepped out into the street and blindly hurled the contents of a bucket all over him.

Father Mac simulated a smile of sympathy. Peter sighed and stood there, soaked. He glanced at Assumpta, who look agonized at what she had done. She clutched her bucket, mouthed the word 'sorry', and dashed back into the bar.

✝

A few miles away, on a mountain roadway, Donal and Liam had finished tying a wooden crate to the back of Quigley's low-loader. Inside the crate was a live ram. Quigley, in a straw hat and a sporty checked shirt, was fastening the tailgate when Eamonn the hill farmer approached, carrying one of the artificial sheep he had created.

'Eamonn, no,' Quigley said.

'Ah, Mr Quigley...'

'Eamonn, I do not need a wooden sheep. I have a real one.'

Eamonn pointed at the crate. 'What about him?'

'What about him?'

'He needs one,' Eamonn said.

'What?'

'He's grown attached to her.'

'Well...' Quigley went round to the driver's door. 'She'll have to wait till he gets back. This is a festival, not a fertility rite.'

Quigley got in the lorry and drove off with Liam and Donal in the back comforting the ram. The festival area was a stretch of land opposite St Joseph's. When Quigley arrived there was frantic activity on all sides. Tents and marquees were going up, scaffolding for stalls was being erected, platforms were under construction and children were jumping all over a fully-inflated bouncy castle.

Quigley parked beside a large platform with a high scaffolding tower erected at its centre. Timmy-Joe Galvin was up in the tower, adjusting the winch on a decorative crate.

Quigley got out of the cab and slammed the door. 'Timmy-Joe,' he shouted. 'What are all those kids doing there?'

Without waiting for an answer, Quigley rounded on the children, clapping his hands and waving his arms at them. 'Go on! You're not supposed to be here!' he yelled. 'Get away! We're not open yet!'

'Mr Quigley,' Timmy-Joe called. 'Hang on. We're testing the rig...'

Quigley heard but didn't acknowledge his mistake. He turned to Donal instead and told him to go to Kathleen Hendley and get a box of cabbages, or whatever it was sheep ate.

Back in Fitzgerald's, meanwhile, the plumber had been and tackled the emergency. Order was restored and the leaking had stopped. The regulars watched Assumpta work at the top of a ladder with a staple gun, tacking ceiling paper back into place around a damp patch that would take months to dry out.

The topic of conversation in the bar was not the water damage, however, but the live ram Quigley was using as the centrepiece of the festival. Siobhan, in particular, found the scheme offensive. Her mood got no better when Brendan said he didn't think Quigley was being cruel to the animal.

'Of course it's cruel,' she said. 'How would you like to sit in a crate for three days and nights with only a cabbage for company?'

'Better than lying on a plate with a cabbage for company,' Brendan said.

'Which is where it's going to end up!'

'Will you shut up about the stupid sheep?' Padraig pleaded.

'Ram,' Siobhan said.

'Apart from anything else, it's embarrassing.'

Assumpta came down off the stepladder and folded it. 'Embarrassing?'

'Crowning the sheep,' Padraig said.

'Ram!' Siobhan snapped.

'Ram.'

'Down in Kerry,' Assumpta said, 'they crown a goat.'

'Exactly,' Padraig said. 'It's plagiarism.'

Assumpta looked at him. 'The goat's going to sue?'

'I don't know why they don't just crown a bottle of stout and be done with it,' Brendan said. 'I mean,' he added, his voice rich with sarcasm, 'that's the whole point of an Irish festival, isn't it? Isn't it, Assumpta?'

She glanced sideways along the bar. 'What are you looking at me for?'

'You're not the only pub in town now,' Padraig said, teasing.

'You're not the only customers.'

The regulars looked around them to see who else might be waiting to spend their money with Assumpta. There was nobody else in the place.

Assumpta got edgy, in spite of trying not to. 'Are you seriously suggesting I'm concerned about a glorified Portakabin out on the Dublin Road with a three-day licence?'

'Could be a lucrative three days,' Brendan said.

Assumpta went toward the kitchen with her ladder. 'I'm not afraid of competition,' she snapped. In the doorway she paused, staring at Siobhan, who was gazing glumly at the counter. 'Siobhan, if you're going to be wearing that face all day, would you put a bag over it?'

Siobhan banged her glass on to the bar and walked out. Padraig and Brendan, silently mirthful, followed her.

It was Siobhan's intention to go to the festival ground and see for herself what indignities were being inflicted on the ram. So that was what they did, all three. They stood by the big central platform in the warm sunshine and watched as Timmy-Joe Galvin hoisted the ram in its decorative crate slowly up the scaffolding tower, supervised by Brian Quigley.

'Ah, this is not right,' Siobhan shouted.

Peter wandered across, wearing a grey T-shirt with his priest's black trousers.

'Father, look what they're doing to that ram,' Siobhan said.

Padraig nodded, mock-sorrowful. 'You should have given the poor old creature a blessing, Father.'

Peter tried to fit in with the merriment, but his misery was poorly concealed.

Brendan looked up at the crate, which was now in position at the top of the tower. 'Hail sheep! We who drink stout salute thee!' Brendan and Padraig gave the ram a synchronized gladiatorial salute.

Peter was looking at the crate from the side, able to see the ram through the mesh fitted on the end. Something about the narrowness of the tower and the flimsy-looking lattice made the arrangement look precarious.

He called to Quigley on the platform. 'Are you sure it's safe up there, Brian?'

Timmy-Joe thought Peter was shouting to him. 'What?'

'Never mind whether it's safe or not,' Siobhan yelled, 'He shouldn't be up there at all.'

Timmy-Joe was getting confused. 'You want him down, then?'

'No, not before the crowning ceremony tomorrow,' Quigley said. 'And then he goes straight back up again.'

'That animal is going back up the mountain now,' Siobhan said.

'No,' Quigley told her. 'In three days.'

'No! He's terrified!'

'He's terrified because you keep on shouting!

'Father!' Siobhan turned and appealed to Peter. 'Will you make him take it down?'

Peter was already walking away. 'I can't make him.'

'Let him try,' Quigley muttered.

Padraig asked Quigley what he wanted this stupid festival for anyway.

'Because every other town in Ireland has one, that's why.'

'And drunkenness,' Brendan said.

Padraig nodded. 'And vandalism.'

'I don't believe you people,' Quigley said. 'The parish council made a democratic decision – '

'You have them all in your pocket, anyway,' Padraig said, his lips scarcely moving.

'Who said that?' Quigley demanded. 'Who said that?' Bewildered innocence gazed back at him. He glared at Siobhan. 'The ram stays.'

Shortly afterwards, as Peter was entering St Joseph's, Siobhan walked past on the other side of the railings. 'Thanks a million,' she shouted, without looking at him. 'All creatures great and small, eh?'

✝

As Assumpta drove her van in the countryside outside town she saw Peter at a small wayside grotto set back from the road. She stopped and got out.

'Have you, er…' She pointed at his T-shirt. 'Have you dried out yet?'

'Just about.'

'Want a lift?'

'No thanks.' He turned and waved his arm at the grotto. 'Who looks after this place?'

'Anybody and everybody I suppose. Why?'

'I've never seen anyone.'

'Because you've only been here five minutes.'

'Ten weeks,' Peter said.

'There you are, then. What do you think of the grotto?'

The small cave with a statue of the Blessed Virgin at its centre was like many others Peter had seen.

'One of a kind, eh?' Assumpta said.

'Oh yeah?'

'Oh, you bet.' It was a wind-up, Peter saw, but she did it with style. 'There was talk of getting RTE down here, but well, too late now.'

'Uh-huh.'

'Do you know, no matter how bad the light, no matter how long you stare at it, and no matter how much drink you've taken…'

'Go on.'

'That statue will not move a whisker.'

'That's impressive.'

Assumpta was frowning at Peter. 'Are you all right?'

'Mmm?'

'You seem a bit – hey, it's none of my business.'

Peter stared at the grotto. 'They want me to go back home,' he said.

'Why?' Assumpta looked concerned for a second, but she covered it promptly. 'What for?'

They need me back at the coalface.' Peter shrugged. 'I'm not sure.'

'Well.' Assumpta turned and walked back toward the van.

'What do you think?' Peter said. 'I should fight it?'

'I'd watch your back if you do,' Assumpta said, affecting unconcern.

'The Bishop's OK.'

'I meant Father Mac,' Assumpta said.

✝

Later, in his full black suit, with a fresh black shirt and clerical collar, Peter drove his stately Jowett out to Cilldargan to see Father Mac. As always, the parish priest saw him in his study. He was busy, he said, but he could spare a few minutes.

'So,' he said, and gestured regally for Peter to say what was on his mind.

'I just wanted to know if there is any way that I can stay where I am.'

Father Mac tented his fingers carefully, allowing a silence to develop. 'Father,' he said, 'when we spoke, was I unclear in some way?'

Peter hesitated, conscious that he was being frozen out. 'Well, yes,' he said. 'A little. You told me it wouldn't be your decision but suggested if I had some popular support – '

'Popular support?' Father Mac's expression suggested the words had tainted his mouth. 'What do you think the Church is, a democracy?'

'Well I just thought, if you were to back me…'

'I've done my best for you, Father. I'm afraid your Bishop is adamant.'

'I see.'

'So you're going home,' Father Mac said, with the distant smile of a stranger. 'Isn't that something to celebrate?'

Peter made himself smile.

Since it was a fine day Father Mac decided to see Peter off the premises. They walked out to where the Jowett was parked at the top of the gravel path.

'What time are you locking up St Joseph's during the festival?' Father Mac said.

Peter asked him what he meant.

'I was thinking five o'clock.'

'What?' Peter still didn't understand.

'To be on the safe side.'

'Father, a lot of people won't even be home from work.'

'It's not them I'm worried about. It's the drunks and blackguards down for the festival.'

Peter smiled, a touch of deference before he complained. 'Father, what's the point in having a church if it's going to have to be closed?'

'At least it'll be intact,' Father Mac said acidly. 'And since when have we had queues to get into St Joseph's in the evening?'

'What have numbers got to do with it?' Peter opened the car door. 'We don't have a box office.'

'You have a tongue in your head, Father, I won't miss.' Father Mac turned away. 'Five o'clock,' he said, and stamped back across the gravel to the house.

Peter got in the car and drove off, fuming.

TWENTY-five

Siobhan was back in the bar, furious at Quigley for what he was doing with the ram, and mad at Peter for doing nothing to support her when she tried to stop Quigley. Padraig and Brendan, on the other hand, had come back to the bar even more cheerful than when they left. They discussed Quigley's iniquity as lightly as any other everyday occurrence.

'Crowning an animal isn't the only idea he's stolen,' Padraig said. 'He wants to run a race through the town.'

Assumpta brought their sandwiches and banged the plates down in front of them. She looked uncommonly distracted. Siobhan stared at her bleakly.

'How's that theft?' Brendan said.

'The runners have to carry trays of stout.'

'What?' Brendan looked surprised. 'Like the Galway Oyster Festival – the bartenders' race?'

'That's right,' Padraig said. 'Except in this case he wants to run it with publicans.'

'Well, he can do it without this one,' Assumpta said. She turned away, then turned back. 'Why publicans?'

'I think he wants to win,' Padraig said.

'Excuse me…' Assumpta was still looking at Padraig. 'To win a publicans' race, isn't the minimum qualification – '

'To be a publican? Yes.'

Assumpta looked at the three of them coldly. 'What's going on?'

'That, er, glorified Portakabin out on the Dublin Road?'

Padraig said.

'Yeah?'

'Quigley's Bar and Grill.'

Assumpta was shaken. She didn't try to hide it.

Brendan smiled at her. 'What did you think, Assumpta – this festival was for your benefit?'

She pulled off her apron, threw it down and stamped out of the bar.

Ten minutes later her van drew up in front of the long, plain, rectangular structure with the lettering 'QUIGLEY'S BAR & GRILL' on the front. She got out and looked at it for a minute, letting her temper build. Then she marched inside.

Donal was on the telephone behind a flimsy makeshift bar. Liam was rolling a beer barrel into place behind the bolted-on pump fittings. Assumpta had seen plenty of cheap, nasty, improvised pubs in her time, but this was one of the tackiest. Quigley, nevertheless, was surveying it with obvious satisfaction as Assumpta walked in.

'You kept this quiet,' she said.

'Assumpta!' Quigley feigned pleasant surprise. 'No I didn't, sure the council told you.'

'Your part in it you did!'

'Oh that's just for the festival. Take a bit of pressure off you.'

She glared at him. 'The one time I stand to make a bit of decent money – '

'Oh but you will, you will, this is just like a...a public service.'

'A public service?'

'Mr Quigley.' Donal had put his hand over the telephone mouthpiece.

'What?'

'The insurance say they'll only offer cover up to 10,000 a night. After that – '

'Ten thousand a night?' Assumpta was staggered. 'You expect to make 10,000 a night?'

Quigley looked at Donal and made a strained imitation of a laugh. 'What is he talking? Pesetas?'

Assumpta was on the verge of screaming. The alternative was to march straight out of there. She took the alternative.

'Assumpta!' Quigley called after her. 'Assumpta, come on...'

He watched her get back into her van. He shrugged and turned back to the bar.

'Are we really expecting to make that, Mr Quigley?' Donal asked him.

Quigley blinked. 'We Donal? What is this we?'

As Assumpta turned the van round on to the other side of the road, she looked across at the bar and saw Ambrose, in shirtsleeves, carrying a stack of empty bottle crates.

'Serving the community, Ambrose?' she called. 'That's good.'

He stopped and flashed her an embarrassed smile. 'Just helping out.'

Assumpta snorted with disgust. She straightened up the steering, slammed down her foot and made the van roar away along the road.

Her day got no better. Later that afternoon she went to try on her bridesmaid's dress. Straight away she complained to Niamh about the unfairness of Quigley's bar being allowed by the council, but Niamh didn't want to talk about that. Her head was full of the wedding. She told Assumpta to get changed into the creation she would be wearing on the big day.

Niamh had spent time, thought and money on the dress, which would not have looked out of place in the social pages of *House and Garden*. The colour – a dark pink that reminded Assumpta of her grandmother's bedspread – in combination with the cut, went right against the principles of current and even recent fashion. Assumpta stared at herself in Niamh's long mirror and, try as she might, her true reaction showed.

'You don't like it,' Niamh said.

'I didn't say that.'

'I can tell.'

'What can you tell?' Assumpta struggled to look enthusiastic. 'I…I love it.'

Niamh still looked doubtful, and that annoyed Assumpta.

'Why shouldn't I love it? It's gorgeous. It must have cost a fortune.'

Niamh smiled ruefully, confirming it, making Assumpta even more annoyed.

'Still,' she said, 'even after Ambrose's cut, the bar and grill will more than pay for it.'

There had been no way to stop herself. She regretted the words as soon as they were out, and she called after Niamh as she stamped out of the room, saying she was sorry, it was a joke. But what she had said, and they way she said it, could not be undone, and Niamh was wounded.

Peter's mood was not helped that afternoon, either, when Siobhan collared him as he walked past the festival ground. The ram was at the top of the tower in its crate, and that fact was a dagger in the vet's heart.

'How would you like it?' she demanded.

'What?'

'Being stuck up in a crate like that all day.'

Peter was in no mood for rhetoric or long-winded arguments. 'Siobhan.' He pointed at the ram, which appeared to be placidly munching its cabbage. 'If you look closely you will notice that that is a ruminant mammal. Not a homo sapiens. It can't think, it doesn't have a soul, and as far as I'm concerned, it might as well be up there chewing a cabbage as out on the mountain chewing the cud.'

Siobhan stared as Peter walked away then turned and came back. 'And what are you having a go at me for?' he demanded. 'There are more important things.'

He marched off, leaving Siobhan deflated. That

evening, in Fitzgerald's, she told Padraig and Brendan what had happened. Assumpta was listening too, as she moved about the bar, cleaning ashtrays, dusting tables, making herself busy to keep her mind off the rotten day's events.

'All I said was, "How would you like it?"'

Padraig asked Siobhan if it could have been the way she said it.

'Father Clifford's feeling a bit sensitive at the moment,' Assumpta said, coming back behind the bar.

'Why?' Siobhan asked.

'He's been told he has to leave.'

Brendan was surprised. 'Has he been sacked?'

'No, he has not been sacked,' Assumpta said testily, 'they just need him more at home.'

'Ohh...' Brendan raised an eyebrow. 'What do you care?' he asked, suggesting that she did.

Assumpta told him to grow up.

'He stayed longer than the last one,' Padraig said.

Siobhan swallowed some of her drink, wishing now she hadn't been so abrupt with the priest.

Assumpta went back to cleaning the ashtrays, polishing some she had done already. It was annoying to her, and getting more so by the minute, that the street outside was thronged with people going to and coming from the festival ground, while her bar, apart from the three slow-imbibing regulars, was empty.

She went outside and looked. There were people everywhere, strangers most of them, presumably with money in their pockets. All walking by.

She went back inside.

'This is the way I like it in here,' Brendan said. He spread his arms to emphasize the amount of empty space.

'Oh, do you?' Assumpta snapped.

'A little oasis. A cocoon out of the storm.'

'Really?'

Assumpta's temper was up. Padraig spotted it. 'Sarcasm alert,' he said.

Assumpta walked up to the end of the bar. 'Incredibly, Brendan,' she said, 'I don't like it this quiet. You see, this is how I make my living. And between people out there who prefer to drink somewhere else, and people in here who take longer to drink a pint than Sonia O'Sullivan does to run a marathon – '

'Three thousand metres,' Padraig said.

'Shurrup!'

Assumpta threw her duster. It landed on Padraig's head. For the second time that day she took off her apron, flung it behind the bar and walked out, shutting the door with a bang.

✞

Quigley's Bar & Grill was already a popular place, if appearances were any guide. Crowds of people struggled to get in, while loud music thumped from the interior above the noise of raised voices and till drawers slamming. Assumpta parked her van across the road and fought her way through the mob outside, squeezing herself into the noisy, crowded, smoky bar. As she made it through the door, Siobhan's Land Rover was drawing up across the road.

Behind the bar, Donal, Liam and Timmy-Joe, in baseball caps and little white waiters' jackets, were struggling to keep up with the clamouring demands of customers two- and three-deep, who were waving money and empty glasses at them. Quigley sat further down the bar, at a big circular table, wearing a stetson hat and a business suit with a string tie. He was in a game of five-card stud with a group of men who looked like farmers.

Behind Assumpta, Siobhan, Padraig and Brendan piled in.

'Would you look at this!' Padraig yelled, astonished at the size of the crowd.

'What has this place got?' Siobhan said. 'It's a right kip.'

'My God...' Brendan pointed to a banner-size sign over the bar. 'Would you look at that.'

It read: DRINKS HALF-PRICE DURING HAPPY HOUR. HAPPY HOUR ALL NIGHT.

Padraig and Brendan grinned at each other and moved towards the bar. Assumpta fought her way to Quigley's table and bent down behind him as he sneaked a look at his hole card. She addressed the rest of the table: 'He's got a Queen in the hole.'

Quigley rounded on her. 'Are you out of your mind?' he shouted. 'What are you trying to do?'

'I could ask you the same question.'

'Ah, get real, will you? I'm a businessman.'

'You're something beginning with B, you lousy – '

A card player across the table broke in angrily. 'Are we playing cards here or what?'

Assumpta stared. It was Father Mac.

'Yeah, right...' Quigley wagged a finger at Assumpta. 'You behave yourself or you're barred.'

Quigley sat down as a drunk walked up to Assumpta, breathed in her face, called her 'sweetheart' and asked what her hurry was. She raised her foot and brought it down sharply on top of his foot. He howled.

'Right!' Quigley shouted. 'You're barred!'

Assumpta ploughed her way to where Siobhan, Padraig and Brendan were standing.

'Are you with me?' Assumpta shouted.

'Of course we are!' Siobhan yelled.

Quigley glowered over his shoulder at Siobhan. 'Given up on the sheep, have you?'

'Right then,' Assumpta said to Padraig and Brendan, taking their glasses and putting them on the bar, 'You're barred too! Come on!'

They all walked out, Padraig and Brendan openly sad at the loss of their drinks.

✝

Early in the evening Peter put through a telephone call from the sacristy at St Joseph's to Father Randall, his old parish priest in Manchester. They had a brief conversation, during which Peter learned that although he had been told he was needed back home, the story received in Manchester was that he hadn't fitted in at Ballykissangel. Peter did nothing to reveal how angry he felt, and he did not argue with Father Randall's assumption that there had been some simple misunderstanding.

Shortly afterwards, as he was leaving, he found a drunk lying in the porchway of the side door.

'This is a church,' Peter said angrily.

'Ah, come on, Father…'

Peter hauled the man to his feet and pushed him out on to the path. 'Get out of here before I lose my temper.'

The drunk shuffled away and Peter closed the outer door and put the key in the lock. He heard someone on the gravel path and turned. It was Assumpta.

She looked mildly shocked. 'You can't be serious.'

'What?'

'Locking up. It's only seven o'clock.'

Peter tried to be patient. 'I should have done it two hours ago.'

'Really? Spiritual guidance off during a festival, is it?'

'Assumpta, am I missing something? What do you want up here?'

'Same as anybody else…' She sounded almost tearful. 'A bit of peace and quiet.'

Peter saw she was distressed. His tone softened. 'There's more to it than that.'

'I had 16 years of it, Father. I just want…' She gave a weary shrug. 'I've done enough arguing for one day.' She turned to go. 'Thanks anyway.'

'No, wait.' Peter unlocked the door. 'We're very big on peace and quiet.'

He stood aside and Assumpta walked into the church. He followed and watched her take a seat at the back, near a stained-glass window. He leaned on the wall by the door and waited. Finally Assumpta turned to him.

'Look, Father – '

'Assumpta, I'm due at Niamh's, but – '

'If I want to talk, right? No, I know what you're going to say and I don't want to be rude.'

After a pause, Peter said, 'It's what I do.'

'I know.'

'It doesn't make me a hustler.'

He turned and left the church. A few minutes later he was with Niamh, going over the details of the Nuptial Mass. Since ordination he had made it a practice, when talking to people about to be married, to emphasize the significance of various parts of the service that were so familiar that the meaning had become submerged. And then there was the optional matter of obedience.

'You won't get many women saying obey,' he told Niamh. 'Nowadays it's love, honour and respect.'

'Respect?'

'That's right. Then you give each other a high-five.'

Niamh smiled faintly. Her heart wasn't in the session. Perhaps, Peter thought, it was because this was her second time. 'We've done all this,' he said, putting down the Mass book.

'I know.' Niamh looked at Peter. 'I've upset my bridesmaid.'

'Not as much as your father has.'

'You heard.'

'Don't worry,' Peter said. 'I'll talk to her. She knows how fond of her you are.'

Niamh sat back. 'Are you really going?'

'Looks like it,' he nodded.

'Why?'

'Oh…' Peter shrugged. 'Square pegs, round holes. You know.'

'Says who?'

'Niamh.' He smiled at her with great fondness. 'You're 48 hours from the most sacred commitment of your life. Can we concentrate on that?'

TWENTY-SIX

When Peter got back to St Joseph's there was no sign of Assumpta. He walked down the aisle, thinking she might have moved closer to the altar. As he passed the seat where she had been when he left, he trod on broken glass. He looked up. There was a hole in the window.

'Assumpta?' He ran round the church looking for her. 'Assumpta?'

She wasn't there. He went out again, locked the door behind him and ran all the way to Fitzgerald's. The bar was deserted and there was no-one in the kitchen. He stood for a moment, wondering if he should look upstairs, then he heard a noise by the back door. Assumpta came in dragging a couple of crates. She had her back to him and was grunting with the exertion.

'You could have waited, Assumpta.' Suddenly bereft of the worry, he felt foolish. 'The least you could have done was shut the door behind you.'

'I had to go.'

'Of course.' He was annoyed now. 'You have a pub to run, right?'

'That's right, Father.' Assumpta dragged the crates another couple of feet then lifted the top one and turned with it. 'It's a dirty job, but somebody's got to do it.'

'Oh my God.' Peter saw she had a dressing on her forehead over her left eye.

'You're just not reaching the kids of today, are you?' she said.

Peter stepped closer. 'What happened?'

'I was sitting too near a stained-glass window.'

Assumpta crouched and began loading bottles from the crate onto shelves under the bar. 'I think it was the stone that caught me. Lucky or what?'

Peter was full of concern. 'Are you OK?'

'Oh, I'm fine.'

'I was worried.'

'Oh yeah?'

'I saw the broken glass. I couldn't see you.'

'Assumpta shook her head. 'You can have too much peace and quiet.'

'But who would…?' He realized he was embarking on a fatuous question and stopped. 'Did you see the doctor?'

'No,' Assumpta smiled. 'It was definitely kids, I heard them running off.'

Peter reached out. 'Let me look…'

'Ahh! Stop!'

He cupped her face between his hands. 'Just hold still.' He peeled back part of the plaster to examine the cut.

'Ow!'

It was clean-edged, but he could see tiny fragments of gravel in the corners. 'Have you cleaned this wound?'

'What are you, a healer now?'

'I feel responsible.'

'You're forgiven,' Assumpta said, her face still cupped between his gentle hands.

'It's my church.'

'Oh yeah?'

'Let me do this properly,' he said, taking hold of the end of the dressing. Assumpta began to whine in anticipation. 'Two minutes,' he promised, and pulled the dressing off.

'Aagh!' Assumpta punched his arm and winced with pain. 'God!'

They went into the kitchen. Peter bathed the cut, dabbed it dry with clean lint, made Assumpta howl again when he dabbed on antiseptic, then told her to hold back her hair while he got a clean plaster ready.

'Nearly finished.' He stripped the backing off the plaster. 'Tell me, are you angry with Niamh?'

'I was.'

'She's very fond of you.'

'Father, when I gave up the Church I made an effort to give up guilt as well, OK?'

'OK.'

'OK? I was angry with her because she didn't tell me what her father was up to.'

'Didn't the council tell you?'

'Yes, but they didn't tell me it was him.'

Peter put the new plaster over the cut and smoothed it into place.

'The application came from one of his companies. It didn't mention his name.'

'Ah.'

'I mean… ' she fingered the dressing, 'there's competition, and there's Quigley.'

✝

At that moment Ambrose and Niamh were at the festival site, eating hot dogs and watching children enjoy themselves on the swings and in the bouncy castle and on the roundabouts. Niamh had told Ambrose about the falling out with Assumpta, and how his own involvement at Quigley's bar had obviously upset her.

'I was only helping him out.'

'I know,' Niamh said, 'and it's decent of you. But it's…how it looks.'

'To Assumpta?'

'Yes, for one. But it's also…' Niamh frowned. 'I don't know. I just don't want my father to think that all he has to do is snap his fingers and there you are.'

Ambrose stiffened. 'Is that what he thinks?'

Niamh sighed. 'I know how his mind works.'

Late that night Ambrose, in uniform, paid a visit to Quigley's Bar & Grill. He did not go in. Instead, he stood for a while, noting the size of the throng outside, then peered through the open door, seeing the jam of bodies at the bar, at the tables, and occupying most of the spaces in between.

He went round the back and had a look at the pad-locked door. As he stepped nearer it he kicked over a cluster of empty bottle. A wooden shutter covering a window beside him was pushed up on a prop, letting a surge of music escape on a cloud of blue smoke.

'Ambrose?' It was Quigley at the window. He pushed his head out of the gap, squinting into the gloom. 'What are you doing out there?'

'Doing my job, Brian. And you couldn't keep that noise down a bit, could you?'

'Ah, don't spoil the fun. Come in for a drink when you're finished.'

'I don't think so.'

'Well, please yourself.'

Quigley closed the shutter. Ambrose took another close look at the padlocked back door. He shone his torch on it. Then he flipped open his notebook and began to write.

☦

Peter was awakened by the sounds of shouting from the festival ground. He listened. He could hear some-thing gently knocking against metal. Then there was more muffled shouting and the bumping on metal again.

He got out of bed and went to the window. Siobhan had climbed the scaffolding and was up beside the ram's crate. Assumpta stood on the platform, apparently pleading with her.

Peter was tired. He wanted to go back to bed. He looked again at the scene across the way and felt the weight of responsibility settle on his shoulders.

He put on a sweater and chinos and went across the

road. As he approached the scaffolding, Siobhan was telling the ram, loudly, that she was coming to get him.

'How much has she had?' he asked Assumpta.

'Is there a metric measure called skinful?'

'Very funny. And who served it to her?'

Assumpta's face turned to stone. 'Don't judge me.'

'How does she think she's going to get down from there?'

Assumpta looked at him.

'Oh, no...'

She went on looking.

'No way...'

Finally he gave in and crossed to the scaffold tower. Climbing it was reasonably straightforward, but as he got higher he was aware that getting down, even with only himself to worry about, would be hazardous. How he would get Siobhan down at the same time was something he couldn't so far imagine.

When he was halfway up he called to her, trying to stay quiet and make his voice travel at the same time.

'Siobhan? Siobhan!'

She looked down from her perch beside the crate. 'Do not try to stop me,' she said.

'Is there a plan here?'

'Yes.' Siobhan nodded sharply. 'You try to stop me, and I push you off.'

'I won't try and stop you,' Peter promised, continuing to climb.

When he drew level, Siobhan handed him the end of a rope. He took it, and between them they started to lower the crate. The ram bleated a couple of times, loudly.

'Oh, great,' Peter grunted.

'It's a ram,' Siobhan said with the careful diction of the drunk. 'What do you expect it to do? Bark?'

At an hour when he should have been tucked up asleep, Peter was actually working harder than he had for years. Once the crate with the ram inside was lowered, and the two of them were back safely on the ground, Siobhan directed him to take one end and between them they struggled and heaved and finally got the crate and its contents into the back of the Land Rover.

Siobhan then made her way, gasping and panting, to the driver's door with the keys dangling from her hand. Peter went after her and took hold of them.

'I don't think so,' he said firmly.

Siobhan tried to focus on him. 'What?'

'You're drunk.'

'So call the guards.'

'I can't let you drive.' He managed to pull the keys away from her.

'Give me the keys,' Assumpta said. 'I'll drive.'

Siobhan looked past her to Peter. 'I'll still need you to help me get him out.'

Peter looked as if he might cry.

Assumpta pushed Siobhan into the vehicle ahead of her. 'Come on if you're coming,' she told Peter briskly.

He looked at the vehicle. 'Where am I supposed to...?'

The only space was beside the crate. He opened the back door and slid in. As they pulled away he stared glumly out of the window. Beside him the ram bleated a couple of times.

As they passed Quigley's bar, loud music still poured out of the place. People with drinks were standing outside, lights were blazing and business appeared to be as vigorous as ever.

'My God...' Peter slid forward and put his face between the two front seats. Siobhan was fast asleep. 'What time is it?'

'What difference does it make?' Assumpta said. 'He has the guard in his pocket.'

She drove on for a quarter of a mile then turned off the road, taking a narrow mountain track. On the way they passed one of Eamonn's wooden sheep, standing on a hillock that gave a view of Quigley's bar in the distance.

'Eamonn says she's a very good listener,' Assumpta murmured.

She stopped a few yards further on. Siobhan was deep into her sleep. Not even vigorous shaking would wake her. Between them, Peter and Assumpta struggled with the crate, inching it to the back of the vehicle.

'There was a time when they'd transport you for this,' Assumpta grunted.

'What?'

'Botany Bay.'

'Sounds good to me.'

They paused to gather their strength, then, with a tremendous effort, lowered the crate to the ground. When it was safely down Peter raised the door on the end. With a minimum of encouragement the ram emerged and ran off into the night.

'See ya,' Peter gasped.

He leaned on the top of the crate. So did Assumpta. For a minute they did nothing but get their breath back. In the dark, Peter became aware that Assumpta was looking at him.

'Don't you want to go back home?' she said.

'Home doesn't come into it.'

'What does?'

'You go where you're told.'

'But where do you want to go?'

'Where I'm wanted,' Peter said.

After a moment Assumpta said, 'Did you talk to Father Mac?'

'Yeah.' He couldn't hide the bitterness. 'I mean, what is his… '

'Problem?'

Peter made a small, rueful smile.

'You are,' Assumpta said.

'What have I ever done to him?'

'You rock the boat.'

That surprised Peter. 'What – because I'm English?'

'No. Worse than that. What you do is, you encourage people to think for themselves.'

Peter smiled awkwardly, feeling he was being praised. But Assumpta had more she needed to say. When she spoke again her voice was level and calm, but there was intensity in her words.

'What you do – the whole lot of you – is holding this country back. But as priests go…'

She hesitated.

'Yeah?'

'We could do a lot worse.'

It was a close as she would come to saying she liked him. With that much established, Peter felt it best to get the talk back to their reason for being out on the mountain at that hour.

'Quigley's not going to like this,' he said.

'Tough.'

He stood up from the crate, smiling. 'I've got an idea,' he said. 'Hang on a sec.'

He strode off down the road.

TWENTY-SEVEN

At 8.30 am the following morning Ambrose drove out to Quigley's Bar & Grill in his police car. After stepping on a half-eaten hot dog, which he scraped off on the grass verge, he marched smartly up to the door and knocked. The door was opened by Liam, who was unshaven and bleary-eyed.

'If you're looking for Mr Quigley, he's gone into town.'

'Never mind.' Ambrose handed Liam a brown sealed envelope. 'When he gets back give him this. It's official.'

At noon, in bright, warm sunlight, Brian Quigley took the platform at the centre of the festival ground and faced an attentive crowd of men, women and children. With the aid of a microphone and a good amplification system, he proceeded to tell the story of 'The Ram of Ballykay'.

'Transport yourselves back, ladies and gentlemen, to a time when the invader stalked our land, when the Norman army, having conquered Britain and half of Europe, has landed in Ireland too. And now they've made their way to Ballykay.'

Peter, in his priest's uniform minus the jacket, joined Assumpta, Siobhan and Padraig where they stood near the platform, listening to Quigley as he stepped up a gear.

'But while the town slept, the ram of Ballykay didn't, and down from the mountain he came, his lungs bursting but his heart refusing to yield...'

'What is he talking about?' Siobhan asked.

Assumpta said she thought it was for the tourists.

Peter leaned down to speak close to Assumpta's ear.

'Father Mac said sorry about your eye. He's praying for you.'

'Oh, hallelujah.'

Quigley described how the ram's tiny hooves clattered across the cobbles to warn the populace of the invaders across the river.

'Haven't I heard this story before?' said Siobhan.

Padraig nodded. 'Puck Fair in Kerry – only there it's a goat.'

'...And so, stirred into wakefulness by a ram many people believed was chosen by God himself,' Quigley went on, 'the people gathered themselves and their army and put the invading Strongbow's army to flight...'

Brendan joined the group. 'Quigley's on good form, isn't he?'

'He's on something,' Assumpta said.

'And that is why, ladies and gentlemen,' Quigley said, winding up for the climax, 'we put aside three days a year to pay tribute to our own king of the beasts – the ram of Ballykay.'

Assumpta let out a snort of derision as Quigley picked up a gold cardboard crown and to a smattering of applause Timmy-Joe began to lower the crate. When it was halfway down somebody let out a mock bleat and the crowd began to laugh.

Quigley had to step nearer the edge of the platform to get a better look. People were roaring with laughter now. Finally, he was able to see what was so amusing. Instead of his ram in the crate, there was one of Eamonn's wooden sheep.

Turning angrily towards the crowd, Quigley searched the faces for a culprit. Siobhan had stepped smartly behind Peter and Assumpta.

'I've heard Dublin is quite nice this time of year,' she said.

'She's right,' Peter said.

Assumpta grinned at Siobhan. 'Missing you already.'

✝

The door of Fitzgerald's was pushed open and Assumpta strode into the bar, followed by Quigley, Niamh, Peter and Ambrose.

'What are you asking me for?' Assumpta demanded. She stood with her back to the bar, confronting the others. 'How should I know where his stupid ram is?'

'She knows where Siobhan is!' Quigley shouted.

'Siobhan is in Dublin,' Assumpta said.

'Don't listen to that, Ambrose!' Quigley was agitated, dodging around Ambrose, goading him. 'Go on!'

Assumpta gave Ambrose a tight, bitter smile. 'I think your boss wants a word.'

'Assumpta!' Niamh was shocked.

Ambrose said he would pretend he didn't hear what she said.

Assumpta nodded. 'And I'll pretend that you haven't been turning a blind eye to his 24-hour shebeen.'

'What?' Ambrose looked startled.

Quigley stepped forward, defending himself. 'Quigley's Bar & Grill is not a –'

'Bar and grill?' Assumpta shouted. 'A pair of crates and a microwave hardly constitutes a bar and grill!'

'Dad!' Niamh howled. 'Assumpta! Please! I'm getting married tomorrow!'

Peter tried to mediate. 'Assumpta –'

'You keep out of this.'

'Assumpta Fitzgerald,' Ambrose said, 'I'd advise you to moderate your language.'

She scowled at him. 'I'd advise you to do your job if I thought it would make any difference.'

'"Not that I want to spoil your wedding, Niamh",' Niamh said, her voice trembling.

'One more word out of you, Assumpta,' Ambrose warned, his own control at a stretch now, 'and I swear –'

'You'll do what? Do what he tells you?'

'Right,' Ambrose said, stepping forward.

Peter stepped in quickly and caught Assumpta by the shoulders. 'Come on, away…'

Assumpta struggled. 'Get your hands off me!'

Peter held on and guided her towards the kitchen. 'She didn't mean it, Ambrose.'

'I did! I meant every word I said! Get your hands – who do you think you are!'

Peter shoved her into the kitchen and shut the door. He leaned on it and waited for her to settle down.

She held up a bunched fist. 'I swear, you are that close…'

'Listen to me!'

'He's trying to destroy me!'

'No he's not,' Peter said.

'You saw his bar last night – it was heaving.'

'Here today, gone tomorrow.'

'You really believe that?' Assumpta's eyes glittered with anger. 'You really think he'll close it down when the festival's over? Come on, you know Quigley, he's nothing but a scheming – '

'Assumpta! Stop it, will you? You make him sound like Don Corleone.'

'Without the morals!'

'Well,' Peter said, 'I think you're wrong.' He stood away from the door. 'I'll prove it to you.'

Later that afternoon Peter drove out to Quigley's Bar & Grill. As he parked his car Quigley was inside, having just read a letter on official notepaper. He read it again and slammed it on the bar.

'You say Ambrose delivered this?' he asked Liam.

'Yeah.'

'Ambrose?'

Liam paused with a frankfurter halfway out of the microwave. 'Yeah. Ambrose.'

Quigley still looked as if he couldn't believe it. He turned as Peter came in.

'I want to talk to you about Assumpta,' he said.

'To be honest with you Father, right now I have other things on my mind than Assumpta Fitzgerald. Anyhow, what is it to you?'

'She's a parishioner.'

'In your dreams.'

'She thinks you're out to destroy her. Just tell me she's wrong.'

Quigley shrugged. 'It's just business.'

'Tell me she's wrong.'

Quigley narrowed his eyes at Peter. 'Why don't you stick to what you're good at?'

They stared at each other.

Finally Quigley picked up an empty bottle by the neck and said, 'I'll tell you what I will do, though.' He spun the bottle like a throwing knife in a clean arc across the bar, into a wheelie bin full of empties. 'I'll make her an offer she can't refuse.'

Half-an-hour later, Peter followed Assumpta into the kitchen at Fitzgerald's. He had put Quigley's proposition to her and now she was thinking about it. She took a tub of margarine from a cupboard and slapped it on the table.

Suddenly, she stopped what she was doing and looked at Peter. Her mind was made up. 'All right,' she said. 'Tell him he's on.'

'Assumpta…'

'No. I want to do it. Everything in writing though, yeah?'

'Assumpta, listen to me. This bet stinks.' Peter might have put the proposition to her, but it didn't mean he was happy with it.

'He's going to put me out of business sooner or later anyway…'

'Well if that's true, why is he doing it?'

'He's a gambling man.'

Peter nodded. 'But he's not stupid.'

✝

A little over an hour before Niamh and Ambrose were
due to be married, the scene in Quigley's home was one
of chaos and undulating panic. Niamh stood in her bedroom in her white bridal dress, visibly distressed, with
the hairdresser and dressmaker both working on her at
once. Assumpta was there too, in her pink bridesmaid's
dress, trying to be calm and worrying for Niamh, who
was wound up to a point where one more wrong vibra-
tion would set her howling.

Donal wandered in with a bundle of wrapped presents.

'Do you mind?' Niamh shouted.

'Well, where will I put them?'

'I don't care. Give them to the missions. Just get out.'

Liam knocked and entered. 'The photographer was
just wondering – '

'What?' Niamh screeched. 'If he could come in here
and take a few pictures?'

'Well, no – '

'Dad!' Niamh shouted out to the hall, tears gathering
in her eyes. 'Will you get a grip out there? Half the town
seems to think it can wander into my bedroom!'

Quigley stuck his head into the room. 'What?'

Liam tried to explain what the photographer wanted.

Niamh began to shake.

'All right!' Assumpta shouted, taking over. 'That is it!
You, scram!' She chased Donal and Liam out, then
turned to the hairdresser. 'Out. I know you're not fin-
ished, you'll have time.' She turned on the dressmaker.
'You too. Please. Five minutes, I'll try and placate her.
Please go now.'

When they had all left Assumpta closed the door. She
looked at Niamh. 'I'm sorry,' she said.

Niamh blinked back her tears. 'It's all right.'

Assumpta went forward and they embraced. 'It's
going to be fine,' she said. 'It's going to be fine.'

By 3.00 pm St Joseph's was packed. Everyone was in best clothes, the women multi-coloured, the men wearing carnations in their buttonholes. As Ambrose and his best man Timmy-Joe waited nervously for the arrival of the bride, a clipboard was being passed around the congregation. Each person glanced at it and signed it almost without thinking.

At a minute past three, just ahead of Siobhan, who hurried down the side aisle and squeezed in beside Padraig, Niamh arrived on the arm of her father. She looked stunning. Ambrose turned and was moved almost to tears at the sight of her. It was a richly emotional occasion for Peter, too: this would probably be his last major ceremony before he left.

The service went without a hitch or flaw. Even towards the end, at the point when couples were likely to fluff their lines, Ambrose and Niamh spoke calmly, looking into each other's eyes, meaning every word.

'Niamh, do you consent to be my wife?'

'I do. Do you Ambrose consent to be my husband?'

'I do. I take you as my wife and I give myself to you as your husband.'

'I take you as my husband and I give myself to you as your wife.'

Assumpta, standing with Timmy-Joe behind the couple, was having trouble maintaining her calm. She glanced at Peter and saw how sad he looked, in spite of his smile.

Speaking in unison Niamh and Ambrose said: 'To love each other truly, for better for worse, for richer for poorer, in sickness and in health, all the days of our life.'

Peter placed his hand over the joined right hands of the couple. 'What God joins together,' he said, 'man must not separate. May the Lord confirm the consent that you have given and enrich you with his blessings.'

As the couple emerged into the sunlight they were cheered and showered with confetti. In the flurry of joy and well-wishing Quigley glared at Ambrose. Niamh saw him.

'Dad,' she said, 'Stop it.'

Quigley was suddenly all innocence. 'Stop what?'

'You know very well what. He was only doing his job.'

'Well...' A smile slowly brightened Quigley's face. 'I hope he isn't going to make a habit of it.' He reached out and shook Ambrose warmly by the hand.

Peter came out and fell into step beside Assumpta. 'Are you fit?' he asked her.

'As I'll ever be.' She crossed to Niamh and hugged her. 'Congratulations.' She turned to Ambrose. 'Treat her right,' she said, 'or I'll have you locked up.'

'I will,' Ambrose said, and blushed as Assumpta kissed him.

Then she turned to Quigley. 'Will we do it?'

'What?' he stared at her. 'Now?'

'I don't want it hanging over me.'

Quigley nodded. 'Let's rock.'

They went directly to their separate bars. Quigley's seconds – Liam, Donal and Timmy-Joe – pulled pints of stout for him and helped him put on his gym shoes, remove his morning coat and roll up his sleeves. At Fitzgerald's, Assumpta's seconds – Dr Ryan, Siobhan, Padraig and Brendan – pulled pints of stout and lavished moral support as Assumpta changed her bridesmaid's shoes for white ankle socks and trainers. Peter provided a small service, too, though more covertly than the others.

Quigley and his seconds arrived at Fitzgerald's and together the combatants walked to the bridge, where a banner that read 'START' was slung across the width of the road. Quigley and Assumpta stood side by side, each holding a tray with three full pints of stout. The streets, all the way from the start to the finishing line outside St Joseph's, were thronged with eager spectators. Ambrose, wedding suit or no, was keeping order around the starting line as officiously as any on-duty policeman.

Peter stood at the side of the bridge with a starting pistol. Brendan and Padraig were beside him.

'Ready?' Peter said.

Quigley and Assumpta nodded.

Brendan said, 'They're taking this awful serious.'

'Get set…'

'Is there a lot of money in this, Father?' Padraig said.

'No.' Peter raised the pistol high. 'Just their pubs.'

He fired. Quigley and Assumpta took off, their pint glasses sloshing and splashing as the crowd shouted and cheered them on.

They rounded the end of the bridge neck and neck and straightened out on to the main street. Assumpta maintained a good lead until halfway up the slope, when Quigley began to overtake her. They battled on, moving fast, all but running, and 10 yards from the church Quigley was 5 feet in front.

He turned his head to see where Assumpta was and he stumbled. One of his glasses fell over, splashing stout everywhere. Assumpta swerved past him. She kept her eyes on her tray, gripped the rim as tight as she could and put on a final spurt. The tape broke and she sailed through to victory. The regulars cheered while Quigley still tried to put right the mess on his tray.

Before the shouting and the cheering had died away Assumpta walked over to Quigley and said, 'Now that's it, right? Finished.'

He nodded, his face impassive. 'I'm a man of my word.'

As Quigley walked away, Peter approached Assumpta. 'Congratulations,' he said, beaming.

Assumpta was elated. She patted him briskly on the chest. 'I never thought I'd have to thank a priest.' Her look, brief and flashing, was warm and sincerely grateful.

✝

The wedding reception was held at Fitzgerald's. By 7.00 pm the place was heaving. The same band that had provided the music for Niamh's 'Hardly a Wedding Reception', U3, was on the stand, playing loud enough to rattle the windows. Niamh danced energetically with Ambrose and numerous other couples tried to keep up.

Brian Quigley and Peter were at a quiet corner of the bar.

'Fair play to you, Brian,' Peter said. 'You kept your word.'

'I did.'

'Some gamble.'

Quigley looked down at the bar for a moment. 'For her,' he said.

Peter frowned. 'Not for you?'

'Ambrose closed me down yesterday. Fire regulations. I had nothing to lose.'

Peter considered that. He began to laugh.

'You're taking it very well,' Quigley said.

'I'm just pleased that I don't have to feel guilty any more.'

Assumpta appeared behind the bar.

'You're a very lucky woman,' Quigley told her.

'Well...' Peter said, 'luck didn't come into it.'

Assumpta handed Peter the tray she had used in the race. Three empty glasses stood on it. Peter took it and brought it towards Quigley. Abruptly he turned the tray sideways. The glasses stayed where they were.

Quigley stared at it. 'You stuck them down?'

Assumpta laughed. 'Do you not recognize a miracle when you see one?'

Quigley shook his head, dumbfounded.

Shortly afterwards Peter slipped away. Assumpta saw him go, and at the first opportunity she went outside, too. Peter was across the road, sitting on the steps outside Kathleen's shop. Assumpta went across and sat beside him.

'So,' she said.

'So.'

'You having a good time?'

He nodded sadly. 'You bet.'

'I'll miss you.'

Peter was touched.

'If you decide to go,' Assumpta added.

'Too late. That battle's been fought and lost.'

'I don't think so.' Assumpta handed him a wad of rolled-up sheets of paper. They were covered in signatures. 'Nearly the whole town's signed it,' she said.

Peter looked at the petition. He opened his mouth but nothing came.

'They all want you to stay, and just so he knows it I'm sending this to the Bishop. Now I don't know if it'll make any difference, but hey, I'm on a roll.'

Peter was leafing through the sheets, reading the names. When he looked up Assumpta saw he was crying.

'I don't know what to say…'

'It's no big deal.'

'Yes it is.' He brushed his sleeve across his eyes.

Assumpta shrugged. 'Whatever.'

It was several seconds before he could speak again. He looked at Assumpta. 'I never thought I'd have to thank a landlady.'

She smiled.

'What about you?' Peter said. 'You said they all wanted me to stay. What about you?'

Assumpta nearly smiled, but her eyes remained serious. Finally, without a word, she got up and walked back to the bar.

Peter stayed there for a while and leafed through the pages of the petition. Then, as the dusk gathered and it became too dark to read, he sat and gazed across at the bright warmth of Fitzgerald's, hearing the music and the endless laughter.

✝